TALES FROM WHERE THE ROAD ENDS

BY KEVIN F. McCARTHY

Jeannie and Dave

Hope you enjoy these Stories.

K. F. McCarthy

CONTENTS

Victoria

The wind was out of the west and blowing at a steady thirty-five miles an hour. It kicked up sand into swirling little clouds that wound their way down the main street and collected in odd corners, around car tires and against curbstones. By 3:00 p.m., when the factory on the far side of the railroad tracks let it's first shift go for the day the wind was building and had begun to howl through the high tension wires that paralleled the tracks.

"It's going to blow tonight," JD said, looking up at the pale, almost purple sky.

"It's fucking blowing right now," Bobby said. He was walking bent forward, shielding his face from the wind and sand.

"This? This is nothing. You wait, by midnight tonight this winds going to be howling past your house. You'll think there're Banshees out and about."

Bobby stopped at his truck and turned to face his friend, using the hood of his sweatshirt to shield his face, "You don't think the power'll go out do you?"

"Good chance, wires could go down anywhere between here and Green River, or a hunk of sage could get up high enough to tangle in a transformer and short her out, happens all the time." JD let out a short bark of a laugh, "welcome to the high desert my friend."

Bobby looked at him for a moment longer then swore and yanked open the door to his rusted out Ford 150. He hopped in and shut the door before too much grit could get in with him, not that it would have much changed the appearance of the trucks interior. JD waved over his shoulder as he walked to his own vehicle, a 1989 Buick sedan that was big and rusty and that he had bought brand-new from a dealer over in Salt Lake back in better times. The engine cranked grudgingly to life and he heard a distinctive clunk as he dropped the gear selector into drive. The Buick was most likely on its last legs and he couldn't really complain, twenty some years was a lot to get out of a car. He pushed the thought from his mind as he drove through the dust. When the thing finally gave it up he would park it out back and get to watching it rust into the ground. He would then find another means of transportation, probably an old used beater because one thing he was sure of was that the days of walking into a dealership and walking out with a new car were pretty much over for him.

Bobby drove slowly along a dirt track in the opposite direction, too unsure of the dust to break twenty miles an hour. He kept his left hand on the wheel and used his right to twist the right-hand knob on the radio, trying to find a signal. All that came up through the dash speaker was static and a low wine. He finally snapped the radio off in disgust and sat back, lighting a cigarette. He thought about turning the wipers on but figured it would just smear the dust across the glass and make it worse. The windshield washer thing hadn't worked in who knew how long, it sure as shit didn't work when Bobby had bought the damn truck. His house, or rather, the house he was renting, was out at the end of a long winding dirt track. You could still see town from his front door and it was even close enough to walk, if you had a mind, and a spare thirty minutes, but right outside his back door the true desert began. At night the lights of town were there blinking in the near distance outside his front windows. Outside his back windows was darkness so solid it sometimes seemed like a wall to him. On clear nights, and most nights were clear, even the moon and the star field wheeling above the roof didn't seem to be able to dispel all the black out there.

He wheeled the truck into the bare spot beside the house that served as a driveway and shut her down. He sat listening to the engine tick for a moment, looking out at the blowing dust. By morning it would probably work its way into the engine compartment of the truck and it would be a bitch starting. Finally, he put his head down, got out of the truck and scurried around to the front of the house, slitting his eyes against the dust. He got inside the door, got it shut and shook himself like a dog to get the grit off.

The house was just three rooms, a living area, kitchen behind that, and a bedroom to the left, running the length of the small structure and ending in a bathroom that hadn't been updated since the house was built forty years ago. The building squatted on a square of cinderblocks and sagged in the middle so that the living room and bedroom floors had a dip to them. It was dreary both inside and out and Bobby had done little to brighten it up. The living room had an ancient couch with sagging issues of its own, a threadbare armchair, scarred coffee table, and a battered old floor model Magnavox that actually had a pretty clear picture, even if the color did have a habit of blinking in and out.

Bobby went into the bedroom and discarded his work cloths, throwing them over a straight back chair while he listened to the wind howl around the eaves of the house. After a quick shower, the water pressure was almost non-existent; he went into the kitchen at the rear of the house and peered out the back door windows. The wind was indeed still climbing and in the swirling dust he couldn't see ten feet past the back steps. At some point someone had built a low wall of cinder blocks in the back yard to mark the rear property line, maybe they'd been expecting a building boom in the neighborhood, it was invisible now from the back door. For no reason at all Bobby checked to make sure the door was locked then turned away and opened the fridge, got a bottle of beer and twisted the cap off as he walked into the living room. The Magnavox always took awhile to warm up so he pulled out the on/off knob then stood sipping his beer and looking out the side windows at the dust piling up on the hood of his truck.

The factory he and JD worked at made office file cabinets of all goddamned things and business wasn't good. Bobby could have predicted that three months earlier when he'd been hired on. You buy a file cabinet, put it in your office, and forget about it. It wasn't like they broke down after a few years or anything for Christ sake. Bobby had kind of been waiting to be laid off for a couple of weeks now and had been thinking about heading someplace with palm trees and beaches. He'd had enough high desert to last him a lifetime. And there was another thing; every once in awhile he would look over at JD, who worked next to him on the metal stamping machines, and think about how JD had been working there, on that very spot, doing that very job, for over twenty fucking years! He couldn't imagine that, he just couldn't get his mind around it at all. He'd been there a few months and by lunchtime each day was ready to throw back his head and just scream at the rafters. He estimated, when he thought about it at all, that he'd held more than a hundred menial jobs of one sort or another over the years, all over the country, and this was one of the most mind numbing he'd ever had, which was saying a lot. If he didn't get laid off soon he was going to have to take matters into his own hands, give notice, and head off down the highway. He had bought the old Ford sitting outside being buried in sand when he'd landed in town; it would be interesting to see how far it got him before it finally packed it in for good. He'd left more than one heap by the side of the road in his day, walking away without a look back. If the thing managed to get him as far as the coast that would be fine and dandy.

JD pulled into his own driveway and shut down the Buick. His house was on the opposite side of town from Bobby's. It sat on the corner lot of a neighborhood street lined with similar small tract houses all built after the war and JD owned it outright. He and his wife had bought it together in 1979 and taken out a thirty year note. JD had paid the note off and gotten the deed two years before. His wife had not bothered to wait around to witness that little milestone, she had lit out for California in 1985 and that was probably ok because by that time they had been tired of looking at each other anyway. JD supposed that, technically, they were still married because he had never heard a word from her since the day he'd gotten home from work and found her gone. She'd still been there a few hours after he'd gone to work when he'd called home during his break to remind her to leave money out for the paperboy, she'd sounded normal and right as rain and had said she would take care of it, he's said thanks and he'd see her that night and gone back to work. Later he would wonder if she'd already written the note he found on the kitchen table when they'd spoken on the phone or if she'd done it after that. For some stupid assed reason he'd always hoped that she'd done it after, it didn't seem as bad somehow. And she never did leave the money out for the paperboy. Now and then he still wondered where she was and how she was getting on....truth be told sometimes he still missed her.

He let himself in through the kitchen door and dropped his lunch bucket on the table. Turning lights on as he went he walked to the larger of the two bedrooms, he used the smaller one for storage, and changed out of his work cloths. Then back to the kitchen to make a quick dinner that he ate in front of the TV. When he was finished he sat in his old barcalounger and watched a sitcom, not really paying attention to it. The chair his wife used to sit in while they watched TV together was still to his right, on the other side of the TV table. He never sat in it.

He saw the way the kid looked at him at work and he knew what the kid was thinking; poor pathetic old man, standing there doing that same mindless work for twenty years, and how sad is that. The kid may have been surprised to find that JD agreed with him, JD thought he would be. But what the kid didn't know was that JD had just over forty grand in a metal box under the floor boards in his closet. Not enough to live happily ever after surely, but enough to get him out of this dead ass town and get him started fresh somewhere else, somewhere with a pulse. He also had twenty years of pension coming to him if he retired, it was a piss poor pension plan but it was something, it would help. The factory had been steadily slowing down over the past five years and JD fully expected the conglomerate that owned it to shut it down entirely in the next year or so. When that happened the town would just curl up in a ball and die. It wouldn't happen overnight, things like that never did. But five years from now there would be nothing left but crumbling buildings and empty streets. Hell, it may only take two or three years. JD had no intention of hanging around to watch that little drama play out.

He'd been born and raised in the town, gone to the elementary school over on Blackburn that was all boarded up now, gone to the regional county high school in Green River, played football, been a big man on campus. Someone had told him recently that the town sent less than a dozen kids to that high school now, they had to walk up to the interstate to catch the bus every morning. He'd married his high school sweetheart and they'd had big plans back then, hadn't they. The town was doing fine back then, it would never be a metropolis to be sure, but it was doing fine, people were still actually moving in instead of the other way around. He and his wife had lived in an apartment over the hardware store on Main Street at first, another building that was now empty and boarded up, and then a larger apartment just off the center. JD had gotten a job with Latitude Scientific out by the interstate and it had been a good job, there had been talk of them sending him to school for a degree and maybe re-locating him to their plant in California after that. Latitude Scientific had developed and manufactured lenses for any and all things that needed lenses and things were looking good for JD. But then things got slow and Latitude said that the work force in town didn't have the level of education they needed to recruit from and they moved their R&D department out to the coast. Any talk about sending JD to school stopped after that. Two years later Latitude said that business was bad and they were shutting down the plant entirely and consolidating, moving everything to their California facility. JD had applied for a position at that facility but they had told him that they didn't need him, they had enough un-skilled labor out there already...unskilled labor.

They had just bought the house and things looked bad for awhile, other companies were leaving town too and JD's wife had mentioned for the first time that maybe it would be a good idea for them to do the same. But then JD landed the job at the file cabinet company and it was a union job with a pension and benefits and it had seemed like a godsend to him. They were able to keep the house and JD had thought that things had worked out ok. His wife had thought differently though, she had still thought that heading off down the road was a good idea and after a year of haranguing him about it she finally took matters into her own hands. He came home from work one day, it had been a Friday, looking forward to BBQing in the back yard on Saturday night and watching football on Sunday, to that brief note on the kitchen table and the small pile of stuff next to it; house keys, credit card, health insurance card, checkbook, she had taken nothing but her cloths, a few personal items, and the small amount of cash she'd been able to put aside since she'd first begun thinking about leaving. Her leaving the checkbook had been more of a dig than anything JD thought because there had only been about eight dollars in their account at the time.

The note had been short and totally lacking in sentiment, the town was dying, he was dying with it, she had chosen not to. If he was smart he would leave too. JD had expected to hear from her and he had rushed home from work every night for weeks to wait by the phone, didn't leave the house on weekends unless he absolutely had to. Surely there would at least be a call to let him know she'd gotten somewhere safe and was starting over, he had even written out a list of things he wanted to talk to her about, things that he still wanted her to know. But the call never came, not a word. He knew that things had been bad between them toward the end but she was his wife, they had known each other since first grade for Christ's sweet sake. He had no idea were she was or even if she was alive or dead, sometimes it kept him up nights, just wondering about it.

TWO

The power went out at Bobby's house at ten twenty-two that night. He had been well into the second hour of the nine o'clock movie and even though it was one he'd seen before, it pissed him off royally. With no lights and no TV he set the Big Ben wind-up alarm clock he'd found in the house when he'd moved in and went to bed.

A little after two am the wind began to truly shriek around the little house and it woke him up. He got out of bed and stumbled into the kitchen for some water. The power was still out and from the sound of things Bobby wondered if the frigging house might come right off its cinderblock foundation. Little drifts of desert sand were forming under the back door and at the kitchen windows, forced through the cracks by the power of the wind. He'd have to clean all that shit up in the morning, and he could just imagine what kind of shape his truck was in right now, sitting out there in the open. No fucking way it was going to start in the morning and he would have to walk to work.

He drained the glass of water and lit a cigarette, leaning against the countertop, listening to the howling going on outside and waiting for the roof to come off. It occurred to him that he may have waited just too damned long to head on down the road.

The wind woke JD up too. He rolled over, pulled the covers over his head and tried to go back to sleep. After a few minutes he finally sighed and climbed out of bed. The house was creaking and groaning from the wind and he thought of the kids' house, standing alone out there in the open outside of town. This wind must really be pounding the hell out of that old shitshack. He went to the fridge and got some orange juice then sat down at the kitchen table, lit a cigarette, and listened to the wind. Somewhere down the street something came down with a pretty loud bang. Hopefully whatever it was had been at one of the houses that was no longer occupied which, truth be told, was most of the houses on his street.

A mile outside of town, were the true darkness of the desert took hold, a woman stood among the sagebrush. She was wearing a cotton dress that was being whipped by the wind to the point of almost being torn from her body. Her long dark brown hair swirled around her face and danced around her head. She didn't seem to notice the wind though, she simply stood and looked toward the town even though from that far out its darkened buildings were invisible in the storm.

Finally she began walking in that direction. Fifteen minutes later the outline of Bobby's little house appeared out of the darkness and swirling sand. She stopped again and stood for several minutes, looking at it, still oblivious to the storm around her. Finally she went to the back door and knocked lightly against the glass.

Bobby had butted his cigarette and was thinking about going back to bed and trying to sleep when, amazingly, there was a tap at the kitchen door. His first thought was that the wind had blown something against the glass but then it came again, harder this time, and he walked over to the door and peered out through the glass. Even more amazing, there was a woman standing out there in the storm, her dress pressed hard against her body, her hair being whipped into a halo around her head. She saw him looking out at her and she smiled.

For a moment, just a split second, something inside Bobby told him to just go back to bed, just walk away from the door. Instead he pulled the door open, letting the storm howl past him into the kitchen. The woman stepped in quickly so he could shut the door again, pushing it against the wind. It had only been open for a few moments yet the kitchen floor now had its own sand dune.

The woman shook out her hair, which struck Bobby as incredibly sensual, then turned to face him and smiled again.

"I'm sorry about the mess," she said and her voice was low and a little throaty, he found it almost as sensual as the hair thing had been. "Thank you for letting me in."

"What were you doing out there in the middle of the night?"

"I broke down out on the road so I just started walking and got lost in the storm, thank god I finally saw your house.

"You would have seen the town eventually," Bobby said, "It's just past here a bit. You are pretty damned lucky though; you should have stayed with your car."

"I know, it was stupid of me, but...it was just kind of scary sitting out there alone with the storm all around me. After awhile I couldn't stand it any longer." She adjusted the thin cotton dress she was wearing and Bobby noticed how it clung to her body, he didn't think she was wearing anything underneath it at all, and she was barefoot.

"What happened to your shoes?"

She glanced down at her feet for a moment then smiled sheepishly at him, "I must have lost them wandering around out there, I hadn't even noticed."

Bobby wasn't sure how you could not notice something like that but he didn't say anything. It then occurred to him that they were still standing just inside the back door. "I'm sorry," he said to her, "would you like to sit down? You must be thirsty, I have soda and beer, or water, the tap water actually isn't that bad here." He was babbling a bit so he shut up.

"Thank you," she said, "but actually, I wonder if you might let me clean up a bit, I feel like I have sand in every crevice of my body."

"Of course," he replied, "You can take a shower if you want, I can show you were it is. It isn't much I'm afraid, the water pressure is terrible, but the water heater is gas so the power being out won't matter, so you'll get hot water if you just wait a while," he was babbling again so he shut up again.

Ten minutes later he was sitting in the living room in candle light, drinking a beer, listening to his shower run, and picturing the woman in it, naked. It had taken her a long time to turn the shower on after he'd shown her the bathroom and then she let it run for a long time. Just as he was thinking that the water shut off, probably the hot water ran out. A few moments later she came into the living room. She was wearing the cotton dress again and her hair hung damp down over her shoulders. Bobby notices that with her hair wet she looked younger than he'd first taken her for, probably only in her early to mid twenties. She was tall and slim, with a very attractive body which was still showing pretty well through the thin cotton of that damned dress. He had noticed when she'd first come through the back door that she was attractive but now he saw that she was more than that, she was beautiful. She had high cheek bones and a strong chin, with long auburn hair framing a perfect face. He thought that she could have just stepped off the cover of a fashion magazine, even with the wet hair and battered dress. He put his hands in his lap as she sat in the chair across from him because he was beginning to get an erection.

"That was wonderful," she smiled at him, "I feel much better. I used your soap, I hope you don't mind."

"No," Bobby said, suddenly imagining her running his bar of soap across that body. He kept his hands in his lap, "not at all. Would you like something to drink? And I can give you a t-shirt and some sweat pants or something to wear if you want."

"No, this is fine," she smiled at him again, "but I would like some water if it's not too much trouble."

Bobby got up and turned away from her quickly to hide the growing bulge in his jeans but he caught a little smile on her face and wondered if she had seen it anyway. He went into the kitchen and got her a glass of water then returned to the living room, watching her to see if she looked down at his crotch, she didn't. She was sitting in the old beat up armchair with her back straight and her bare legs together, the pose struck him as very prim and proper, she took the water and thanked him.

He sat back down on the sofa and it suddenly occurred to him that it was the middle of the night, and he had to go to work in a little over four hours. "You can stay here tonight if you'd like," he told her, "I can sleep on the couch and you can have the bed. In the morning you can call for someone to go out and get your car. There's only one service station left in town but they have a tow truck and they're pretty honest about repairs and stuff."

"Thank you," she said, "that's kind of you. I can sleep on the sofa though, it will be fine."

"All right, I think there's a spare blanket in the closet, I'll get it for you. I don't mean to be rude but I have to get up for work in the morning so I do need to get some sleep."

"I understand, I'm sorry to have kept you up like this, I'll be fine out here, you go and get some sleep."

Bobby got the blanket for her along with one of his pillows and left the candle going for her in the living room. He left the bedroom door open and told her to feel free to use the bathroom if she needed to then he climbed into bed and knew immediately that he wasn't going to be able to sleep at all. Not with her right in the next room wearing nothing but that damned dress.

THREE

JD was still sitting at the kitchen table smoking. He knew he wasn't going to be able to sleep anymore that night so he didn't bother trying. He'd heard several more loud crashes outside but so far his own house seemed to be staying in one piece.

When the sun started to come up he looked outside and saw a debris strewn street. There weren't many trees in town but there were plenty of trash cans and pieces of lawn furniture, shrubs, even a mail box or two, littered up and down the little side street he lived on. People had been leaving town for years as company after company shut its' doors and now there were more empty houses on JD's street than occupied ones, including the one abutting him and the one directly across the street. He could remember summer days in years past when there would be kids playing up and down the street, people mowing their lawns, barbequing in their back yards, living. Now the street was usually quiet and deserted, the driveways empty and just a handful of windows lit up at night.

JD put the coffee on and took a shower while it was perking. Breakfast was a bowl of cereal and two cups to try to get his motor running. Doing an eight hour shift on three hours sleep was going to be a bear and he considered for a moment calling in sick then dismissed it. The last time he'd called out sick from the plant was six years ago when he'd had the flu so bad he could barely make it from the bed to the bathroom. His job might be mind numbing and the plant might be on the verge of closing its doors, the last one in town to do so, but they still paid him real money to do a job so he damned well was going to do it.

When he went outside the sand immediately hit him full in the face so hard that he wondered that the Buick still had any paint on it. He got the door open and got in as fast as he could, tossing his lunch bucket onto the passenger side as he went. He brushed the sand out of his hair and put the key in the ignition betting with himself as to whether or not the old girl was going to start. She caught on the first try and JD shook his head in amazement. The Buick was on its last legs, there was no getting around that but it apparently didn't intend to go down easy. He pulled out of his driveway being careful to avoid a length of gutter pipe in the street. The only other car he saw was the Rievers old Ford parked in their driveway with a large sage brush caught on its rear bumper, whipping around in the wind. He only saw one other car on his drive to the plant too, a Sheriff's cruiser driving slowing along a side street. He'd thought he'd have trouble with seeing his way but the wind was blowing so strong that the sand wasn't able to stick to anything at all including his car windows. He tuned through the radio while he was driving but all he got was static.

Bobby woke up without ever realizing that he'd fallen asleep. The first thing he noticed was that the wind was still howling around the house, if anything it had gotten worse. He remembered the girl then and it occurred to him that he didn't even know her name. He got up and used the bathroom then went out into the living room. She was asleep on the sofa, curled up on her side with the blanket wrapped around her, her hair spilling down over his pillow. He went to the window and looked out at his truck, there was no sand on it now, the wind had grown too strong for that. No way was that thing going to start. He turned from the window and she was watching him which made him jump a little.

"I didn't know you were awake," he said, feeling a little stupid, again.

"Just now," she said. She sat up, swung her legs out from under the blanket and stretched her arms over her head and he just about fell in love right then and there.

"I was going to make coffee," he said, "would you like some?"

"I'll make breakfast for you if you'd like," she said, "what do you have?"

"Not much really, I usually just have coffee then get something in the cafeteria when I get to work. There may be some bread in there but not much else."

"You go get ready for work," she said, standing up, "I'll see what there is."

"The power is still out but the stove runs off of propane so it will work," he said. "I can light it for you."

"I will manage, you go on and get ready, I don't want to hold you up."

Bobby went back into the bedroom, showered and got into his work cloths. When he walked into the kitchen she had the coffee ready and was toasting some bread over a stove burner using shish kabob skewers that he hadn't even known he had.

"Sit down," she motioned to the table and he did, noticing that she had also swept up the sand that had been on the floor from the night before. She put a cup in front of him and poured the coffee. A moment later she put two pieces of toast and a jar of jelly on the table then began toasting two more pieces of bread.

"I can give you a ride to the service station," Bobby told her, "on my way to the plant. Although in this storm they may have their hands full. My own car might not even start."

"I don't want to make you late for your work," She replied. "It can wait."

"It's no problem; you don't want to leave your car out there on the interstate for too long, it'll disappear. What kind of car is it?"

"It's a brown car, with a white top," she put the toast in front of him and sat down across the table.

"Aren't you going to eat?" he asked her.

"I had some, with my coffee while you were getting ready," she said.

"Well, I could at least take you out to your car to pick up your suitcase so you have something else to wear."

"But then you would be late for your work. You've already been very kind to me; I don't want to cause you any trouble. Why don't we wait until you finish work, maybe the storm will be gone by then as well."

"What are you going to do while I'm at work?"

"If it would be all right I can stay here, as I said, the storm will probably be gone soon, I'll just wait."

Bobby hesitated for a moment and she nodded, "If you would prefer that I not be in your house while you are not here I understand, I can go somewhere else."

"Where could you go, back to your car, in this storm? No, you can stay here, I have some books I can leave you to pass the time, if the power ever comes back on you can watch TV."

"I did not sleep well last night because of the wind," She said, "I will probably just rest."

"Ok, whatever you like," he stood up and put his cup and plate in the sink and saw that the sink was empty. She stood with him and smiled and he noticed again how the cotton dress clung to her and that in reality, she was wearing next to nothing. He got some old paperbacks out for her, along with a few magazines that had been in the house when he had moved in and he hoped that she wouldn't stumble across the Playboys he had in his nightstand in the bedroom. At first the thought of leaving her in the house alone while he went to work seemed very strange but as he got the things together for her and explained to her about the TV having to warm up he began to get used to the idea. His shift at the plant would certainly be different knowing that there was a beautiful woman waiting for him at home, and a scantily clad one at that.

She was standing in the middle of the living room smiling at him as he went out the front door and he had the crazy urge to cross the room and kiss her on the cheek but he walked out into the storm instead. The blowing sand hit him in the face and he swore under his breath, put his head down and ran for the truck. Just opening the drivers' door, getting in, and closing it left a drift of sand on the dash board. He swept it off with his hand and a healthy portion of it disappeared down the speaker vent. He put the key in the ignition, held his breath and cranked it. The starter wined for a few moments then the engine caught and came choppily to life. He pumped the gas a few times until he was sure it was going to keep running then he backed out of the driveway and headed for town.

FOUR

JD swung the Buick through the gates of the plant and down to the employee lot which was less than half full. He parked in the first row and ran for the employee entrance with his head down. Just before he went through the door he saw Bobby's pickup come through the gate.

The employee entrance to the plant let you into a short hallway with a locker room on one side and a time clock bolted to the cinderblock wall on the other. JD punched in then walked down the hallway and into the cavernous factory. There was a small knot of guys standing and talking just outside the supervisors' office along the wall to JD's left. The fact that JD could actually hear them talking was because the plant was quiet, none of the machinery was running, and only one in three of the huge overhead lights was on. JD walked over to the group, already pretty sure of what he was going to hear.

Bobby came through the employee entrance and punched in, shaking himself to get rid of the sand he'd picked up during his run from his truck. He emerged from the hallway and immediately noted that the plant was quiet, and darker than usual. JD was walking toward him from the managers' office and Bobby went to meet him.

"Stand down kid," JD said, "we won't be working today."

"Powers out?"

"Yup, and the backup generator is older than dirt, they expect it to give up the ghost any time now. Once that happens we won't even have the lights that're on now never mind trying to run the line machines."

"They could have called us before we drove in here," Bobby groused.

"Said they tried, phones are down all over town, and all they're getting on their cellulars is static."

"Pain in the ass", Bobby muttered, he was hourly which meant he'd just lost a days pay. Then he remembered that there was a woman at his house who could pose for Playboy if she wanted to, and then it occurred to him that he still didn't know her name.

"Come on into the break room," JD said, "I'll buy you a cup of coffee before the genny craps out; I'm not ready to head back out into that shit storm again just yet."

Bobby really wasn't either, woman or no woman, so he followed JD into the plants grubby little break room where they got cups of coffee from the machine and sat down at one of the scarred Formica tables. There were a couple of other guys in there doing to same. It seemed no one was all that anxious to go back out into the dust storm. Even in the break room, in the center of the huge two story factory, they could still hear the wind howling outside.

"How long does one of these frigging storms last," Bobby asked.

"Usually not more than a day or so," JD answered, "this one'll probably blow itself out by nightfall. I might head out to Green River if the driving isn't too bad, beats sitting around the frigging house all day, if you're interested."

"Can't," Bobby said, "I have someone at my house," he told her about the woman showing up in the middle of the night."

"You're bullshitting me," JD snorted, "A beautiful woman walks out of the desert and knocks on your kitchen door, a scantily clad beautiful woman, get the fuck out of here."

"She's at my house right now," Bobby replied, "You're welcome to come over and meet her. I'll introduce you, even though I still don't know her damned name."

"No shit, she's really there."

"No shit, I thought I was in an old Penthouse Forum letter for awhile there. I told her I'd take her over to the service station after work to see about getting her car towed off of the interstate."

"Where was she headed?"

"Don't know."

"Well where is she from?"

"Didn't ask, I was mostly just staring at her tits and her legs and convincing my self that she was really there. Sounds like she's from back east though."

"She just walked across the desert in the middle of a dust storm and found your house. She's goddamn lucky she didn't wander off the other way, someone would stumble across her bones in ten or twenty years."

"You best watch yourself," one of the guys at another table said, "she could be a banshee, come out of the desert in a storm, in the middle of the night like that. Not a natural thing is it?"

"What the fuck is a banshee," JD asked him.

"A ghost, a mean one who wanders the earth looking to do harm to mortals, they're usually beautiful woman."

"You're thinking of your ex-wife," JD said to him, "all except the beautiful part that is."

"They scream in the night," The old guy continued as if he hadn't heard, "that's were the expression comes from. Did you hear screams out there in the desert before she showed up?"

"I didn't hear anything but the fucking wind trying to take the roof off of my house," Bobby told him. "She's not a ghost, she made me breakfast for Christ sake. She's just a woman whose car shit the bed out on the highway and who made a stupid decision to try to walk into town.

"I'm just saying," The old man replied, "you watch yourself around her, that's all."

"Oh I'll watch her like a hawk," Bobby assured him, "especially as long as she's wearing that dress. Unfortunately I'm going to go home, give her a ride to the Sunoco, they're going to fix her car, and then I'm never going to see her again, except in my dreams."

"Your wet dreams," JD laughed.

"Yeah, that's for sure," Bobby said and stood up. "So I guess I should go get her and get it over with, since I'm not going to be making any money today."

"Ask her for a blow job before you drive her over to the Sunoco," one of the other guys said, "it's the least she can do don't you think?"

"Hell, ask her if you can tear off a piece," another said, "why not shoot for the moon," and they all laughed.

"Get a picture of her at least," JD said, "so we can all see what she looked like."

"Yeah, a naked one, full frontal."

"You guys are real class acts," Bobby said. He tossed his coffee cup in the trash and walked out of the room. If anything it seemed that the wind had intensified as he walked out to his truck, something he wouldn't have thought was really possible. He wondered once again if the truck would start but it did, again grudgingly, and he headed for home.

JD left a few minutes later, after spending some more time making fun of the old man's banshee theory. There just wasn't anything else like blue collar lunch room humor to brighten ones day. He steered the Buick through town and out to the interstate with the intention of going to Green River for a few hours but once he got to the open terrain of the highway he couldn't see twenty yards past the

Buicks front bumper so he bagged the idea and drove back into town. He doubted any of the guys at the Sunoco were going to be willing to take the wrecker out to Bobby's lady friend's car with conditions what they were, they were probably going to have to wait the storm out first, and Bobby would have some more time to get to know his house guest. JD considered heading over to Bobby's to meet the little lady, under the guise of telling him about the terrible conditions on the highway of course. He decided it was a good idea and headed in that direction, noticing as he drove through town that there was just no one out and about, he hadn't seen one other vehicle on the road since he'd left the factory. People were hunkered down waiting it out and JD supposed he would end up doing the same but the thought of spending the day alone wandering around his empty house didn't really appeal to him. No, he'd definitely stop by Bobby's and visit for awhile, and meet the supermodel himself.

FIVE

Bobby swung the Ford into his driveway and shut it down. He had stopped at one of the few remaining markets in town on his way home, been surprised that it was open, and bought some stuff to make sandwiches, some more beer; warm of course, some soda, some canned goods and some munchies. All in case the woman wanted to stay for lunch before they hit the Sunoco and he supposed it would be a good idea to have some damned food in the house either way.

He got out of the truck with the bags and bolted for the front door. Just as he got to the door it swung open and she was standing there in that dress smiling at him. She closed the door behind him and then followed him into the kitchen as he explained to her that he didn't have any work that day because of the storm. He put the bags down on the table and turned to face her.

"I thought we could have some lunch and then I'll drive you down to the service station to see about your car," he said.

"That sounds fine," she replied, "I'll fix it for us if you'd like to go and change out of your working cloths."

He frowned for a moment at the term 'working cloths', she'd said that earlier too, but nodded and told her what kind of sandwich he wanted then went into the bedroom to change. When he came back she had set the kitchen table with silverware and napkins and his sandwich was on a plate waiting for him. She had placed a glass by his plate and put a bottle of beer and one of soda next to it, both unopened. Her own plate was across from his and was empty; there was a half full glass of soda next to it. He said down across from her and told her everything looked very nice and she smiled at him, she smiled at him a lot he was noticing.

"Aren't you eating," he asked her as he opened the bag of chips and dumped some onto his plate.

"I picked a little was I was preparing yours," she said, "I'm not really that hungry."

"All you had for breakfast was a few pieces of toast; I would think you'd be starving by now."

Before she could answer someone knocked at the front door. Bobby went and opened it and JD rushed in out of the storm.

"I thought I'd stop by and give you an update on the storm," he said loudly, leered at Bobby then craned his neck to try to see into the kitchen.

Before Bobby could reply the woman entered the living room and walked toward them and JD just stared, first at her face and then at the dress, and what the dress barely covered. She had pulled her hair back into a ponytail and tied it with a piece of string she'd found somewhere and it just served to highlight her face even more, her high cheekbones and perfect features.

JD caught himself and looked back into her eyes then smiled at her.

"Ma'am," he said, holding out his hand, "I'm JD, Bobby's oldest and dearest friend, at least in this town. I'm pleased to make your acquaintance, Bobby has told me all about your unfortunate experience last night in the storm and I am glad to see that you came through it ok and hope that your vehicle will be good as new as soon as possible."

She smiled back at him and Bobby thought JD was going to melt right there in his living room. She shook his hand, thanked him for his concern and invited him to join them for lunch, which he readily accepted. When Bobby and JD were seated at the kitchen table the woman removed her plate and glass and insisted on making JD a sandwich at the counter.

"In regards to your car," JD said to her as he poured himself a warm beer, "I'm afraid I have some bad news," he related his experience on the interstate in his attempt to go to Green River. "I just don't think those old boys at the Sunoco are going to be able or willing to go and fetch your car until the storm lets up some, you just can't see anything at all out there at the moment."

"That is too bad," she replied, "but I wouldn't want anyone to risk being injured just to help me so if I must wait then that is what I will do."

"How far down the interstate is your car anyway," JD asked her.

"Oh I couldn't guess, in the darkness and with the storm what it was I have no idea how far I wandered before I saw this house. I do know that I was out there for some times and had begun to fear that I wasn't going to find anything at all."

"But how did you know there was a town here in the first place," JD asked.

"I saw the signs on the road," she said, "and I thought it was just a short way, people don't realize how endless the desert is do they? And how easy it is to become lost in it. I am very lucky to be here."

"Where were you headed for?"

"California," she said a bit abruptly and put his sandwich down in front of him then sat down between the two of them.

"Aren't you going to have anything else," Bobby asked her.

"I'm fine," she smiled at him, "I don't eat much,"

"No doubt how you maintain your fine figure ma'm," JD smiled at her. "Were you going to California to visit or to live?"

"Oh, to live, my whole family is moving out there from the east, I will meet them there."

"By family do you mean husband, kids, that kind of family?"

"I am not married, my mother and father and my brothers and sisters will be there."

"That sounds fine," JD said, "Say, you know I didn't catch your name, makes me feel like we haven't been properly introduced yet," he smiled at her.

"My name is Victoria."

"Well that's a pretty name, do you go by Vicky?"

"No, I go by Victoria."

"Oh, it's kind of an old fashioned name though isn't it?"

"Is it?"

"Not really," Bobby said, "I went to school with a girl named Victoria, we were kids though and we all called her Tory."

"Is your full name Robert?" she asked Bobby.

"It is but my mother was the only one that ever called me Robert."

"I think Robert is a fine name," she said, "You should go by it."

"Not at the plant," JD said, "wouldn't fit at all, you'd look like you were putting on airs is what."

"The plant is the place you both work?"

"Yeah, we make filing cabinets, for offices," Bobby told her.

"Probably not for much longer though," JD added.

"Why is that?"

"Business is bad," Bobby explained to her.

"You wouldn't have noticed because you haven't seen it yet," JD said to her, "but this whole town is dying. Ten years from now I doubt there will be anything here at all but empty buildings."

"But there has always been a town here," she said, "why would it die?"

"How do you know there's always been a town here?"

"I read about it, when we were planning our route to California. There was a shootout here, on the main street of town."

"That was over a hundred years ago," JD laughed, "ancient history."

"But it was famous," she replied, "I read about it, wouldn't people come here to see where it happened?"

"Like I said, it's ancient history. It's not like Tombstone down in Arizona, no one remembers it anymore. Hell, the west is full of ghost towns; this will just be one that held on a little longer."

She got up from the table and turned to face the counter. After a moment she began to wash her dish in the sink. Bobby caught himself staring at her ass and turned to face JD, who was doing the same thing. Bobby cleared his throat and JD looked at him, shrugged his shoulders and smiled then took a bite of his sandwich.

JD hung around for an hour after they'd finished lunch, until Bobby was ready to throw him out. He finally got up to leave and Bobby offered to take Victoria down to the Sunoco anyway, to be sure they couldn't do anything yet but she said that it was ok, she could wait. So JD left and Bobby found himself alone with her with no TV, no electricity, nothing to do but talk which is what they did and he learned that her least favorite subject was herself. Other than saying that she had been born and raised in Philadelphia she just wouldn't be baited into talking about herself at all. She did however ask him many questions about himself, wanting to know little details about the most mundane episodes of his life. He found himself telling her pretty much his entire life story and she seemed geinuinly interested in hearing it. He actually found it very flattering, especially since he'd never considered his life to be all that interesting, and neither had anyone else.

He offered to take her into town to buy some essentials to hold her over until she got her luggage from her car but she said she was fine. It was then that it first occurred to him that she had arrived at his house without a single possession except for the dress she was wearing. No purse, no ID, no money, nothing. He asked her about it and she simply said that she had left her things in the car, that she'd been so upset by the storm that she had acted stupidly. Bobby offered to loan her some money but she said again that she was fine. And all the while the storm raged on around the little house.

SIX

JD drove home through the storm thinking about the girl. There was something about her that didn't seem right to him, the fact that she had just wandered out of the desert in the middle of the night not withstanding. She was probably one of the most beautiful women JD had ever met but then again, he'd lived most of his life in this one horse town so he might not be the best judge of what constituted world class beauty. But, the woman was undeniably stunning, even with in old sun dress with her hair in a pony tail. But there was just something…off about her, something disjointed. He couldn't put his finger on it and he knew it was going to drive him absolutely batshit until he did.

He turned down his street and immediately noticed that one of the few trees it boasted was now lying across it at a ninety degree angle. Fortunately his house was a corner lot, the first house on the left as you came onto the street so the tree was no problem for him. The thought hit him that the town maintenance department, or what was left of it these days, was going to have a hell of a time cleaning up after this blow. The fact that there were many streets in town that were totally deserted now would help but still, it was going to be a bitch kitty of a chore to clean everything up. It had occurred to JD a few times recently that they should ask everyone who was left living in town to all move in toward the center, to consolidate so that the municipal departments had less ground to cover. Hell, he knew one guy that he played cards with who was the only one left living in an entire neighborhood that was on the edge of town. Whenever they played at his house it was always creepy leaving at night, driving past house after house that was empty and dark, and would be that way now forever. Yes, he thought that the time for leaving was definitely drawing nigh.

The first thing he noticed when he entered his house was the smell coming from the fridge. He had forgotten to empty it out and everything inside was turning. He got a trash bag from under the sink and started tossing stuff from the fridge into it. When he got to the freezer he cursed out loud because a half gallon of Rocky Road ice cream had leaked all over the damn place. He got a roll of paper towels to clean it up.

Some of the things the woman had said, or rather, some of the things she hadn't said, had seemed strange; no last name, no details at all about her trip, who she was, what she did for a living, none of that, none of the usual small talk that people made when they were getting to know one another. But there was something even more basic than that, more ground level that bothered him. She didn't talk like a normal person, he just couldn't put a finger on it beyond that but she just seemed out of place somehow, almost like she was a foreigner or something but she didn't have an accent and she'd said she was from Philadelphia hadn't she?

He finished with the fridge and did a quick circuit of the house to check for damage from the storm and to look out his windows at the damage in his yard. The sand was so thick that he couldn't see much but it didn't look that bad. He had a couple of Yucca trees in the back and a Hibiscus in the front yard and all were still standing so that was fine. He got a warm beer from were he'd left them on the kitchen counter and sat down in the living room to drink it.

See, the thing was, he thought, the woman really was drop dead gorgeous, and it was obvious that that was all Bobby saw when he looked at her. That worried JD a bit. He had been around the block a few times and while he had lived most of his life in East Bumfuck Wyoming married to the same woman, he also knew a few things about the world, and the woman just didn't seem right to him. He hadn't gotten a bad vibe off of her per se, just a wrong one. And Bobby didn't see that, not at all, Bobby just saw that face, and those legs and that was it. Christ, no one just walked out of the desert in the middle of a dust storm with no ID, no purse, no shoes for shits sake, nothing but an almost see-thru little gingham sun dress and a sketchy story. It just didn't happen. Could it happen? Sure, almost anything could happen, but it just didn't happen, not really. If the woman had been normal, if she had been like everyone else he'd ever met, well then, he'd have found it a hell of a lot easier to buy her story. And that was what it finally came down to wasn't it, he just didn't buy her story. He thought about getting back into the Buick and driving back over to Bobby's but what the hell was he going to say to him, that the stunning young woman shacking up with you is an alien or something? Yeah, that would go over big. And as much as he liked Bobby and regarded him as a friend, they had only known one another for a few months. Push came to shove and JD knew damn well that the kid would listen to his little head instead of his big one.

Then he thought about driving out along the interstate and looking for her car. It didn't matter if she couldn't remember where it was or how far she'd walked. She couldn't have walked that damned far, not in this storm. So the car had to be fairly close to town and it was just a four lane interstate, not like the thing would be hard to find. But, the storm hadn't slacked off at all since he'd tried to drive to Green River early that day, if anything it had gotten worse. If he went off the road out there and got stuck then he'd be the one trying to walk back into town and he was just too old and too smart for that shit.

So, it looked like what he was going to do was sit there and drink warm beer and hope that Bobby would be ok and the woman would just move on when the storm lifted. Hell, it wasn't like the kid was rich, or even had anything worth stealing, not that JD knew about anyway. He just hoped that if the kid got up the nerve to make a move and she said no he would be smart enough to let it drop. This was a jerkwater town but it did still have a Police Chief and two sworn officers and rape was rape. He knew how he'd feel sleeping in the same house tonight with that woman and shit, he was an old man. In the end there was nothing he could really do no matter how much he thought something was wrong with her other than just hope she moved on before Bobby got to find out what it was.

He got up to get another warm beer. If he did decide to stay in this shithole town for awhile longer then first thing Saturday he was driving over to the Sears in Green River and buying himself a portable frigging generator.

They'd talked all afternoon and then Victoria had gone into his room and slept for a few hours. He'd wandered back and forth from the living room to the kitchen and back replaying their conversation in his head and wondering if the entire thing was really happening. When she woke up they'd had a dinner of sandwiches and warm drinks because the power was still out and she still didn't really eat much. Truth be told Bobby couldn't swear that he saw her eat anything at all. After that they'd sat in the living room and talked some more and she was still closemouthed about her life but she continued to pump him for information about his. Bobby sensed that something about her was strange, not to the extent that JD did because JD was right, Bobby was looking at her through star struck eyes, but it had sunk in that she wasn't your ordinary run of the mill woman. He'd never known a woman yet who could sit around for twenty four hours without her purse or her makeup or her id or something more than a sun dress. None of it seemed to bother Victoria and once again, she seemed fascinated with his life. Bobby was also smart enough to realize that he was extremely flattered, and a little flustered by such attention being paid him by someone who looked like Victoria. It was like an SI Swimsuit model had not only suddenly showed up at his house, but also found him to be the most fascinating man alive. He'd decided that it wasn't hurting anything and he was going to go with it.

As it got later he also made the decision, again, that he was definitely not going to make any kind of move on Victoria. For one thing he though it would be incredibly unfair of him under the circumstances, her being trapped here in his house by the storm. For another he was pretty sure that she would shoot him down. She had seemed totally unconcerned about being stuck here with him like this, she had seemed that way from the moment she'd arrived. She was completely at ease in his house, with him. Even with that though, he had gotten zero come hither vibes from her since she'd been there, not a twinge. Which told him that while she was comfortable with him, she was not interested in taking things to the next step. He could be wrong about that, god knows he had been in the past but, he was having a good time with her, was flattered by her attention, and he wanted things to remain pleasant, he wanted to have a good memory after she left, probably the next day, and went out of his life forever. Besides, a woman like her wouldn't come on to a guy like him. Not that he wasn't good looking because he thought he kind of was but, he was a factory worker who lived in a rented house that was just a few jumps up from a shack and he drove a beat down old pickup truck, he was pretty sure she had done better.

So, when the time came to go to bed he had set her up with the sofa again, he offered a second time but she still refused to take his bed, and he had gone to bed, alone, hoping that he'd be able to go to sleep with her in the next room.

He was lying awake in bed, hands behind his head staring at the ceiling and thinking about her when she came into the bedroom and stood by the doorway.

"Robert," she said softly, "The storm is dying."

"It is," he replied, "looks like you'll be leaving soon."

"Yes, it looks like I will be leaving soon." She crossed the room then and stood over him at the edge of the bed. She looked down at him for a long moment then unbuttoned her dress and let it fall around her ankles. He hadn't moved a muscle and he stared up at her, she was so beautiful she looked almost ethereal, like she wasn't even real. And then she slowly lowered herself down to him and she was very real.

He awoke in the morning to sunlight shining in through the bedroom window. The storm was gone, and so was Victoria. The bed beside him was actually still warm from where she'd been sleeping and he checked the bathroom door then listened for sounds from the kitchen of her maybe making breakfast. When he heard nothing he got out of bed and it took him just seconds to confirm that the house was empty. He went outside and walked all the way around the house but there was nothing but desert, and the town in the distance. He actually called her name a few times, already knowing somehow that there would be no answer. He went back into the house and noticed that the power was back on and the phone was working. He called in sick to work then went back into the bedroom, sat on the edge of the bed and just looked at the impression her body had left on his sheets, the indentation of her head on the pillow, and the single long brown hair in the center of it.

After awhile he got up and got dressed and went outside and walked around the house again. This time he saw the footprints in the sand, small prints of a barefoot person that led in a straight line away from his back door and into the desert. He began to follow them, walking to the side so as not to disturb them and he realized that he was afraid of what they would lead him to but eventually they simply stopped. He stopped too and looked around, then he walked in a half circle around the last print, further and further out until he was sure there couldn't be any more. He returned to the spot were the footprints just stopped, a left footprint, the last in the line and then...nothing. He looked back and saw that he was about one hundred yards from the low cinderblock wall that marked the end of his property, and the end of the town, the end of civilization. He was standing in the middle of the desert, surrounded by nothing but sage brush, sand and emptiness. He stood there for a very long time, not wanting to leave because this was the last trace of her. Finally the sun began to get to him and he returned to the house. He gently took the one long brown hair from the pillow and placed it carefully into a plastic sandwich bag from the kitchen. He put it in his pocket then sat down at the kitchen table to contemplate the rest of his life.

PART TWO

The file cabinet factory closed six months later, after giving its employees just a few weeks notice that their jobs were disappearing. By that time more people had left town and JD was the only person living on his street. On the last day at the plant where he'd spent twenty years of his life JD signed the paperwork for his pension, the plant was owned by a huge conglomerate so his money was safe, and walked out to the Buick without looking back. He found that he had no desire to look back and that struck him as both profoundly sad and incredibly liberating all at the same time. In the coming weeks he would go out of his way to avoid driving past the plant, shuttered and dark and dead. And still more people left, until the town began to resemble what it was to become, a ghost town, the buildings slowly giving in to the desert until, a hundred years from now there would be almost nothing left.

A week after the plant closed JD and Bobby met for a beer at the one bar that was still operating in town, Stukey's, just off the highway. Stukey's got enough trade from traffic passing on the interstate to hold on, at least for awhile. But the writing was on the wall for the bar just like it was for the Sunoco and the market and every other business left in town. On the day that JD met Bobby there they were the only patrons at the bar.

"So when are you pulling out," JD asked him after they'd rehashed the death of the plant and were starting on their second round of draft beers.

"Don't know," Bobby replied, "I haven't really made any plans yet."

"Bobby, there's nothing to stay here for, twenty years ago there were twelve thousand people in this town, five years ago that was down to five thousand, right now I'd say there are maybe two hundred left give or take, a year from now there won't be anyone at all. Hell, you were laid off a month ago, what are you waiting for?"

"Just haven't decided what I'm going to do next, that's all. How about you?"

"I'm pulling out of here next week, lock stock and barrel. I don't have to worry about selling the house, who the hell'd buy it. Heading to the coast, shit maybe I'll bump into my wife somewhere out there," he barked out a laugh then took a pull on his beer. "Why don't you come with me," he continued, "we could convoy, see which one of our shitboxes makes it the furthest."

"Thanks but I think I'm going to hang around awhile longer," Bobby said."

JD faced the bar and took another pull on his draft then swirled the bottom of the glass around in the water ring it had made on the bar, "She's not coming back," he said finally, "I'm not sure she was really here in the first place."

"She was here," Bobby replied softly, "and I know who she was too."

JD turned to face him, "You hear from her?"

"No, but I found her, right here in town."

"The fuck you say, if someone who looked like that was in this town I would have heard about it, everyone would have heard about it."

Bobby drained his beer and put the glass on the bar, "I'll show you," he said to JD, "We can take your car."

A few moments later, having followed Bobby's directions, JD was driving down Main Street.

"Pull in here," Bobby said when they'd almost reached the end of the business district.

"She works at City Hall," JD asked him as he swung the Buick to the curb.

"No, but she's there."

City Hall was a hundred and twenty year old two story brick building with worn wooden floors that creaked when you walked on them and huge faded murals along the wide empty hallways. It had been built in the towns' youth, its heyday, when the future was limitless and everything was possible. Once it had been a bustling and industrious place. Now it was a tomb. The murals depicted the glory days of the town, railroads, cowboys, even the famous gunfight on Main Street that no one remembered anymore. Most of them were so darkened with age that you could barely make out the details. It occurred to JD that the town should try to sell them to some museum before they shuttered the building for the final time. It was a shame to think of them remaining here after the last person left, waiting for time and the desert to erase them.

Located on the dank and low ceilinged basement level was the town assessor's office, locked up tight, probably for good, and the town historical department, a tiny office at the end of the hall. About ten years earlier the powers that be in town had decided that the way to keep the town alive was to make it a historical mecca for old west enthusiasts and tourists, like they had done with Tombstone down in Arizona. They had opened the historical office and appointed a town historian; some old biddy names Agnes Crook, who had probably arrived in town on a Conestoga Wagon herself. Of course the idea amounted to nothing, no one came, and the town continued to grind toward its inevitable end. But Agnes had hung on, in her little office surrounded by all the historical stuff that people had donated and that the town had dug up from its old records. And there Agnes sat, in the basement, alone, waiting for visitors that were never going to come. JD only hoped that the last person to leave town would let Agnes know so she wasn't left down here all by herself, wondering why it was so quiet.

"She's the new town historian," JD said as they walked toward the little office. "Agnes has finally assumed room temperature."

"Funny," Bobby said, "Agnes is actually home sick, I was here earlier today, but the town clerk opens the office every morning in case anyone wants to look at the old records."

"And you've been looking at the old records?"

"I have," they entered the little office, there was a tiny desk against the far wall, neat and orderly, and empty, and a scarred wooden table in the middle of the room, it's surface bare save for one old leather bound book. The walls were lined with shelves stacked high with books and folders and file card boxes. It all looked neat and orderly, and dusty.

Bobby motioned him to a chair on one side of the table, JD sat down without a word, he was really looking forward to seeing where this was going. Bobby sat down on the other side of the table and looked at him for a moment.

"Was the woman Agnes's long lost niece," JD said finally, "come to town to see if old Aunt Agnes was still above ground?"

"What got me started," Bobby began as if JD hadn't said anything, "was thinking about how Victoria's footprints just ended out there in the desert. I mean, how could that happen? She was no where in sight, it's not like she got picked up by a helicopter. So after I got laid off last month I came here and asked Agnes if there were any stories like that in the town's history."

"Stories like what," JD said, "Banshees out in the desert appearing and disappearing? Jesus Bobby, instead of coming down here to the dead files room you should have been getting the sweet fuck out of town as fast as you could."

"Do you want to hear this or not?"

JD sat back in his chair and folded his arms across his chest.

"Ok," Bobby said, "so I asked Agnes and she told me that the desert around here is dotted with pioneer graves because this was a main wagon train route to California and when a settler died they would just bury them right there on the spot. Some of the graves are still marked but many of them aren't, you could walk right by one and not know it. She also said that there were old stories about the ghosts of some of these people roaming the desert. The early settlers here would see or hear them out there, mostly at night."

"The high desert can be a damned creepy place at night," JD said, "I'll give you that. But you don't really think they were seeing ghosts do you?"

"They did, Agnes does, her father saw one once, when they lived on the outskirts of town. A man dressed like a pioneer and carrying an old flintlock rifle came to their door one night and asked if they knew the way to Green River. When Agnes's father came to the door the man turned and walked away then just vanished. Agnes and both her parents saw it."

"So you had a sexual encounter with a ghost?" JD gave him a look, "is that where this is going?" Have you written in to Penthouse Forum yet?"

Bobby sighed and leaned forward over the table. He pulled the old leather bound book toward him and opened it to a marked page. Then he spun it around and pushed it over to JD. JD looked at him for another moment then looked down at the book.

There were two sepia toned black and white photographs, one on each page. The first was an image of a family posing in what was obviously a photographer's studio, dressed in their finest nineteenth century duds. The mother and father were in the center, very stiff, very formal, no smiles. Lined up in front of them were six children ranging in age from about five years old to early twenties, four boys a little girl, and a young woman. The young woman was on the far right, her left hand on her mothers shoulder, looking at the camera with an implacable gaze that made JD a little uneasy. It was Victoria.

He looked up at Bobby then looked at the second photo. This one depicted a Conestoga wagon, what they used to call a Prairie Schooner, on a muddy street in some frontier town, parked in front of a mercantile store. A woman that looked like the mother in the first photograph was sitting on the wagons drivers' seat, staring at the camera. The father was standing in the mud in front of her, his hand resting on the Conestoga's front wheel. Both had the same stoic looks on their faces as in the first picture but with a difference this time. JD thought he saw something beneath their formal expressions, something that looked a little bit like fear, or maybe desperation. The little girl was in her mothers lap and the other kids were ranged in front of the wagon, all looking into the camera. The young woman...Victoria...was standing at the back of the wagon, arms at her sides, staring into the camera. She was a bit out of focus, she must have moved her head when the photographer exposed the negative plate, but JD could still make out the look on her face. The look on her face said that she wasn't afraid of what might happen to her because she already knew, and she was resigned to it. It was the look of someone who knew they were doomed. It made JD very uneasy. He looked up at Bobby again across the table.

"The caption is on the next page," Bobby told him, "but I'll sum it up for you so you won't have to read it, I know it by heart. The Starbuck family, father, Josiah, mother, Lizbeth, kids, Josiah Jr. Jacob, William, Henry, Suzanne, the little girl...and Victoria. Originally from Philadelphia, making their way to California to start a new life, seems Josiah had been in banking back east and the bank he'd worked for had failed. There was some talk of improprieties among the bank officers, including Josiah. True or not, and he denied it of course, his reputation was ruined. Kind of funny in this day and age huh? So he felt he had no choice but to move his family to San Francisco where he hoped to start over with a clean slate. The were on the Oregon Trail, the one that runs right through here, with a dozen or so other families, a small wagon train by the standards of the day, when they ran into some trouble about eight miles south of here.

"Indians?" JD asked him.

"The Indians were all pretty much on reservations by that time. No, apparently what happened was that the Starbucks original wagon train had fallen apart, cold feet, finances, whatever, and so they had hooked up in Kansas City with a wagon train that was primarily made up of a clique of families from Mississippi along with a few stragglers, like the Starbucks. Well Josiah Starbuck was a very opinionated man who wasn't shy about sharing his opinions with others. He was also used to giving orders. He was also a northerner, a Yankee, among a bunch of southerners less than twenty years after the end of the Civil War. Tensions between him and the southern clique started right away and by the time they got this far along the trail it had reached a head. As the story goes, one night Josiah got into it with the leader of the group, a man named Lee, no relation, and Mr. Lee decided he'd had enough of Josiah's uppity Yankee bullshit and buried a knife in his chest, killing him dead.

"Doubt he was the first person killed by a fellow traveler on the trail," JD commented.

"Probably not," Bobby agreed, "but now they had a problem you see, their leader had committed murder. Josiah hadn't been armed so there's no way it was self defense, the rest of his family had seen the entire thing so there were plenty of witnesses. The clique was in a real tight place."

"So," JD asked quietly, "how did they get out of this real tight place." He was pretty sure he already knew.

"They walked the rest of the family out into the desert at gunpoint and killed them, one by one. By all accounts Victoria was the last to go and some of the single men in the train wanted to keep her around for awhile, for recreational purposes, but the men with families were against it so they killed her too. But not before she'd watched the rest of her family murdered then been forced to stand there alone in the darkness next to their bodies for at least a few minutes while the men debated whether she'd be raped and then murdered, or just murdered. The only thing she was reported to have said during those few minutes was that she was a virgin and preferred to die that way. She got her wish. They buried the bodies in the middle of the desert in unmarked graves and went on their way.

"Jesus," JD said under his breath.

"Yeah," Bobby agreed.

"But if they all died how did anyone find out about it," JD asked him.

"One of the other families that had joined up in Kansas City kept their mouths shut until they reached California but as soon as they did they went to the nearest Federal Marshal and told their story.

In the end two other families in the train backed them up, they all said that they would have stopped it but they'd been outnumbered by the clique and so there was nothing they could do. Over the next few years' people tried to find the graves but they were unmarked and it's a big desert. Eventually the story was just forgotten. Best estimate is that they were buried somewhere just south of here, not far off the original trail.

"So," JD was looking at him closely, "you think it was Victoria that came to your house that night, or rather, Victoria's ghost, looking to lose her virginity?"

"Tell me that's not her in those photographs," Bobby said, "look at them again and tell me that. And there's more."

"What?" JD said, still watching him.

"The second photograph, look at it again, look at the dress she's wearing in it."

JD looked down at the photograph again then up at Bobby.

"It's the same dress," Bobby said softly to him, "It's the same dress she had on when she came to my house that night. It was a lot shorter, she would have looked pretty odd wearing a full length dress wouldn't she have, and in that photo she's wearing under garments and it's buttoned to her neck, but it's the same goddamned dress. Look me in the eye and tell me it isn't."

"It looks the same," JD said quietly.

"And Agnes told me a story," Bobby went on, "An old town legend about this beautiful woman that would appear when there was a really bad windstorm and try to talk to people in town. A woman with long brown hair wearing a gingham dress. No one's seen her in decades but there were at least four or five times that people claimed they spoke to her and many more that saw her out walking during the height of a storm."

"Any of them get lucky?" JD asked him.

"There was no car broken down out on the interstate," Bobby went on, "I checked. Her footprints just stopped a couple of hundred yards from my house, they just stopped. And she was walking south, toward where the graves are supposed to be.

JD sat and continued to look at him for a long moment then sighed. "I've seen some shit in my day kid," he said. "I know you probably don't think I have cause I've lived in this one trick town all my life but I have. And I've heard of lots more." He looked down at the book again then back at Bobby. "It does look like her, just like her, and the dress does too, although the picture's in black and white so you can't tell the color. You think she came to you with it the way it was because she wanted to know what it was like to do it with someone?"

"That's exactly what I think," Bobby said, "And for some reason she picked me. In all the old stories she just tries to talk to people, or just stares at them, none of them mention her dress being so skimpy and none mention her trying to have sex with anyone."

"Ok" JD said, "So say I buy this story, say I believe that the woman who came to your house was Victoria Starbuck, murdered one hundred and thirty some odd years ago and buried out there in the desert in an unmarked grave. So ok, it happened, you met her, she got to know what it was like to not be a virgin, you got to be with a beautiful woman, and then she left. She's gone, your job is gone, and this town is getting gone real fast. Which brings us back around to my original question, why are you still here?"

"Because I think Victoria and I have unfinished business," Bobby replied softly.

JD continued to look at him closely, "What," he said, "You want to find her grave? Give her a proper burial? That's a needle in a haystack buddy, you'll never do it."

Bobby shook his head, "I did think about that but you're right, it's a big desert out there. No, that's not it."

"Then what are you..." JD stopped and leaned back in his chair, "Holy shit kid, you think she'll come back. You're going to wait around this shithole for the next big windstorm to see if she comes back."

Bobby didn't reply, he reached across the table, retrieved the book and turned it to face him.

"Kid, think about this," JD said, "This is fucking looney tunes. You could sit out there in that shack for decades waiting for another windstorm the size of the one that happened that night. Trust me, I've lived here my whole miserable life and storms like that don't come along but once every twenty years or so. And even if one came next week, you don't know that she'll show up, she got what she wanted, maybe she's at peace now, maybe she isn't going to walk out anymore. You can't sit here and wait for something that isn't ever going to happen. You're a young man, go find a real live woman somewhere, in California, and screw her brains out. Hell, find ten and screw all their brains out. If you're right, and I'm not saying you are mind you, but if you're right, this woman is long dead. You're not. Chock it up to a very strange but very pleasant experience and move the fuck on!"

"I can't," Bobby said simply, "I think this is what I've been looking for all this time I've been wandering around, and I'll never find anything like it again. And you're right, the town is dying. What if she comes back and there's no one here?"

"You actually mean to stay," JD said in awe, "you actually mean to sit out there and burn your life away on the chance, the crazy chance that a dead woman will show up again so you can spend one or maybe two nights with her.

"You've spent you're entire life here," Bobby said to him, "what were you waiting for?"

"Touché kid," JD replied and got up from the table. Bobby got up too and held out his hand, "I didn't mean any disrespect by that you know," he said.

"I do know," JD said and shook his hand. He started to turn from the table then stopped, "one thing," he said, "the men who killed her and her family, where they ever caught?"

"No," Bobby replied, "the Marshalls looked for them but by that time they had scattered. It was the old west and anyway, who knows how hard they looked."

"Maybe that's why she walks," JD said, almost to himself.

"Maybe."

"Keep your phone hooked up," JD said, "For as long as you can anyway. When I land somewhere in California I'll give you a call, so if you come to your damned senses you can come on out and visit, or stay." He walked to the door of the little office, looked back at Bobby for a moment, started to say something, thought better of it, turned and left. Bobby listened to his footsteps echo down the hallway then up the stairs and then out of the building. He heard the door shut behind him with a hollow bang and then quiet settled through the old building again. Bobby sat back down at the table and looked at the two photographs.

EPILOG

Bobby drove the pickup along Main Street, deserted now; the buildings all either boarded up or just left as they were. He passed the hardware store above which JD and his new bride had lived in their first years of marriage. JD had talked a lot about those times while the two of them had stood side by side at the metal stamping machine in the now deteriorating file cabinet plant. Sometimes when Bobby drove past he thought about stopping to check out the apartment above the hardware store. JD had talked about it so much Bobby was kind of curious to see what it really looked like. And no one would care if he broke into the building to take a look, it was empty, they were all empty. There was no one left to care. Maybe one of these days.

He passed City Hall, also empty and boarded up now and he *had* let himself into that building after everyone was gone, just once, to go down to the little office in the basement to retrieve the book with Victoria's pictures in it. Agnes hadn't been there so apparently someone had told her that it was time to go. She'd left the office door wide open when she'd left for the final time though, as if she'd known that Bobby would be back. He wondered when that had been; what day she had actually left the town she'd lived in for so long. He wished he'd known because he would have liked to have said goodbye, and thanked her. That bothered him a little.

He drove on past Main Street, past the Sunoco, closed and shuttered too, one of the last businesses to go, past abandoned neighborhoods, houses with blank windows and empty driveways. The last business to close had been Stukey's, just as JD had predicted. Bobby had been coming back from Green River one afternoon and swung into Stukey's for a beer only to find it locked up tight. He missed going down there nights to sit at the bar, watch a game and make small talk with Wayne, the owner, and whoever else may have wandered in. The last dozen or so nights he had been the only one at the bar. He'd never had a chance to say goodbye to Wayne either.

Bobby drove on and finally parked the truck in the little worn area to the side of his house that served as a driveway. He retrieved his groceries, bought at the Red Lion in Green River, from the trucks bed and went in through the unlocked front door. He didn't bother to lock his doors anymore, didn't seem to be any reason to. A few months ago there had still been five other people, old timers mostly, living in town, he would see them from time to time and wave. But he hadn't seen anyone at all for quite a while now and he was pretty sure that they were gone and he was the last. Or maybe one or two of them had simply died in their houses and were there still, their bodies mummifying in the dry desert air. The old guy who had been his landlord was one of the last to head out, he had stopped by before he'd left and told Bobby that he could have the house, wasn't worth a damn anyway. Bobby hadn't asked him for a deed or a bill of sale or anything. There didn't seem to be any need.

Bobby put his groceries away and thought about JD for a moment. Phone service to the town had been cut off a year or more ago but before it had JD had called him from California, some little town on the coast near San Diego. He had told Bobby that the weather was beautiful and so were the woman, that even an old fart like him was getting some action on a regular basis and he told Bobby to get his ass out there pronto. Bobby had written down his address and phone number, he thought he still had them around the house somewhere but he wasn't sure. He hadn't seen the slip of paper for quite awhile.

He made a living, after a fashion, off of the town. There was a flea market in Green River every weekend and Bobby had a couple of tables there. He sold stuff that he got by going through the empty houses and businesses in town, stuff that people had left behind. Nothing big, nothing very valuable, but enough to provide him with food money and gas money which was all he really needed. And every once in awhile he came across a real jackpot, a TV that still worked, or a stereo or small kitchen appliances, it was amazing sometimes what people didn't bother to take with them. He worked on the Ford himself down at the city DPW garage where the exiting city employees hadn't bothered to take most of the equipment and tools. So far he had managed to keep the old truck running. When the electrical power had been turned off to the town he'd found a big old generator on wheels that he'd brought home and built a shed around at the back of the house. He had actually been a little relieved when the power had been shut off because there had been times before that when he'd be driving around town near dark on a scavenging trip and would see lights on inside a house, once or twice even the wavering blue light of a television set left on. It would creep him out to a fair thee well.

And other times he would catch movement out of the corner of his eye, at a distance down a side street or at the corner of a building and it was probably sagebrush or coyotes but still he would wonder, if Victoria could be real then wouldn't there be others? Maybe one of the men killed in the famous gunfight, or a settler who died too young from disease. And sometimes the nights were bad, the silent husk of a town on one side, the endless darkness of the desert on the other and a cold wind blowing around the house. He would think about her out there, in the dark, in an unmarked grave where no one ever went. Sometimes the nights were bad.

He was getting by though, and while at first the empty town had bothered him, he was pretty much used to it now, maybe even had come to rely on it in some ways. He had no idea what was going to happen eventually, he didn't know who owned the municipal buildings in town, if anyone, or if the state would come in and level them, so far no one had shown the slightest interest in doing anything with the town. He was alone there, day after day and night after night.

Maybe it didn't matter anyway because there was a storm coming, a big storm. A year ago he had bought a multi-band weather radio at the Sears in Green River that ran off current and off of batteries. It had been announcing a huge sand storm since this morning and it was heading right for Bobby's little house. So maybe nothing else mattered now.

By the time he'd put his groceries away the wind was out of the west and blowing at a steady thirty-five miles an hour. It kicked up sand into swirling little clouds that wound their way down Main Street and collected in odd corners of empty buildings and against curb stones on empty streets. On the other side of town the front door of a house that Bobby hadn't closed tight after one of his scavenging raids blew open and sand began to collect in the entry hall, there was nobody there to care. By 3:00 pm the wind was building and had begun to howl through the high tension wires that paralleled the unused train tracks that ran by the now abandoned factory where Bobby and JD used to work.

By the time Bobby finished his dinner, or tried to, he was too excited to eat much, the wind was howling through the eaves of the little house. He looked out the front windows toward where the lights of the town used to be; where now there was nothing but darkness, then looked out at the sand beginning to build up on the hood and in the bed of his truck. He walked through the kitchen to the rear door and stood there looking out at the stygian darkness of the desert through the sand swirling up against the glass. He made sure the door was unlocked then he sat down at the kitchen table to wait.

Flying Home

He was feet wet about ten minutes after taking off. He didn't actually see the coast of France slide by beneath him because it was obscured by cloud but he knew it was there. After takeoff he'd climbed the Mustang to 10,000 feet for the trip home but as he approached the Channel the solid grey overcast above him had begun to come down, forcing him to descend in little increments so that by the time he got over the Channel he was at 7,000 feet. He had filed VFR upon leaving Abbeville and while the Mustang was fully rated for instrument flying he really didn't care to amend to IFR and go on instruments if he didn't absolutely have to. The World War Two fighter didn't have an autopilot and it was not much fun to fly on instruments.

When he'd left Abbeville the weather had been closing in a bit but not so much that he'd thought about scrubbing. The forecast for the next few hours wasn't much better showing deteriorating conditions but he was sure he could make it back to Biggin Hill before things got really dicey. He had certainly flown through worse in his time and besides, plan B would have been sleeping on the floor of a seventy year old hangar in Abbeville.

Not going on an IFR flight plan also allowed him to a fly a straight line home; his route was taking him from Abbeville straight across the English Channel making landfall at Hastings on the southeast coast of England, over the Kent countryside toward London and landing at Biggin Hill. The Mustangs cruising speed was 300 miles per hour and the distance from Abbeville to Biggin was just about 115 miles so, he was looking at roughly twenty-five minutes wheels up to wheels down. It occurred to him, flying a World War Two fighter as he was, that during that war the German fighter jocks based at Abbeville, and famous fighter jocks they were, and the RAF boys stationed at Biggin Hill, just as famous, were not very far away from one another. Must have made things very dicey back in 1940. Of course he was from the United States so to him everything in Europe seemed like it was very close to everything else.

Once he was out over the channel the cloud cover broke up a bit but as he neared the English coast it began to close in again. The waters of the channel were slate grey and perfectly flat and he thought about how many planes were down there under that placid surface; Spitfires and Messerschmitt's and B-17's and even Mustangs, some with their pilots still in the cockpits. Benny Goodman was probably down there somewhere, and Amy Johnson, and so many others. He didn't bring his Mustang over to Europe often but when he did, and he flew over the Channel, or the land were the Zuider Zee used to be he thought about it. Being a World War Two aviation history buff and flying a warbird it was hard not to.

He'd come over this time for a warbirds fly-in at Abbeville, the first they'd ever held there. The chance to come back to Europe with his Mustang and participate in an airshow at the famous German fighter base was too good to pass up. Back in the day the Abbeville Boys of JG26 with their yellow nose 109's were the scourge of the very airspace he was currently flying through. The airfield was just a backwater now, a sleepy little aerodrome with a few general aviation aircraft, one paved and two grass runways and an old Mystere fighter sitting atop a pylon as a gate guard.

It had been well worth the trip, over a hundred warbirds had participated including an honest to god Messerschmitt 109G, the only one in the world still flying, and a handful of beautiful elliptical winged Spitfires, one with an authentic Battle of Britain pedigree. His Mustang had been parked on the grass with the 109 on its left and a P-47 Thunderbolt on its right and he'd been in absolute warbird heaven for two days.

Most of the aircraft had left earlier that day but he'd hung around for a while talking with the owner of P-38 Lightening who was staying with friends in the area for a few days. He'd helped him push the Lightening back into the hanger that had once housed those famous yellow nosed 109's then decided he'd better get it in gear and back to Biggin Hill where he had friends and where he hangered the Mustang whenever he was in Europe. Biggin Hill with its own long history, probably the most famous RAF fighter base from the Battle of Britain it was now a busy private aviation field with its own gate guards; mock-ups of a Spitfire and a Hawker Hurricane guarded the fields' entrance, mock-ups because the real thing had become too scarce and too expensive to serve as gate guards. In the Mustang it was a quick hop from one base to the other so the weather hadn't particularly concerned him.

He estimated he was just a few minutes from making landfall, if it had been a clear day he would be able to see the coast by now, when the ceiling dropped even lower. In a few spots bright spears of sunshine streaked through and splashed reflected light on the surface of the water. He looked up at the ragged holes torn in the cloud cover above him, sucker holes they were called because you would go up through them, chasing the sunlight and blue sky and then they would close up behind you leaving you above a solid deck of overcast and no way down through it if you didn't know how to fly instruments.

So he eased the Mustang ever lower, trading altitude for visibility and the flat gray surface of the channel came closer and closer while long tattered tendrils of even grayer cloud slid past his canopy. He was down to four thousand feet now and hoping he wouldn't have to go any lower.

The cloud grew even heavier as he approached the coastline, the streamers of cloud around the Mustang getting thicker. He turned up the rheostat on the instrument panel to brighten the gauge lights then made sure that his outside navigation and ant-collision lights were working properly. Water vapor was beginning to stream across the outside of the canopy, pushed into tiny wiggling rivulets by the slipstream. He peered through his windscreen looking for the coastline and checked his RNAV instruments for the hundredth time to be sure he was riding the radio beam that was taking him to Biggin Hill.

A shadow caught his eye off the Mustangs right wingtip, just ahead of him, heading in the same direction, and close. He was overtaking whatever it was so he kept the Mustang straight and level and watched the shadow as it drew closer to his wingtip. When it finally broke out of the ragged streamers of cloud his mouth fell open. He'd been a warbird enthusiast for twenty years and had owned the P-51 for half of that time so he was used to being around rare old aircraft but the one currently flying off of his right wing was another matter altogether. At first he thought it was something else and that his eyes were playing tricks in the wet mist that surrounded both aircraft. But there was no mistaking the long narrow wings, the lattice like sides of the fuselage and the triangular gunners' window in the waste.

He was looking at a Vickers Wellington, a British twin engine medium bomber from the war and he had never seen one before, not even in a museum. The closest he'd ever come was building a model of one when he was a kid. It was flying on the same heading he was and must be on its way home from Abbeville like he was. He couldn't for the life of him recall seeing a Wellington at the show but there had been a group of aircraft parked along one of the old abandoned runways away from the hangers and he hadn't had a chance to get over and look at them, it must have been parked over there. If he had known he would have made it a point to walk over because a Wellington would be as rare as the 109G that had been parked next to his 51. Now he was angry at himself for not taking the time to explore more of the show but he never like to leave the Mustang alone for long at those things, a few times he had and come back to find kids climbing all over it and trying to get the canopy open.

He was definitely going to get a good look at the Wellington now though because it was edging closer. He looked it over admiring the camouflage paint scheme, it was war era, probably '41 or '42, and as it got closer he saw simulated battle damage on the rear fuselage and tail as well as the starboard engine nacelle, someone had done a hell of a good job on the thing. As he pulled up level he throttled back hard and the big twelve cylinder Rolls Royce Merlin engine crackled and growled up in front of him. Top speed in the Wellington couldn't be much over 200 miles per hour, significantly slower than the 51's cruising speed so he slowed as much as he could to keep the Mustang abreast of the bomber. As he drew even he saw someone sitting in the pilot's seat, complete with leather flying helmet. He owned one of those himself and wore it when he was flying the 51 in shows but he removed it and went back to modern earphones the rest of the time, the leather helmet was kind of uncomfortable.

The pilot turned and looked at him then waved and he waved back then pointed to his ears indicating the radio but the man shook his head and made an X across his earphones with his finger, their radio was out. Not surprising, a lot of these warbirds used as much original equipment as possible to keep the aircraft in wartime configuration. He himself had the 51 loaded with modern radios and RNAV equipment but not everyone went that route, some warbird owners were real purists. He nodded that he understood. The pilot then pointed ahead of both aircraft and shook his head then shrugged his shoulders. They were lost because of the cloud which was pretty much all around them now. So they were real purists, probably original radios and no modern RNAV equipment, they definitely should have stayed in Abbeville for the night if they were operating with such rudimentary equipment. Then again, they'd probably thought, as he had, that the weather would hold long enough to get home.

He signaled that he understood then motioned for them to follow him and the pilot nodded his head and gave him a little salute in way of thanks. He pulled the 51 a bit ahead of the Wellington but took care to stay close; in this kind of weather they could lose sight of one another's aircraft very quickly. He wasn't happy about flying the 51 this slow in weather but there wasn't much he could do about it if he wanted to stay with the Wellington. The bomber had been built for distance, and to carry bombs, not for speed.

They flew on for a few minutes and the cloud around them didn't get any worse although it didn't get any better either. He glanced over at the bomber again and noticed that it was trailing smoke from its starboard engine now. He eased back a tiny bit on the stick and the Mustang lifted up above the bomber so he could get a better look. He had noted the simulated battle damage on the nacelle when he'd first seen the bomber but now he noticed that it was extensive. He also noticed that the radial engine was definitely trailing smoke and possibly some type of fluid. He dropped back down on the bombers port side and waggled his wings to get the pilots attention. When the leather helmeted head turned toward him he motioned toward the far side of the bomber and the starboard engine. The pilot nodded twice and kind of shrugged his shoulders. So, the battle damage may be simulated but it appeared they may be having a real issue with one of their engines. Possibly an oil or glycol leak. He was more than a little surprised that they hadn't shut the engine down to save it. Fifty year old radial engines didn't grow on trees these days and he assumed that the Wellington, like most twin engine bombers of the day were capable of flying on one engine. The pilot may be reluctant to go to one engine while they were still over water though, and of course if they did shut it down they would have real trouble staying with his fighter.

He looked down at the Mustangs instruments and RNAV to determine their location which was approximately ten miles out from the coast. They had slipped down to 3,000 feet too. He waggled his wings again and motioned for the bomber pilot to make a slight course correction to the north which he did alongside the Mustang. When they reached the coast, invisible below them he motioned to the pilot again, making a little walking gesture with two fingers and the pilot nodded and smiled. They were over the Kent countryside now, headed northwest toward London.

A few moments later the soup they were flying through cleared a bit and just ahead and below them was a castle with a moat around it. The countryside of England was still dotted with castles but few of them still had moats around them. He first thought of Hever Castle but this one was much bigger than Hever so it was probably Leeds Castle. He was studying it when the Wellington waggled its wings and he looked over at it. The pilot motioned to him that he knew where he was now and was going to turn west from here. He motioned back that he was continuing on toward London. The bomber pilot nodded, gave him a thumbs up and waved his thanks.

The Wellington dipped and crossed beneath him turning west as it did. It was losing altitude rapidly and just before it faded into the mists of cloud he saw its landing gear coming down. He knew that there weren't any airports in the area, not in that direction anyway, the owner of the Wellington must be a very well off collector with his own private strip to operate the bomber from...must be nice.

He throttled back up and continued on toward London and Biggin Hill which was located in the outskirts before the city. He should be wheels down in just a matter of minutes which was good because the weather was beginning to get really dicey. If he'd had much further to go he would have definitely called ATC for an IFR clearance. Eight minutes later he entered the landing circuit at Biggin Hill and a few moments after that he was taxiing in toward the hangers. It was raining.

PART TWO

Biggin Hill Airport had probably been the most well know Royal Air Force fighter base during World War Two. It was located in Kent, on the southwestern outskirts of London so it had taken the brunt of the fighting in the Battle of Britain. Unlike a lot of airfields from the war that were now farmland Biggin Hill not only survived into the 21st century but was a thriving airport for corporate and private aviation.

He was putting the Mustang away for the night when something occurred to him. If the Wellington had been at the airshow and he'd caught up to it shortly before they'd reached the English coastline then it must have taken off from Abbeville an hour or so before he had. His 51 cruised at three hundred miles an hour and the Wellington's cruising speed had to be much less, hell its top speed probably wasn't even close to that, he found out later that it's top speed was actually listed at 235 miles an hour. So that meant that the Wellington would have taken off while he was in front of the hanger trading stories with the P-38 owner and he was damned sure he would have noticed a Vickers Wellington taking off.

Well maybe the Wellington hadn't been at Abbeville at all, maybe was just a coincidence that he'd caught up with it on the way home. He had never put much faith in coincidences though and what where the chances that he would just happen to run into a Wellington over the English Channel? In 1943 very probably, in 2014, highly unlikely.

He finished with the Mustang, talked with the hanger manager for a few minutes then caught a ride around the perimeter road of the airfield to another hanger on Churchill Way. He kept his Mustang in a little hanger tucked away in the northwest corner of the airfield because they took good care of it and the hanger rates were reasonable but it was a long way from anything else on the field.

Robert Stanford, the friend he stayed with whenever he was in the area worked a short distance away for a corporate fixed base operator at the field but he also volunteered his expertise at the Heritage Hanger, a World War Two museum located on the field that boasted the largest collection of flyable Spitfires in the world along with an honest to god airworthy MKI Hawker Hurricane.

Robert worked right next door to the Heritage Hanger and since it was after 5 pm he knew he'd probably find him there, hanging out and talking shop. He would love to own a Spitfire himself but with the asking price for an airworthy one well north of a million US dollars these days he supposed he'd have to be happy with just the Mustang. Of course he could get about the same price for the 51 and then buy a Spitfire but he'd owned the Mustang for a long time and had become attached to it, it was his baby.

Robert was indeed sitting outside the red hanger that housed the museum talking to an older gentleman who he remembered as an employee of the museum. He joined them, sitting down in one of the wicker chairs outside the hanger's office.

"So how was the show?" Robert asked him.

"Worth the trip, that's for sure, I was parked right next to a 109G. I tried to talk the owner into letting me take it up but he wouldn't hear of it."

"Can't blame him there," Robert said, "That's a rare aircraft if ever there was one."

"I suppose," he said then added; "Speaking of rare aircraft, over the Channel on the way back I ran into a Vickers Wellington headed in the same direction and a bit lost. I thought he must have been at the show as well but it's odd because I never saw him there."

"A Vickers Wellington, are you sure? Might it have been something that looked like a Wellington, the weather is getting a bit filthy up there."

"It was a Wellington, I'm sure of it. I was flying right off his wing. When we spotted each other he formed up on me and followed me across until we spotted a landmark in Kent then he peeled off and dropped down to land somewhere.

Robert shook his head for a moment then replied, "don't mean to doubt you old boy but to the best of my knowledge there are only two Wellington's still in existence in the world and they're both in museums here in the UK, one in the RAF Museum and one in the Brooklands Museum." He turned to look for the Heritage employee he'd been talking to earlier and who had wandered off a bit to begin closing the hanger doors. "Woodley, you know anything about someone restoring a Vickers Wellington to flying condition?" He turned back, "Woodley knows every warbird in the UK, flying and static, he's like an encyclopedia on the matter."

The older man approached them wiping his hands on a rag after getting the hanger door closed. "A what now?" he asked.

"A Vickers Wellington, in airworthy condition."

"There are only two surviving Wellington's in the world and neither has been off the ground in fifty odd years, both in museums on static display."

"What about someone finding one somewhere and restoring it?"

"That'd be fine and dandy were there one anywhere to be found but there isn't or I would have heard of it. Certainly would have heard of one being restored. And as far as wrecks go the thing with the Wellington was that a good deal of it was made of light aluminum you see, worked in a lattice structure for strength. That type of material would not last long, a wreck found now probably wouldn't be anything but the engines, landing gear and cockpit, you'd have to build the thing from scratch and far as I know there are no plans left to do that, very complicated internal structure you know. Who saw a Wellington?"

"I did," he replied, "I was flying next to one not two hours ago, coming back across the Channel from Abbeville."

"Well son, what you might have seen was something else made up to look like a Wellington, an Anson or Dakota or something, but there's no way it was an honest to God Wellington, unless you saw a ghost." The old man turned and walked back toward the other hanger door which was still open and needed closing.

They sat and looked out across the airfield for a few moments as it got dark, watching a Falcon Jet taxing out to take off.

"So," Bob said at last, "Off to the house for dinner? Suzy's expecting us."

"I know it was a Wellington Bobby, I was right next to it."

"Well let's nip back to the house, they're closing up here. I've got plenty of books that will have pictures of Wellingtons in them, we'll have a look."

Robert and his wife lived less than a mile from the airfield on Arthur Road, they were there in five minutes and Robert's wife Susan did indeed have dinner on for them. After dinner they sat out on the patio behind the house which had a long narrow back yard facing the field. Every once in a while a biz-jet flew past in the near distance on final approach into Biggin Hill.

Robert had brought out a stack of books, the internet might have been easier but he was a book man all the way. It took him only a minute to put several of them in front of him opened to wartime photos of Wellingtons. He looked them all over then nodded his head, "that's it, that's the type I saw, right off my wingtip. No mistake Bobby, that was what was flying next to me for a good fifteen or twenty minutes." He pointed to one of the pages that had color charts showing the aircraft with various paint schemes, "That's the color scheme it was wearing, brown and green camouflage on top, jet black on the bottom."

"Do you recall the squadron markings on the side?"

"I do, EH-T; echo hotel tango."

Robert pulled a book out of the stack and thumbed through an index in its pages, "That was 109 Squadron, they flew Wellingtons out of Boscombe Down, Amesbury from '40 to '42, special ops squadron. I don't see anything on T for Tommy but I can do some digging, sure I'll come across it."

"So someone restored a Wellington who isn't part of the warbird community and painted it the colors of this 109 Squadron. It even had simulated battle damage."

"You say that it formed up on you over the Channel?"

"Yes, the pilot gestured that his radio was out and they were lost, not surprising, some of these hardcore warbird people put as little in the way of modern avionics in their aircraft as possible to keep them authentic, you know that. He followed me the remainder of the way across and once we were over Kent and spotted a landmark through the cloud he waved and dropped down, I saw his gear coming down just before I lost sight of him."

"What was the landmark?"

"Leeds Castle, I'm pretty sure."

"There aren't any airfields around there, where was he landing?"

"I thought of that too and just assumed that he was some rich collector who had his own private field next to his manor house or something like that."

"And you say it had simulated battle damage?"

"On the tail and around one engine, the engine was actually throwing smoke too, nothing too serious but that's why he was probably anxious to get down as quickly as possible."

Robert gazed off above the trees at another jet coming in to land, "let me do some digging," he said finally. "I can't believe that someone could be stooging about in a Wellington without everyone knowing about it but maybe Abbeville was his coming out party. I'll have something for you well before you leave the field tomorrow."

"Great," he said, "I'd really like to get a look at the thing and take a few photos before I head home."

The following day he had breakfast with Robert and Suze then caught a ride to the airfield with Bob when he went to work. He hung around the Heritage Hanger for a while drooling over the Spitfires and trying to talk them into letting him take one up in exchange for them having a go in the Mustang. When that didn't pan out, and he began to feel like he was underfoot, he walked the perimeter of the field to the hanger where his plane was. They had serviced it overnight and it was ready to go although he didn't have plans to take it anywhere that day. He had an appointment for lunch scheduled the following day, after that he would probably head back to the states.

He was sitting in the little office inside the hanger when on a whim he picked up the phone and called Abbeville. The airport manager, also ground mechanic also groundskeeper at the little field answered on the first ring.

"Joachim, it's Carl Anderson, I had my Mustang in the show yesterday."

"Ah yes, Mr. Anderson, I remember your wonderful aircraft, is everything all right?"

"It is, I had a great time and will be there again should you have another. I just had a quick question, I was wondering if there was a Vickers Wellington at the show yesterday. It's a British bomber from World War Two."

"Yes, I know it but there was not one here yesterday, I'm sure of it."

"I didn't actually see it at the show Joachim; I saw it in the air after I took off from your field."

"That is a large coincidence to be sure," Joachim replied and he heard the rustle of papers over the line. "I am looking at the list of entries for yesterday's show," Joachim told him, "And the landing register as well and I'm afraid I was right, there was no Wellington here yesterday Mr. Anderson."

After he'd hung up he sat and looked at his Mustang for a while, thinking. He was still doing this when Bob called him on his cell and asked if he could meet him at the Heritage Hanger. So he walked back over to the red hanger and Robert was waiting for him out front by the row of cane chairs, he was holding a folder.

"Sit," he said to him, "I've found something that you may or may not believe."

"That sounds interesting," he said, "and fast as well, you just started looking this morning."

"I have a friend who is an RAF historian, in service so he has access to very nearly any records he cares to look at. He found something and emailed it to me several hours ago. I spent some time researching it myself then called you."

"So did you find the Wellington?"

"Yes and no."

"Ok..."

"There is no restored Wellington anywhere that I can find any trace of. All the records I've found still point to the two aircraft in museums here in the UK as the only surviving examples of the type."

"But I know what I saw Bobby."

"Indeed, I then looked at the possibility of someone having built a clone aircraft, something that looks like a Wellington but isn't. No joy there either I'm afraid. Then I remembered what you had mentioned about simulated battle damage and I went in another direction. I called my friend the RAF historian and had him do some digging for me and he came up with this," he waved the filed in front of him.

"And what's in there?"

Robert handed it to him but began to speak again before he could look at it, "it's an after action report from summer 1943, the 109 squadron Wellington T as in Tommy or, EH-T, came back over the channel with battle damage to her tail surfaces and her port engine. She made a forced landing at an emergency field in Kent, not far from Leeds Castle, the crew came away unscathed, all except the tail gunner who had been wounded in the action over France that crippled the aircraft."

He opened the folder and looked down at copies of the pages from an archaic report, its text faded and in some places almost unreadable.

"The pilots' narrative is on the last page," Robert went on, "all about how his instrument panel was shot up, radios come a cropper, how he got lost over the Channel, and how an American Mustang shepherded him home. He passed away on May 5th 1987 by the way, I had my friend check."

He turned to the last page and read the narrative. When he'd finished he sat for a long while and looked out over the airfield.

"This says that the Mustang was unpainted, bearing the designation O-QP, with a red nose and rudder and "Red Dog XII painted on the side along with the initials CJA just under the canopy."

"It does," Robert said.

"That's my aircraft," he said.

"It is," Robert agreed.

"He closed the file and placed it gingerly on his lap, as if it may bite him. "I was just now speaking with the manager of Abbeville about coincidences," he said softly.

"Did he claim to have a Wellington at the show then?"

"No, there was no Wellington; he checked the fly-in roster to be sure."

"So what are you thinking?" Robert asked him.

"What the hell are you thinking?"

"I also did a little research on emergency airfields," Robert said ignoring his question, "The one in the report was a small emergency field just south of Kingswood in Kent. That would make sense if he left you over Leeds Castle and dropped his gear, the field would not have been far off."

"So you're saying you think I ran into T for Tommy coming back from a mission…in 1943? You want to explain to me exactly how that works?"

"Not everything can be explained and not everything in the world is known to us is it? I have a story for you, been in my family for years, believe it or not as you choose. You've heard of the invasion of Dieppe, Normandy that the allies tried in August of '42?"

"Vaguely, it was a dress rehearsal for D-Day that went badly wasn't it?"

"Very badly, August 19, 1942, allied forces came ashore at night at Dieppe and were pushed back off the beach by the next morning; over three thousand either killed, wounded or captured by the Germans. Terrible show all around. Of course once the war was over Dieppe went back to being a resort city on the French coast, once it was rebuilt that is. Which was why on August 4, 1951 my grandmother and her friend were on holiday there, two English ladies enjoying the sea air and the French cuisine. Until the night of August 4th that is, when they were awakened in the middle of the night to the sounds of a horrific battle occurring on the beach by their hotel. They looked out and saw nothing and yet for several hours they listened to explosions and gunfire and the screams of the wounded, until around 7 am the following morning when it petered out into silence. They found later that their hotel was in the very spot where the allies came ashore, and that the time they first heard the battle and the time that it stopped coincided exactly with the time that the battle had actually occurred."

"That actually happened?"

"My grandmother, and her friend, swore to it till their dying day. I never knew my grandmother to tell a lie a day in her life either."

"Did anyone else hear it?"

"Just them, that time at least. Who knows if it had happened prior to that."

"Or if anyone's seen my Wellington before," he added quietly.

"One question now," Robert said, "in keeping with coincidences and all, is your Mustang painted after one that would have been here in 1943?"

"No, it isn't, it's painted for a fighter flown by a Major Louis Norley, 334 Squadron. He was with the 4th Fighter Group stationed in Germany in 1945 so even allowing for that amazing a coincidence the original wouldn't have been anywhere near southern England in 1943, it wouldn't even arrive here from the US for another year or more. Besides," he looked down at the after action report again, "those initials just under the cockpit, those are my initials, I painted them there myself when I bought the Mustang. They wouldn't have been on the original."

"Well," Robert said, "there you have it then."

A corporate jet was spooling up across the airfield and they both fell silent watching it make its way toward the runway in the gathering dusk.

And he was suddenly very aware of the warbirds sitting in the hanger behind him, and of the men who had once flown them, not to airshows, but to life and death situations, to war.

His Mustang had come off the production line in 1945 and had never left the United States during the war; it had never seen a shot fired in anger. Some of the aircraft behind him had though; the Hawker Hurricane in there was an authentic veteran of the Battle of Britain. He'd always believed that he'd given that a lot of thought while he'd attended all those warbird shows over the years but funny thing was; at that moment it didn't seem like he'd ever given it much thought at all.

"So," Robert said finally, "what do you intend to do now?"

EPILOG

He'd rented a Mini Cooper and even that seemed huge for the road he was currently driving on. It was called East Sutton Road but it looked like nothing more than an asphalt covered bike path. If a car approached from the other direction he had absolutely no idea what he would do. He'd come down from London into Kent, through Kingswood, past the Ridge Golf & Country Club and then East Sutton Hill and onto this so called road. There were low hedges on either side of him and beyond them open fields, some of them in use to grow whatever and some just grassy meadowland.

He was looking for a right of way somewhere along this road that would offer access to Willow Wood, his final destination. He finally saw it, a small weather-beaten sign and dilapidated wooden lynch gate on either side of the road, the signs announcing the presence of a public footpath. The gate on his right was larger and looked newer and it opened onto what appeared to be a dirt access road. That at least would solve the problem of where the hell he would park the car. He stopped in the middle of the road, got out and swung the gate open then pulled the Mini onto the dirt track. He closed the gate again and started off across the fields on the foot path. In the distance was a large stand of trees that he assumed was Willow Wood.

The path petered down to a narrow dirt track and finally ended all together at the edge of a very long narrow meadow with a stand of trees on the far side that he still assumed was Willow Wood. According to Robert's research in 1943 this had been an emergency landing field for damaged aircraft flying home to England. He walked a bit into the meadow and stumbled across a concrete foundation almost completely hidden in the grass. Beside it was a small surviving patch of asphalt and lying next to that a long rotted wooden pole that still had traces of white paint on it. He thought that at one time it had probably been a flagpole. He walked the rest of the meadow but found nothing more and finally returned to where he'd begun and stood by the wooden pole on the bit of asphalt, put down by men who were most likely long dead.

It was a very peaceful spot now, a quiet open meadow bordered by trees and far from any houses or real roads. It must have been a very different place in 1943, there would have been men here, and buildings and aircraft, noise and activity. And yet he thought it had probably seemed even more peaceful for the crew of his Wellington, back safe and sound on English soil at last after a long and violent flight, and shown the way home by a helpful American pilot, who wouldn't even be born for another 22 years.

He looked down and noticed a metal cleat attached to the flagpole, about to fall off after so many years left out here in the middle of nowhere. He reached down and pulled it out of the rotten wood, keeping the screws with it. He put it in his pocket then turned and began walking slowly back toward his car.

Cruising the Mall

He was sitting on the bench out in front of Orange Julius when he saw her. She was standing in front of the windows for The Limited on the malls upper level directly across from him but he could still tell that she was hot, extremely hot, and that he'd never seen her in the mall before. He got up and headed across the nearest sky bridge that connected the both sides of the upper level. He thought she'd turn and walk away toward Sears but she didn't, she just stood there looking into The Limited through the windows. Maybe she's waiting for someone he thought; maybe she's waiting for her boyfriend.

He approached her without giving himself time to think about it because if you hung back trying to build up the nerve to approach a hot girl you just ended up never doing it. You had to dive right in before you could consider how badly it could go. The worse that could happen would be getting shot down, actually no, getting laughed at, that was the worse, getting laughed at was a killer. Just before he reached her she turned to face him and he had the distinct impression that she'd known he was coming since he'd left his bench by Orange Julius.

"Hi," he said, "I'm Ray," he'd learned that the direct approach was always the best, just say hi, because a girl who looked like her had probably heard every dumb pick-up line going.

"Susan."

"Nice to meet you Susan, haven't seen you in the mall before, do you live around here?"

"I used to, how long have you been sitting on that bench over there?"

"You noticed me."

"Yes, I noticed you, hard not to."

"I'll take that as a compliment," he replied and she looked at him a little funny so he hurried on to cover his obviously failed attempt at sounding witty, "so you don't live around here anymore?"

"Well, I do and I don't, it's a long story. So you just cruising the mall looking for girls?"

"No, not really, just hanging waiting for my friends to show up."

"So you're cruising the mall looking for girls."

"If I am or not it looks like I found one."

"Yeah, what were the odds."

"Do you want to walk down to the food court and grab something? Or we could go for a ride, my cars right outside."

"Getting into a car with you probably wouldn't be the wisest thing for me to do so how about we just walk for a while and talk."

"That sounds great, let's do that," he couldn't believe it was going to be this easy to hook up with this incredibly beautiful girl, just like that. He turned toward Sears because his car was in that direction, just in case, and they started walking slowly along the concourse. She was wearing a blue dress that seemed a bit formal for the mall but the hem stopped above her knees and she had great legs so it worked for him. And of course she caught him looking at her legs; he blushed and turned away so he didn't see her smile.

"Where do you go to school," she asked him.

"I'm a senior at Redman high, you?"

"I went there too."

"Oh no, that's not possible, I would definitely have noticed you!"

She smiled again, "I'm a little older than you Ray, I was already gone before you were a freshman."

"You don't look older than me," he replied, worried now because if she was too much older she wouldn't be interested in him at all. Older women in high school and college *never* dated younger men, he was pretty sure it was written in frigging stone somewhere.

"Thanks, I guess I'm not really. So what did you want to do after you graduated?"

"Go to college I suppose, that's what my parents are planning for me. Are you in college?"

"No."

That was good, no competition from college guys then, just every other guy on the face of the earth...

"You don't sound like you'd be interested in college," she said.

He shrugged and took in the smell of baking cookies from Aunt Annie's as they passed by it. He thought about asking her if she wanted one but she just kept walking so he did too. "I don't know," he replied, "it's a lot of money for something I'm not even sure I want to do. Why didn't you go?"

"I really didn't have the chance to; did your parents go to college?"

"Yeah, my dad has a degree in accounting for Christ's sake, and my mom has hers in education, she used to be a teacher but now she works for some big corporation in the city."

"Most parents that went to college want their kids to go too," she said, "but even parents who didn't still want their kids' to go. They just want a better life for their kids than the one they had, that's all. You can't blame them for that." She put her head down and looked at the floor as they walked.

"I don't," he replied hurriedly because she looked like she was getting sad for some reason, "my parents are all right, I just don't want to take their money if it's just going to be wasted. They work hard. Do you get along with your parents?"

"They're both great," she said, "I was lucky to have them for parents. So if you're not interested in college then what would you want to do? Just hang around here for the rest of your life?"

"Hell no, I can't wait to get out of this town, other than this damned mall there's not a thing to do around here but ride around in cars and get drunk.

"So you'd leave it you could."

"In a minute."

"Wouldn't you miss your folks, your family?"

"I could always some back and visit them, they're not going anywhere. Where did you go, you said you don't live around here anymore."

"What I said was that I do and I don't and that it was a long story which it is."

"Well maybe you can tell me about it when I buy you dinner."

She smiled and shook her head in a way that he didn't think meant *no* but in a way that meant she was amused by his offer which, when you thought about it wasn't all that much better than *no*. "Or not," he added quickly, "just a thought."

She glanced at him again the motioned to a bench they were passing and actually it was the bench in front of Orange Julius. He hadn't noticed that they'd made an entire circuit of the mall. "Why don't we sit for a bit," she said to him and they did.

"Do you have a boyfriend?" he asked her then added, "I probably should have led with that huh?"

She smiled again and shook her head, "I don't have a boyfriend, not anymore and under different circumstances I would love to have dinner with you."

"Well that's a start then," he smiled at her. "Maybe you could give me your cell number and I could call you?"

She turned on the bench to face him and study his face. "You really have no idea do you?" she said finally.

"No idea of what?"

"Nothing," she smiled and stood up, "I'm afraid I've got to go now."

"Ok," he stood up too, "I really would like to see you again so, can I have your number?"

"I'm afraid I don't have a phone at the moment but maybe I'll see you here again, I come by from time to time."

"I will be sitting right here on this bench waiting for you," he declared with a bow and she laughed. "I believe you will be," she said then turned and walked off down the mall toward Macy's.

He watched her walk away enjoying every minute of it then sat back down on his bench and eyed the mall around him, waiting for the next cute girl to wander by.

He parked behind the mall near the Sears automotive bays and they walked across the parking lot toward the main entrance that was to the left of Sears.

"Not my idea of the most fun thing to do on a Saturday afternoon Marty," Lori said, in case Marty hadn't gotten the point the first seven times she'd said it on the ride over.

"It won't take long," Marty told her, also for the seventh time. "It'll be fun."

"Somehow I doubt that." She said and Marty chose to let that statement go unchallenged which, with Lori, was usually the best option.

A side door at the main entrance was open and they used it to enter the mall. They were on the first level in a short wide corridor that led to the two story atrium at the center of the mall. They walked to the atrium and Marty led Lori up the steps to the second level.

"This place is filthy," Lori said, "and it smells."

"It won't take long," Marty said for the eighth time and led her away from Sears toward the center of the mall.

"I am not having sex with you in here if that's what you're thinking Martin, so just let that thought go right now."

"That's not why we're here," Marty replied, "Come on, don't you think this is cool?"

"It's a dirty, smelly, abandoned mall," Lori told him, "And there are probably rats, if I get bitten by a rat you're a dead man."

"There are no rats, I've been here before."

"Seriously Marty, a dead man, and it will be slow and painful."

"You could screw me to death."

"You are a pig."

He stopped walking in front of The Limited, "Right there," he told her, pointing across the mall, "see that bench in front of the Orange Julius? It's the only bench they left in the entire mall when it closed, that's where he sits."

"The ghost?" she asked, staring across at the bench.

"Yeah, the ghost, Rodney and Claire saw him, about a month ago, just sitting there looking around. They said he looked real, like anyone else, until he moved and then they realized that they could see the wall behind him, they could see it *through* him. He got up and started walking in this direction and then he was just gone, just poof and gone."

Lori was still staring at the bench, "You're full of shit," she told Marty but there wasn't much conviction in the statement.

"I swear, lots of other people have seen him too, groups of kids have seen him. And if you come here at night you almost always see him."

"I am not staying here till night," she told him and this time her statement held a lot of conviction. "You wouldn't be able to see anything anyway, there's no electricity and all the outside windows are boarded over."

"You have to come when there's a moon, then there's light coming in through the glass domes on the roof."

"I don't care; you will not see me here at night, its creepy enough here right now, fifty empty stores, dust all over everything, SALE signs in windows for sales that happened twenty years ago."

"The mall closed eleven years ago," he corrected her.

"All right, eleven years ago, it's frigging creepy is the point I'm trying to make, and the *real* point I'm trying to make is that I am not coming here at night." She was still staring at the bench across the atrium.

"Don't you want to see him, how cool would that be?"

"Who is he anyway?"

"Who was he you mean, he was a senior who got killed in a car accident on the way home from here one night, apparently this was his hang out, a lot of kids hung out here when the place was open. Anyway, he wasn't even drunk, his car slid on some ice on the road and he hit a utility pole and that was it for him. The whole place closed not long after and his ghost started showing up, before it even closed I think. I guess he's still just hanging around the mall. And sometimes there's another one, people have seen him walking the mall or sitting on that bench with a pretty blond girl in a blue dress but no one knows who she is."

Lori stared at the bench for another moment then turned away, "Well he's not there now and I'm leaving, this place gives me the creeps, and I keep smelling cookies!"

Job Security

In Boston jaywalking was a sport; sometimes it was a contact sport. Bob Grumman was a true Bostonian and would walk out into the street against the light with the best of them, daring a motorist to hit him. He did this three times on his way to the company's new building pissing off a half dozen motorists and almost getting tagged twice. During the walk he compiled in his head a list of the people he knew who he wished *would* get tagged, and soon. It was kind of a long list.

The new building was an old building on Water Street on a short block in the heart of Boston's financial district. Just across the street was a T station which would make the public transportation people in the office very happy. The building had gone up in the 30's and was constructed of pale grey granite that was now dirty pale grey granite. It had originally been built as a bank for a financial company now long gone and forgotten. It was nine stories of ornately carved stonework with iron trim and a first floor that was two stories high to facilitate the bank that had been the original tenant. It was on a corner lot so while most of the building was on Water Street the entrance was right on the corner and actually on Devonshire.

He let himself in with a key and left the tall heavy doors unlocked behind him. The first floor of the building held over 16,000 square feet of what could be utilized as retail or office space. The huge front area had 18 foot ceilings and was brightly lit by very large windows. Bob's company intended to transform the space into a fashionable lobby/reception area. Behind this was a series of smaller connecting corridors with small offices off of them. The ceilings here were much lower and the walls plain white plaster. This area ended in a large empty room that was dominated by an enormous circular vault door in the rear wall. The door measured nine feet across and hung on two hinges that were each two feet high and three feet across. Immediately inside was a set of steel grates that swung open inward, beyond those the vault itself, one huge steel room the size of a studio apartment with two small rooms off of that that had once held safe deposit boxes and counting tables. The entire thing had been built into the structure during the original construction which was the only way it really could have been done; it had walls that were four feet thick.

The hinges were rusty now and the doors surface pitted and tarnished but it didn't really matter because a work crew was coming in the morning to frame in the front of the huge door and wall the entire thing in. In a few days there would be nothing there but a blank plaster wall. Bob's company really had no use for a huge rusting bank vault.

He was there that day to do a final walkthrough and make sure that everything from the previous occupants was gone, that the entire space was bare, and that the building was move-in ready. He was also supposed to verify that the vault room was empty then secure the door and seal it so the construction guys could get started the following morning. He put his briefcase down against the wall by the vault door and began his walkthrough. Eventually he would have to do the same on each of the 8 floors above his head that contained over 36,000 square feet of office space but he could do that later, after he'd finished what he had to do down here.

He'd been there a few minutes when he heard the front door open and high heeled shoes clocking across the floor in the front space. A moment later Lacie Hendricks appeared at the end of the hallway. She shrugged out of her coat revealing a snug blue dress that was cut long enough to serve as business attire but still short enough to show off her legs. Lacie was a looker, no doubt about that, Bob was reminded of the old adage that beauty was only skin deep but ugly went to the bone. It summed up Lacie nicely.

"Good afternoon Bob," she said coolly, "why are we here?"

"I'm fine, how are you?" Bob replied.

She looked around for somewhere to drape her coat and settled for hanging it on a hook on the inside of a small office behind her.

"You called, I'm here, so I'll ask again, why are we here? Actually, why are you here, why didn't Kyle meet me here himself?"

"He's out of town, he knew I'd be here because he asked me to do a walk through and make sure everything was cleaned up and ready for the move in."

"From a potential VP candidate to handling facilities and housekeeping chores, that does sound about right."

He smiled a bit at the insult, "Kyle asked me to have you meet me here, he wanted you to look at the space and start getting some ideas as to what was going to happen where, apparently you're going to receive a job offer in the not too distant future."

She smiled, a smile that he used to find oh so enchanting and that now caused a slow burning sensation in his gut.

"Did he say that?"

"Why else would he want you to do the walk through with me, I don't think it's because he's trying to get us back together."

She laughed at that, the laugh had the same effect on him as the smile, only more so. "That's funny," she said, apparently on the chance that he'd missed the laugh. Then she gave him what he'd come to think of as the Lacie Look, going from laughing to glaring in a split second. It was amazing really. "You'd better not have said anything to him about us," she said, "or to anyone else either. I'm going to be a heavy hitter in this firm and if you want to keep your prospects in this city alive, dim as they are, you'd better remember that."

"That was always part of the deal wasn't it," Bob replied, "from the beginning. I didn't understand why then but I do now." He leaned against the wall and looked at her, remembering her naked, remembering the things she'd done with him, to him. Looking at her now, smug and victorious in the game that he'd not even been aware she'd been playing."

"Good for you Bob, I thought on the way over here that you were going to use this time alone with me to beg me to come back to you. That would have been kind of pathetic, even for you."

Ok, but while we're on the subject," he smiled amiably at her, "let's just get everything out on the table, so there are no misunderstandings going forward."

She shook her head, and flashed that smile again, "Do you really need to do that Bob? Things aren't crystal clear to you yet? I thought I spelled things out a month ago when you showed up un-announced at my damn apartment."

"I'm a little slow on the uptake," he said, "Humor me."

"Fine, I used you, this is one of the hottest brokerages in the city and I wanted in. I'd applied twice and didn't make it past the trolls in HR, apparently my resume didn't have enough of the right buzz words in it, so I needed to try something else. Kyle isn't the type of man that I could just throw myself at, he gets that all the time, I'd brand myself as just another bimbo. So I found a middle manager kind of guy, high enough up the ladder to help but not high enough to be all that sharp, a worker drone who was kind of a loser with women, and life in general for that matter, who would take the bait without being smart enough to realize that someone like me would never really be interested in someone like them. That was you Bob and you played your part admirably. To put it succinctly, you were a way for me to get in the door. But look at the up side; you did get to fuck me for a couple of months. And don't think I didn't earn this job just by having to endure that!"

"So what if I do talk, what if I tell Kyle exactly what you did."

"Do you really think he'd believe you? Look at you and look at me, come on Bob. Besides, I'm in now, I've got him around my little finger and he'll believe anything I tell him. So you try that Bob and I'll see you out of this firm within a week, I promise, no severance, no nothing. And I'll make it my life's work to see that you never get a job in the financial industry in this town again. Boston's a provincial little city Bob, everyone knows everyone. I will ruin you. So no, you just continue along in your sad little life and in twenty years or so you can retire with a pathetic little 401K and fade away, no one will even notice you're gone."

"But not here right?"

She looked at him for a moment and then smiled that little smile again and that's when he was sure, about everything. "You're smarter than you look," she said finally.

"I've been with the firm for twelve years," he said, "and I'm just going to leave now because it's what you want?"

"Do you think I'm going to come in here every day and see you here, see you looking at me, knowing what's running through what passes for you mind, thinking about what we did together, what I had to do with *you* to get here? And why put yourself through that anyway? Knowing that you'll never have anyone like me again. No, I think it would be best for both of us if you moved on now Bob, find employment elsewhere."

"We're in a recession, jobs in the financial industry are impossible to find in this city."

"You're telling me," she laughed.

"So just like that, I'm out and you're in."

"It would appear so. You still don't get it do you? I get what I want, always, and if you get in my way you'll wish you hadn't. You can't compete with me, you're so far out of your league here that it's beyond comical. So move on and no one will be the wiser and we'll all live happily ever after. Well, Kyle and I will anyway." She smiled sweetly at him.

"So no one knows, no one at all, about us."

"Good God no, and they never will...will they Bob."

"No," he agreed, they never will. "You've got it all figured out, you played me like a pro."

"I'll take that as a compliment. And now that our business is concluded let's get on with this, I have things to do and you really do bore me, you always have." She stood away from the wall and started walking toward the front room.

He fell in walking behind her, admiring the view of her rear end. "Just one thing you didn't really figure into your plan though Lacie," he said while reaching into his pocket.

"And what's that *Bob*," she didn't turn to look at him.

"When you push people too far, they sometimes push back," he drew the stun gun from his pocket, flicked the switch to activate it and pressed the business end against the back of her neck. She let out what he could only describe as a shriek and went down in a heap. He let her have it a second time because really, you just never could trust Lacie at all. She flopped around on the floor for a bit and then went limp. He rolled her onto her back and stretched her out straight, he hesitated for a moment then reached down and pulled her dress up around her waist and yup, her bladder had emptied leaving a puddle on the floor under her butt. It was kind of disgusting and he wondered what he had ever seen in her in the first place. He pulled her dress back down then pulled her arms up over her head, grabbed her by both wrists and began pulling her across the cement floor. She was dead weight and a lot heavier than she looked. He had to stop when he got to the vault door to lift her up and over the raised sill and then again to swing open the grates inside the vault. It was a bit easier then, the floor inside the vault was linoleum that had been polished smooth by decades of foot traffic.

Almost in the center of the vault were two round steel support columns roughly six inches in diameter. They were anchored into the floor and the ceiling. He propped her up against the one deepest into the vault in a sitting position. She started to stir and moan so he hit her with the stun gun again which caused her to shriek again and topple over on her side which he had to admit to himself was kind of comical.

He sat her back up against the column and drew her arms back around it, bringing her hands together. He reached back into his coat pocket, brought out a set of steel handcuffs and snapped them on her wrists, not too tight but tight enough that there was no way she was getting out of them, ever.

He straightened her legs out and considered binding her ankles with flex cuffs, he'd brought some with him but then said the hell with it, she wasn't going anywhere with those cuffs on unless she ripped her own hands off. One of her high heel shoes had come off with that last jolt so he put it back on her foot then stood up and looked down at her. She was moaning and gurgling and coming around so he leaned against the second column and waited.

She straightened up a bit, shook her head to clear it and wacked her skull on the steel column which served to wake her up more quickly. She looked around the vault, tried to stand up and became aware of the handcuffs keeping her arms behind her. She sat with her head down, hair hanging in her face for a moment, then slowly looked up at Bob.

"Take these off of me," she said to him in a tone that told the world she would brook no argument concerning the request, or any other request.

"Sorry," Bob said, "I wish I could but I can't. Those handcuffs are now a permanent addition to your jewelry collection, and I really do mean permanent."

She flicked her head back to get the hair out of her face, careful not to hit the column again and glared at him, "So what's the deal here Bob, you going to rape me? Show me whose boss, is that it?"

"You should be that lucky Lacie...lucky Lacie, that's funny isn't it."

"You've lost your fucking mind. Do you have any idea what I will do to you when I get out of here? Forget about just losing your job, you're going to fucking jail you limp dicked little puke. And they're going to love you there; you think I fucked you over, wait until the guys in Cedar Junction get their hands on you. NOW TAKE THESE THINGS OFF MY FUCKING WRISTS!"

"There's just one small problem with your plans for my future Lacie," he paused to look at her for a moment, making her wait for it. "You're not getting out of here, not ever. Five years from now, on your birthday, when you turn thirty-four, you're going to be sitting right where you're sitting now. And ten years from now when the company probably leaves this building in search of even more office space, there you're still going be, just sitting...right...where...you ...are...now. And one hundred years from now, when they finally tear this building down they may find you, what's left of you anyway, and wonder wow, who in the hell could that be? And what is she doing here? Of course they may not, this vault may just be pulverized and hauled away, you with it. But at least you'll be in sunlight again, after a century of darkness, not that you'll know it."

She sat there breathing hard, her hair in her face, staring at him. "I'll just wait till morning and scream my head off you asshole."

"Soundproof vault," he replied with a little shrug as if to say it's really a shame but there it is. "One of my, how did you put it, menial tasks today, is to check the vault one final time, close and secure the door and put seals on it so the workmen tomorrow know it's been checked and they're clear to wall it in. You won't hear them and they won't hear you. No, I'm afraid this is where you're going to face eternity sweetheart so I'd try to get comfortable if I were you, as comfortable as you can get wearing urine soaked panties that is."

"How long have you been planning this?" she hissed at him.

"Yeah, that's you Lacie, forget about anything else, the most important thing you need to know right now is how long I've been getting the best of you."

"What do you want?"

"I'm afraid I don't understand the question."

"It's a simple question Bob, do you want me to admit that you beat me, you're smarter than me? Ok, fine, you're a fucking genius. Do you want me to forget about you're leaving the company? Fine, done, I'll even tell Kyle that you're an amazing worker and should be promoted. With me in your corner you can go far here, you know that's true."

"And after I let you out you'd just forget all this and be my best work buddy, do you honestly expect me to buy that? Really?"

"I would put it in writing."

He laughed at that, "Well, why didn't you say so! And I would believe you because you've been so up front with me until now. It's obvious that you've had my best interests at heart all along."

"Look," she took a ragged breath and Bob realized that she was fighting panic now, just the beginning of it maybe, but that would change. "I took a shot and you got the best of me, I'm able to accept that and move on, business is business. I'm an adult, I can admit that you've won and move on from there."

He just looked at her and shook his head, and he realized that the time was passing and he was going to have to wrap this up soon. "Not buying it Lacie but nice try, two faced lying bitch right to the end and as much as I'd like to continue along this line because it's actually kind of nice to see you like this I'm afraid I still have to perform the remainder of my "menial" duties and check the rest of the building so, going to have to wrap this thing up sweetheart."

"I'll be your girlfriend again, I will, I'll do anything you want, I'll let you do that thing to me that you wanted to do when we went down the cape together, do you remember? You can do that to me every night."

"I'm doing it to you right now," Bob replied and straightened up from the wall. "Got to go."

"WHAT DO YOU WANT!" she screamed at him, spittle flying from her mouth.

"I would think that would be obvious," he replied, "I want you to die a slow and horrible death in this vault." He turned to leave.

"Kyle will be looking for me," she said, breathing hard, "He'll wonder where I went and he'll turn the world upside down looking for me."

He laughed again, "Are you serious? Kyle will wonder for a while then he'll just assume that you're like every other flighty bimbo that he's known over the years and wandered off to Vegas or something. Believe me, he won't miss you for long, he'll find another just like you within a month's time tops, probably less."

"He asked me to come here tonight, he's going to hire me, he won't just let that go," she cried at him.

"I made that up to get you here," he said gleefully, "I can't believe you haven't gotten that yet. He didn't ask you to be here I did, for this," he swept his hand around the vault. "And thanks to your insistence that we tell no one about our relationship not a single person is going to even ask me if I know where you went."

"You can't just do this; you can't just kill someone like this! You're going to get caught and then you'll spend the rest of your life in jail. You don't want that, I know you don't!"

"Lacie, I know you, obviously a hell of a lot better than you know me. You have no friends, not a single one. You have no family either, at least none that you didn't blow off years ago. There's no one out there who's going to miss you, no one who's going to beat the bushes looking for you, no one. You live in a furnished apartment that you rent by the month; you don't even own a car for Christ's sake. You'll vanish like you were never even here and there's just no one who's going to notice for very long."

"You don't know shit about me, I played you like the loser that you are, and you fell for it all the way. You're too fucking stupid to pull this off."

"Like Larry Hurley, stupid like him you mean?"

She stared at him for a moment, she'd caught her breath again and he could see the wheels turning, kind of like a wild animal trying to get out of a trap. "I don't know who you're talking about," she replied.

"Oh sure you do, good old Larry, worked at that investment firm in Providence, I forget the name, what was it again Lacie?"

"I…don't…know…what…you're…talking…about!"

"You worked there too right? Larry got you in after you'd let him ride you for a while, sound familiar? Does to me. But after you were in poor Larry had to go right? So you arranged for an anonymous call to his wife, and a little funny record keeping in his department to make it look like he was skimming, am I close Lacie? Guess Larry didn't take the hint and quit when you threatened him just like you thought I would huh? I'm not married so I assume if I'd hung around I'd only be answering some touchy questions about diverted funds right?

She had her head down, her hair hanging down on both sides of her face, she didn't say anything.

"Larry went out a hotel window after his wife threw him out, did you know that Lacie? Probably not, I doubt you took the time to keep tabs after he was fired."

"He was a big boy," she whispered into her lap, "He knew what he was doing, I didn't force him to cheat on his wife."

"No, you just enticed him into doing it, geeky guy like that, woman like you? And how about those stray account documents that found their way into his desk and got him fired, he know what he was doing there too?"

"I don't know anything about that," she replied.

"You're a lying bitch. Larry's just the one I found out about, who knows how many more there were. How many more where there Lacie? Were there a lot, I'm guessing there where a lot, what number am I, or do you even remember at this point?"

"Fuck you," she whispered.

"Yeah, that's about what I thought. And what happened with the job? The one that cost poor old Larry his life, why aren't you still there, clawing your way up the corporate ladder? Didn't work out huh? They finally figure out what you really are? That why you're here now Lacie?" She still had her head down and she didn't answer.

He straightened up away from the wall again and picked up his brief case. He reached inside and took out a small standup LED light. "I bought this at a sporting goods store, it wasn't cheap by the way," he told her. "It's supposed to last in continuous use for at least two weeks, maybe longer but I'm pretty sure even the two weeks is a lot longer than you're going to need it," he turned the little light on and put it on the floor a half dozen feet away from her, "Thought you'd appreciate it seeing that it's going to be very dark in here once I shut that door."

"You won't really be able to do this," she said, raising her head to look at him, "you're not this kind of person, this will haunt you and by tomorrow you'll be screaming for them to let me out of here."

"You keep telling yourself that," he replied and began going through her purse. He found her cell phone, dropped it on the floor and crushed hit under his heel then he tossed the purse across the room. "Tell you what," he said and walked around behind her. He reached down and took her wrist watch off then came back around to face her. He propped the watch up against the base of the LED light so she could see it. "So you can keep track," he told her, "It's 2:41 pm now, the builders will be here tomorrow at 8:00 am to start framing in the wall covering the vault, you may even hear a little hammering or something though I doubt it, as I said earlier, this place is pretty much sound proof, but you can keep track on your watch, 8:00 am tomorrow morning, and then 9:00 am and then 10:00 am, keep telling yourself that I'll have a change of heart, that that vault door will swing open again, until it's 8 pm tomorrow night and you're still here, and then 8 am the following day, the wall should be done by then, and you're still here...after that I don't know, this vault may be air tight too but even if it is it's a big space so you probably won't have time to suffocate, but no food, no water," he just shook his head and shrugged, "But I guess you'll find out won't you."

"You'll come back," she said to him, "you don't have it in you."

"We'll see won't we, I really have to be going now, finish those menial tasks you mentioned earlier, I'll leave you to it." He started toward the door.

"You'll come back," she repeated, "You're just trying to scare me, that's all."

He continued on and just before he left the vault she said it again, almost to herself; "you'll come back, you don't have it in you, you're just trying to scare me."

He went around to the outside of the huge vault door and began to push. It was precisely balanced on its huge hinges to allow one person to operate it, and it had been opened not long ago for inspection of the vault but now it wouldn't budge and his heart leaped up into his throat. He leaned into it and really pushed...nothing, and now it felt like he had a lead ball in his gut. He straightened up and stood there for a minute trying to calm down. Lacie wasn't making a sound and he knew she was waiting.

He leaned into the door again and instead of shoving at it just applied steady pressure and it finally began to move. Once he had it going it swung pretty easily and he almost had it shut when he suddenly stopped. He heard a sob from inside the vault but still she didn't speak, waiting.

He left the vault door, walked over to the little office on the far side of the room and retrieved her coat from the hook where she'd hung it earlier. He returned to the vault and squeezed through what was now a very narrow opening.

"I knew it," Lacie said, "so you scared the shit out of me, good for you, you're a big man. Now let me out."

He walked up to her without speaking and tossed the coat at her feet. It landed close enough that she may just be able to hook it with her foot, if she happened to get cold later on. He turned and headed back for the entrance.

"LET MY OUT OF HERE!" she screamed and he kept walking.

He got to the narrow gap and began to squeeze through it; the sun was slanting in from one of the basement windows and glinting off of the steel edge of the door.

"THIS IS NOT HAPPENING!" she screamed after him, "YOU ARE NOT DOING THIS TO ME! THIS IS INSANE!"

He got on the outside and braced himself against the door again.

"YOU ARE NOT DOING THIS TO M—"

He pushed and the door seated into its frame with a loud clunk. There was a wheel at the center of the door that moved the four large cams into brackets set into the door frame. He moved to it and spun it until they were in place then he turned his attention to the combination dial in the door. It was the size of a dinner plate and it had a steel wedge jammed into its edge to keep it from turning because the last person who'd known the combination to the vault probably died twenty years ago. He took out a pocket knife and worked the wedge back and forth until it came free. He put it in his pocket then spun the dial several times. Finally he took two adhesive seals from his bag; he put one over the combination dial and the other along the seam of the door by one of the locking cams. He managed to finish up the rest of his tasks at the building in less than an hour and was home in time for an early dinner.

Bob Grumman was a very happy man. He'd just received his second promotion in the fourteen and a half years he'd been with the company. True it wasn't a huge promotion and he was still working in facilities management but it was a promotion, and more money, a little more anyway. He left his tiny office on the second floor and went down to the mailroom to drop something off before leaving for the weekend. The mail room was at the rear of the first floor; he stood and chatted with the mailroom manager for a few minutes about their plans for the weekend before braving the crowded sidewalks outside the building. He never once glanced at the plain white wall to his right, the one with the vault door behind it.

Riding the Train; Part One

The 10:20 to Boston

One

Jonathan Harkness measured his life by small events; paying his bills at the end of another month, winterizing his little house in the fall, doing his tax return every March, mowing the lawn for the first time in the spring and the final time in the fall, small events that marked the passing of the years and the passing of his life.

Jonathan Harkness measured his life by small events...and yearned deep in his soul for just one really big one...

He kept his yard nice partly because of his neighbors but mostly because it gave him something to do on the weekends. His co-workers spent all week yearning for Friday but for him weekends were just two long lonely days full of hours that had to be filled...that had to be survived. Jonathan much preferred being at work, around other people, socializing and interacting.

He was fairly sure that he was well thought of at work, he joked with his co-workers every day, shared stories, theirs probably true, his not, and he always participated in whatever pool or sports lottery making the rounds. He had actually started watching sports at home so he would be able to participate in the conversations about sports at work and sound knowledgeable. Besides, it gave him something more to do at home that he didn't look at as just killing time; he looked at it as a kind of social homework that helped him fit in with the people at work. He was very diligent about it. He had realized early on that there simply wasn't enough time to keep up with all the professional sports teams in his city and he'd also noted that others seemed to have certain sports that they preferred so, after much study and contemplation he'd settled on football (professional, not college) and hockey as his sports of choice. He'd picked football because it was on over the weekends and helped to pass the time and Hockey because the games were on at night which served the same purpose. He'd also noted that these two sports seemed to generate the most betting pools and fantasy leagues at work.

He had also invented a complex and interesting life for himself outside of work so that he would fit in there too. When others in the office were talking about their vacations or what they did over the weekend he always had stories to share, things he'd done, places he'd gone, time spent with family and friends he didn't have. He kept a little journal of notes in his desk at home to keep track of this fantasy life so he could keep everything straight. He didn't fail to notice though that while his co-workers were happy to tell him about their weekend adventures they never thought to invite him along on any of them. It never occurred to him that his rich, full, and completely invented home life might be the reason why. And vacations were the worst, he took two weeks off a year at different times because that's what everyone else did and for those weeks he wandered around his house trying to come up with projects to take up the time, and stories to tell when he returned to work. He had tried years ago to actually go places on his vacations but he really had few for real interests and he disliked staying in hotels and being around strangers so after several attempts he'd resigned himself to two weeks a year of crushing loneliness and boredom. How he dreaded vacations.

So the years slipped past and as he slid quietly and oh so quickly into his fifties he began to accept that anything other than what he had just wasn't in his cards. A line from an old rock and roll song had begun running through his mind at odd times; "His life had passed him by like a warm summer day".

That lyric was running through his mind on the warm summer day that found him standing on the train platform in South Weymouth waiting for the 10:20 am train to Boston. He normally caught the 8:05 train to Boston but he'd had a doctor's appointment that morning; yearly physical, no problems there, so he was going into work late. And since it was only 9:50 he was the sole occupant of the platform with a silent parking lot full of cars baking in the sun behind him.

So he was standing there alone, the line from the rock and roll song running through his head and he thinking about the fact that his physical was fine and he would probably live well into old age and end up in a nursing home. One of those people no one ever came to visit who sat all day watching daytime talk shows waiting to die. He was thinking these uplifting thoughts when a train appeared far down the line to his right, heading northbound toward the station. As it got closer the barriers at the crossing by the entrance to the parking lot swung down, the lights began flashing, and the train sounded its whistle in warning. There was no train scheduled until the 10:20 so this must be an out of service train heading into the city. Except that when it reached the platform on which Jonathan was standing it slowed to a stop and the doors slid open. He noticed that it was empty, except for the conductor who stepped out onto the platform right in front of him.

"Good morning Mr. Harkness," he said.

"Good morning, do we know each other?"

"We do not, or rather, you do not know me but I do know you. I trust you haven't been waiting long."

"No, is this the 10:20? If it is you're pretty well ahead of schedule, I think a southbound train is going to be coming through here soon."

"We run by no set schedule at all so we are most assuredly not the 10:20. Today we are here to see you."

"To see me," he repeated stupidly.

"Indeed."

"Well...why?"

"Because you are just the type of fellow we're looking for, you have so much potential Mr. Harkness, and yet you have realized none of it. Your life is empty and without any real significance, you spend each day, each month, each year, just marking time waiting for...what? What are you waiting for Mr. Harkness?"

"I don't know."

"Ah, you don't know, a good answer sir, an honest answer from an honest man. May I suggest sir that this is what you've been waiting for, this very train that now sits before you?"

"I don't know, this isn't an ordinary train is it? Do you go into the city?"

"That depends on which city you are speaking of Mr. Harkness, in what time and in what place, and what you are willing to accept as ordinary. We do indeed go to cities and towns and everywhere else you can imagine. We will go to wherever it is that you wish to go so that you may realize that potential that lies dormant within you."

"I'm not sure I understand what you're talking about."

"Of course you don't, this is an entirely new concept for you. I would be dubious of any statement made by you to me claiming that you *did* understand what I was talking about. I would immediately suspect that you were playing me false or trying to look more intelligent than you felt. So allow me to explain, but quickly because while we hold to no schedule we cannot remain here for very long. As you say, a southbound train will be coming through shortly, the Kingston train I believe."

"Yes, it's usually almost empty this time of day."

"Every train that comes through here is always almost empty," the Conductor replied, "Even the full ones."

"Yeah...I'm not sure what that means exactly."

"Mr. Harkness, I think you have likely come to the conclusion that most of the people who ride these trains, almost all of them in fact, are sheep. They are sheep because they spend their days in meaningless tasks with meaningless results achieving nothing save the burning of time. In point of fact I *know* you yourself have come to this conclusion for had you not we, you and I, would not be speaking at all and this train would not have pulled into this station."

"I do that myself," Harkness admitted, "That's pretty much how I spend my life."

"Ah yes, we come to it now don't we sir. We have arrived at the crux of that matter at last. Your honesty is appreciated."

"I wish it were different."

"Of course you do, why would you not. Although all those other people I spoke of, they do not wish it were different, not at all, they like things just the way they are and they strive to keep them just so. They are the people that cut you off in traffic aren't they Mr. Harkness. They are the people who refuse to move to give you free passage whilst exiting the train, the people who hold up the queue at the grocery store talking on their phones instead of taking care of their business, aren't they Mr. Harkness! The fact that you are not *them* is the very reason that we've stopped here today and you and I are engaging in this delightful conversation. We are here to change your life for you Mr. Harkness, change it in ways that you can only imagine. Change it to whatever your heart desires, to whatever you would like to see and do and experience. You need simply to step onto this conveyance and your journey will begin"

He leaned around the conductor and looked at the train again. "Why isn't there anyone else on the train?" he asked the conductor.

"Sheep are not allowed to ride this train sir! And most people are sheep, as you and I have just so recently discussed and come to agreement on. That is why there are so very few people who ride this train. This train is only available to a select group of chosen riders, and you my good man have been chosen!"

"Why?"

"Why not?

"Well, I've never done anything of note for one thing, I'm just someone who goes to work and then home again. I've never done anything heroic or daring or even mildly exciting. I'm just another guy riding the train every day, day after day after day. That's all I am."

"Is that all you wish to be?"

"No,"

"Then board the train and let us be off sir!"

He hesitated for a moment, looking into the train again. "What's it going to cost me," he asked the conductor.

"Have you a monthly rail pass in your possession?"

"I do."

"That is all we need!" the Conductor cried happily."

"And nothing else," Harkness asked.

"What did you have in mind?"

"Oh I don't know, my soul maybe."

The Conductor laughed at that, "I suspect you watch too much bad television Mr. Harkness," he replied, "followed up by too many hastily written works of cheap fiction."

"So then not my soul."

"Not that I'm aware of. But say that were the cost of the ride, just say that, would it not still be worth it? To go anywhere, be anything, achieve great things and lead a life full of wonder and adventure. To have your heart's desire in all things! To leave behind the mind numbing daily exercise that you so laughingly call your life. I mean, you're not using your soul are you? Have you ever even seen it? What has it ever done for you?"

"I knew it," Harkness exclaimed, "I knew it was too good to be true and I knew that you were the Devil!"

"Actually my name is Claude, Mr. Harkness and I must apologize, I'm afraid I was just having you on for a moment there."

"So you're not the Devil, you swear."

"I swear my name is Claude."

"Well all right then," Harkness stopped, not sure where to go from there.

Far off to his left he heard the bellow of a train whistle, then again a moment later and closer than the first one.

"Ah, I'm afraid that is the Kingston train," the Conductor said. "We must be moving on Mr. Harkness, and you must decide. I do so hate to rush you but," he gestured up the tracks toward the sound of the whistle, "as you see, we must be off. Will you be accompanying us on our momentous journey today?"

"I'm not sure," Harkness said, "I have to think about it."

"We may not be back this way again sir, I must warn you of that. This may be your only chance to board this train."

"I have to think about it," he repeated and stepped back, "That's all."

"Very well sir," the Conductor stepped back aboard the train and it moved slowly away from the platform in the direction it had come from. The Conductor tipped his conductor hat then the door slid closed.

He stepped back again and sat down heavily on a station bench. A moment later the Kingston train pulled up to the platform. No one got off.

Two

He thought about the train a lot, he thought about it while he was working, and while he was sharing made up stories about his made up family with his co-workers, and while he was trying to sleep in his tidy little house. He wished there was someone he could talk to about it, to see what they thought, but of course there was no one. So he thought about it some more.

In the end he came to the conclusion that there wasn't much for him to think about. He didn't know anything other than the train shouldn't have been there, that it wasn't a practical joke, and that the Conductor probably wasn't the Devil because he was pretty sure he'd read somewhere that, if asked directly if he was the Devil the Devil had to tell the truth. And in the end he came to the conclusion that it may not really matter all that much who the Conductor was if what he was saying was true. Because wasn't this what he had been waiting for all of his life? The big thing that would wipe away all the endless years of little things, the thing that would make his life mean something? And when the chance to do what he'd always dreamed of doing was right there in front of him what had he done? He had stepped back, that's what he'd done!

And that was why the following day he was back standing on the station platform an hour before the 10:20 to Boston was due. Except that the platform wasn't quite deserted this time because there was a woman there, standing a good distance down to his left. She was wearing casual clothing, not what one would wear if one were waiting for the train into the city to go to work. She had a suitcase resting next to her as well, not a particularly large suitcase, one that would probably qualify as carry-on where she getting on an airliner.

He thought about just leaving because he thought that the special train showing up again was a long shot even if he was there alone and he wasn't. But then he thought he'd just wait because if it didn't come he still had to go to work didn't he. He looked at the woman again and she was looking at him. She nodded to him then turned her head to look out across the tracks again. It didn't occur to him to go and speak to her.

He had only been there a few moments, he and the woman that is, when he heard a very faint train whistle off to the south. He kept looking down the tracks in that direction, they ran straight as an arrow for over a mile before a curve took them out of sight. A tiny light appeared at that curve and came toward him on the tracks and a moment later he saw the train behind it. He realized that for the first few seconds he'd been able to see the light there hadn't been anything behind it, nothing at all, but he didn't think about that because what would be the point really.

The train drew closer to him, and the woman, and he thought; it will just be the Boston train running early, or an express that will blast right past them in a rush of hot air and noise and leave them standing there on the platform. And for a moment he almost wished that was what would happen.

But that didn't happen, the train slowed and came to a stop at the platform and it was the same train and the same conductor got off right in front of him and smiled. Movement to his left caught his attention and he turned in time to see the woman get onto the train. She had taken the suitcase with her.

"Good morning Mr. Harkness," the Conductor said, "So nice to see you again."

"That woman got on the train," he said.

"Yes indeed she did. That is Mrs. Deakins. Like you she has been here before and like you she has decided to ride the train. A sad story I'm afraid, husband's run off with a younger woman, she's suffering from various rather serious physical ailments, Mrs. Deakins, not the younger woman. Will you be joining her Mr. Harkness?"

"I'm not totally sure yet," Harkness said, "I wanted to ask you a few more questions first."

"Of course sir but I must warn you, the Kingston train is due before too long as you well know which does limit our time together. I must also remind you that this is the second time you have had the opportunity to ride the train and warn you that it is an opportunity that will likely not be offered a third time."

"If you can do anything you want why do you have to leave before the Kingston train comes through?" What difference does it make?"

The Conductor just smiled indulgently at him. "You said you have further questions for me Mr. Harkness."

"Yes, I do. So, I've heard, or read somewhere, I don't remember, that if you ask the Devil directly if he is the Devil he has to tell the truth, is that true?"

"You seemed obsessed with my being the Devil Mr. Harkness; do you have a dark twisted side that would like for this to be true? If that's the case we would have to take it into consideration."

"No, of course not, I'm a perfectly normal person."

"If that were true this train would not be here before you as it is, for the second time."

"You don't think I'm normal?"

"Do you? If you were normal you would be one of the sheep that we've previously spoken of wouldn't you? While you've lived that life for nigh on twenty years now Mr. Harkness I do not believe that is your true self. If it were you would not have returned here hoping for another opportunity to board this train."

"I have often felt that there was something big waiting for me, that this wasn't all there was, that's true."

"There you have it!" the Conductor clapped his hands together with a smile. "Shall we embark and thus be on our way then? Mrs. Deakins is waiting after all."

"I'm still not sure," Harkness said and a hint of a whine came into his voice and he heard it and hated himself for it.

"Time grows short Mr. Harkness," the Conductor said curtly, the smile gone. "And I grow weary of your indecision. This is an offer that may well not be repeated, that you will never have again, an offer that is put before very few of your fellow man. Can you say no? Can you go back to your drab, empty life when you have been offered the world? When it is right here, right now, within your grasp simply by your taking five steps forward? Will you be able to live with that decision for the next thirty-one year's sir? Mrs. Deakins knew well the answer to that question and she now awaits us within the train, about to embark on a journey that neither she nor you can even begin to imagine."

He stood there for a long moment, then took one step forward, then slowly moved his right foot back again and stepped away from the train.

"Very well Mr. Harkness," the Conductor said tightly, "In the days to come, as you gaze ahead at the long desolate plain that represents the years of your life yet to live please recall this moment clearly sir, so that you may ponder your decision and lament." The Conductor stepped back onto the train and the door slid closed. A moment later it was gone, back the way it had come.

Three

Jonathan Harkness measured his life by small events, paying his bills at the end of another month, winterizing his little house in the fall, doing his tax return every spring, small events that marked the passing of the years and the passing of his life. But Jonathan Harkness didn't yearn for bigger things, not any longer he didn't. And if the Conductor could be taken at his word, and Mr. Harkness fully believed that he could, he had thirty-one years left to spend not yearning for bigger things.

There was a new betting pool at work the following week and he showed his usual enthusiasm for it and bought in with a vengeance. After all he was just one of the guys. And when another one of the guys suggested gathering at a local pub after work to watch the game and maybe make a few side bets he did something he'd never done before and asked if he could tag along and they all said that was just fine because after all, he was just one of the guys.

He kept riding the train every day too, the nice normal overcrowded 8:05 to Boston and that was fine too. And once in a while he'd think about Mrs. Deakins and wonder where she was and what she was doing, if she was anywhere at all. He had no regrets really; he was good with his choice. The Conductor had never really answered his question.

THE BOAT HOUSES

One

Italy's Bay of Naples is one of the most naturally beautiful places on earth. The Romans knew it and built their vacation villas along its shore over two thousand years ago. Unfortunately the modern city of Naples now occupies that shore and is a classic example of too much of a good thing; it's one of the most crowded cities in Italy, probably in all of Europe. The natural beauty of the hills and the harbor are still there, but they're much harder to see and appreciate among the urban sprawl.

Every morning as archeologist Stahley Kane left her apartment and headed out to work through the city she'd wish she could have seen the bay in A.D. 79 when the cities of Pompeii and Erculano perched along the shore, melding with the natural beauty of the bay instead of smothering it. Before Vesuvius buried both cities under forty feet of ash.

Stahley retrieved her Vespa from her buildings courtyard and launched herself onto the insanity of Naples streets. Attempting to get anywhere in the city driving a car was a fool's errand; a scooter was a much more practical, if riskier alternative. Her building was just a mile from her current dig and even in the cities perpetual traffic jam it was a short commute. She had pulled her long auburn hair back into a ponytail and was wearing shorts and a sleeveless shirt in homage to the heat. She garnered any number of appreciative glances from male pedestrians as she wove in and out of traffic, something she either didn't notice or chose to ignore.

Her destination was what they all called The Boat Houses. In A.D. 79, before Vesuvius, a city called Herculaneum had perched here along the shore of the bay. It had died the same day as Pompeii and forever since had been that cities lesser known step child. The Boat Houses had been situated along the bay shore of Herculaneum though they were now almost a mile inland from the modern harbor. Herculaneum had been her first archeological dig after she'd finished graduate school six years earlier and she'd returned here almost every digging season since, she was fascinated by it. Pompeii, with its famous plaster castes of victims frozen for all time in their death throws and it's long wide open streets got almost all the press and most of the tourists but in truth Herculaneum was in a much better state of preservation and had been a richer town than Pompeii so it boasted amazing mosaics and beautiful villas. Unfortunately, it differed from Pompeii in another respect as well, most of the town was beyond reach because the Romans had built directly on top of the deeply buried ruins and now Naples sprawled over everything. But the ancient shoreline, and the Boat Houses, were accessible as were other small parts of the town and that's all Stahley cared about, there was enough work here to last her lifetime. Sometimes she thought she was more in sync with the ancient inhabitants of Herculaneum, what she called "The Boat House People", than she was with the people that were around her every day.

She reached her destination and parked the Vespa at the edge of the huge pit that marked the boundary of the dig. The ancient shoreline and the Boat Houses were almost forty feet below modern ground level and had had to be excavated. An excavation that had been going on for more than a hundred years now. The bottom of that pit had been Stahley's whole world for five years now. She took the stairs down to the bottom and walked along what had been the shoreline of the bay two thousand years before. Brian Carter was already on site and on his hands and knees working at something in the ground. He looked up when her shadow fell across him.

"It's going to be hot as hell today," he said in greeting.

"Good morning," Stahley replied, "are we having a bad day already?"

"I'm not coming back this early in the fall next year," he said, "it's like an oven down here."

"It beats digging for hominid bones in Tanzania though doesn't it?" She squatted down beside him.

He sat back on his haunches and shook his head, "Jesus wasn't that a frigging nightmare! And not just the heat, there were bugs there big enough to ride."

"And let us not forget the Gobi," Stahley continued, "or that Roman outpost in Libya, heat and terrorists all at the same time."

"Ok, ok," Brian said, smiling a bit, "I get the point, there are worse places and we've been to a lot of them. But you have to admit that it's damn hot, and there's just no breeze down here."

"Brian, you are in one of the most beautiful resort areas in Europe, people from back home pay big money just to come here for a week. And you're working one of the most incredible digs on earth."

"So what's your point?"

"My point is suck it up and stop bitching," she leaned forward and looked at what he'd been working on.

"I think he's a soldier," Brian told her, "he was wearing a short sword and this right here," he pointed at the dirt, "looks like armor. It's weird though because we're at least fifteen or twenty feet out into the bay here."

"Maybe he was trying to get a boat launched," Stahley said, "they found one guy about ten years ago, a fisherman judging by the wear patterns on his bones, still holding onto an oar. That was just over there," she gestured back toward the remains of the boat houses. "And before that someone found an intact boat with three guys hiding underneath it, that was maybe a dozen feet that way," she gestured again. One of the amazing things about Pompeii and Herculaneum was that the archeological digs at both had been going on for decades, over a century in fact. And there were still new things being found all the time. Even the Pompeii dig, which wasn't restricted by having a city built atop it, had still only uncovered a third of the city.

"Yeah, probably," Brian said, "but this guy would have had to have been chest deep in the bay, wearing armor, not a smart move on his part."

"Maybe he was already in the boat and fell out, or jumped out" Stahley suggested. "They were all about to get flash fried Brian, what would you have done?" She stood up and arched her back. "I'm going to pick up again on the guy at the edge of the pit," she said "All I've got so far is feet and lower legs but it looks like a good one."

She turned and started up the "beach" toward her own dig and she was sure that Brian was watching her walk away. She considered putting a little sway into her hips just to irk him but she didn't. She was an attractive young woman, something she was aware of but seldom thought about. She was more than accustomed to men looking at her. Still, she and Brian had worked together for years and he knew Chris as well as he knew her, you would think he'd have seen everything he needed to see by now.

There had only been a dozen or so bodies found in Herculaneum since excavations had begun over a century ago. Archeologists had once taken this as a sign that most of the residents of the town had escaped the eruption of Vesuvius. That had been a safe assumption since the eruption had been going on for twelve hours or more before this area had been touched at all. Pompeii had borne the brunt of the first day's activities from the volcano. Unfortunately, for those early archeologists anyway, while it had been a safe assumption, it had also been wrong.

While digging a drainage ditch one day a local resident had found the boathouses that had been buried for a millennia, that had, at the time of the eruption been located on the bay shore. When those boathouses were excavated it was discovered why there had been so few bodies in the town. On the first day of the eruption many of the people living in Herculaneum had tried to flee along the road to Misenum but several thousand had also come here, to the shoreline, apparently hoping for a rescue from the sea that never came. This was where they died.

Just after midnight on the beginning of the second and final day of the eruption the cloud shooting skyward from Vesuvius became too heavy to support itself and began to collapse. The result was a pyroclastic flow that cascaded down the mountain side like a tsunami. It was made up of molten rock and ash five times hotter than steam and it was moving at sixty miles an hour. It reached Herculaneum in less than four minutes. No one from the town was ever seen alive again.

The people on the beach knew what was coming; they could probably see it coming because the cloud would have been glowing with roiling fire and smoke. By that time they had two or maybe three minutes to live and all that was really left to them was to decide where they were going to die. Most crowded into the boat house stalls in an attempt to fine some sort of cover, still trying to live. Others simply stood on the beach and watched the cloud come toward them. They all died together in a split second, flash fried, their bodies turning to carbon, their bones distorted from the incredible heat and the force of the blast. It happened so fast that they would not have had the time to feel anything; their nerve endings were gone long before a single pain impulse could have reached their brains.

And here they had lain for almost two thousand years, their bones forever frozen in that final terrible moment that happened just after midnight on August 25, AD79. Until someone like her came along to uncover them and give them life again.

She reached her own excavation, almost at the base of the pit wall and very close to where the edge of the bay would have been on that day. She sat down next to it and went to work. As she worked the sounds of the city all around them drifted down into the dig, traffic sounds, radios, people on cell phones, the occasional aircraft overhead. It had always struck her as a bit eerie; the sounds from the modern city above while she worked forty feet below at what once had been ground level, uncovering thousands of residents of the very same city who had died on that spot in a split second. But then after an hour or so in the pit she usually felt closer to the Romans she was freeing from the ground than she did to the people going about their daily lives up above her.

Most of the areas around the boat houses had been excavated over the years but as they kept expanding the dig outward from the structures they kept finding new bodies. Judging by the size of his feet and legs Stahley's latest find appeared to be a male and he'd been facing the approaching surge cloud when he'd died. She worked upward on the legs, freeing them from the earth. The volcanic deposits in the area were fairly soft and easy to manipulate so the work went quickly. Nothing like chipping dinosaur bones out of solid rock. Also, the entire area was now roughly fourteen feet below sea level which softened the ash deposits as well. The pit was only kept dry with the use of pumps that ran day and night. They were fourteen feet below sea level because since the time of the eruption the Mediterranean has raised by that much. Everything changes, especially after two thousand years. By lunch Stahley had reached the skeleton's waist and verified by the pelvic bones that it was definitely a man.

She and Brian usually ate together at the site instead of buying lunch in the city because the lunch crowds, like all the crowds in Naples, were brutal. It was cheaper too. They climbed the wooden steps to the top of the dig and found a spot at the edge of the pit to try to catch the sea breeze. The dozen or so other archeologists working the site, many of them locals, exchanged small talk with them as they passed by on their way into town.

"I have some news for you," Brian said after he'd finished his first sandwich.

"It's really really hot?"

"Guillermo asked me about you yesterday, I think he's smitten."

Guillermo was one of the students from the University in Rome working the dig that season. "He's got to be ten years younger than me," Stahley pointed out.

"I don't think he minds, he wanted to know if you were seeing anyone, and what you did in your spare time."

"And what pray tell did you say to him?"

"I told him that you didn't believe in free time, and that you're madly in love but the guy doesn't seem to be around right now."

Stahley didn't say anything for a few moments; she crumpled up her lunch bag and put it in a plastic bag she'd brought for trash. "That was a pretty shitty thing to say," she told him quietly.

"Yeah, it was," Brian said after a moment, "but it's pretty much true isn't it Stahl?"

"No Brian, it's not."

"Then take Guillermo up on it when he asks, or someone else if not him, or even me, date someone for Christ's sake."

"Dating you would be like dating my brother," she said, her voice still quiet.

"I was kidding,"

"No, you weren't."

"Fine, maybe I wasn't. It's been almost two years now Stahl, how long are you going to mourn?"

"I'm not mourning; mourning implies that someone is dead."

"If he's not dead then where's he been all this time?" he hesitated for a moment, "he was my best friend you know, I knew him longer than you did."

"And yet here you are hitting on his girlfriend."

"Fine," Brian stood up and packed up his lunch stuff, "that's great, fuck you Stahley." He turned and walked off toward the stairs.

Two

She worked the rest of the afternoon on her guy, her head down most of the time hoping that Guillermo had met some hot Italian cutie at lunch. Every once in a while she glanced over at Brian on the far side of the dig. He had his back to her, working on the guy with the sword and the armor who'd been standing in deep water when he'd died, probably thinking that it would save him.

When they quit for the day she hung back, making a production of covering her dig, waiting until Guillermo and his friends left before she headed for the steps. Brian had already left the pit and she'd thought he had gone but he was waiting for her at the top of the steps.

"I'm sorry," she said to him before he could say anything to her, "Buy you an adult beverage?"

"I'm sorry too," he replied, "I need to shower and no offense but, so do you. Why don't I bring a bottle of wine up to your apartment and we can sit on the balcony and look out over the lovely, crowded, odiferous city of Naples."

"Sounds good," Stahley said, they lived in the same apartment building because they'd come over together for the season and it was just easier, she had been lucky enough to score an apartment with a balcony facing the bay. Brian's apartment didn't have a balcony but it didn't really matter because it faced the side of another building. "And make sure it's wine this time," she added as they walked toward her scooter, "Real wine, we're in Italy for God's sake!"

An hour later they were sitting on her tiny balcony drinking wine and eating cheese like a couple of real locals. The sun was setting behind her building casting long shadows across the city to the bay. She was on the twelfth floor so a lot of the street noise didn't make it up to them and what did was muted and indistinct. Her view of the bay was limited by the buildings in between but it was still a view of The Bay of Naples damn it, it worked for her. Her balcony had just enough room for a couple of wrought iron chairs and a little table. They were both sitting back in their chairs with their feet up on the railing. It didn't suck.

"I am sorry for my choice of words," Brian said after they'd talked about other things for a while, dancing around the elephant on the balcony. "But Stahl, it has been almost two years."

"Are we really going to talk about this?"

"I think we should, we have to, I want to."

"Fine," she sighed and took a sip of wine.

"Do you really think he's still alive?" Brian asked her.

"I don't know that he isn't," she said too quickly then sat staring out at the bay for a while and he knew her well enough to wait. "No," she said softly, "I don't. He would have gotten in touch with me by now, no matter where he was or what had happened to him. But to have him just vanish like that, just disappear, it doesn't make any sense to me Brian. It's not like he was on a remote dig somewhere, he was in Boston for Christ's sake! People don't just up and vanish from major metropolitan areas."

"Actually they do," he told her gently, "probably more often than you think."

"Well no one I know ever did."

"Anyway," Brian went on, "the last time you spoke with him he was in Boston, you don't know if he was still there when whatever happened...happened. Didn't Cleo tell you that Chris had been planning on leaving town the last time they'd talked?"

"Cleo told me a whole lot of things, most of which I don't believe at all. Cleo is living proof of that old saw about there being a fine line between genius and insanity. I think he hops back and forth over that line on a weekly basis.

"We've been over this before Stahl; you still think he lied to you?"

"I never said he was lying; I just think he left out a whole lot of the truth. He and Chris were always screwing around with weird shit. I think they actually thought they were going to figure out a way to transport people across space, like in Star Trek. And then UFO's and the Lost City of Atlantis and time travel and endless other crap that they would talk about endlessly into the wee hours. Chris was a perfectly sane, rational scientist when he wasn't around Cleo. When he was around Cleo he turned into somebody else. Somebody I don't think I knew very well."

"Well even if he was lying, or leaving out the truth or whatever, there's nothing you can do about it, you can't prove it, and he's not going to tell you anything he hasn't already."

"I've never really pushed him on it," Stahley said, still gazing out at the bay, "I've never gotten in his face."

"Cleo is filthy rich and marginally insane, I don't think there's anything you can do to him that will make him find Jesus if he has been lying. And why now, why all of a sudden are you obsessing about this again?"

"I'm not obsessing. You brought up the possibility of me dating some Italian child this afternoon and we somehow slipped into this conversation." She took a sip of her wine and thought for a moment. "Also, I've been thinking about him a lot lately," she said finally. "Every day for the past week or so, I don't know why.

"You're always thinking about him Stahl."

"But you see that's it," she replied, "I haven't been lately. I've been busy with this dig, and while this is a place that we both loved we hardly ever worked together here, so I wasn't really...until lately."

"You should try to stop that then," Brian said, "You said it to me this morning, we're in one of the most beautiful spots on earth, except for the crowds, and the noise, the smells, you know, that stuff, and we're working an amazing dig so, you should think about other stuff."

"Now why didn't I think of that," Stahley smiled a bit at him and sipped her wine.

Three

They were sitting on the edge of the dig pit again eating their lunch. Stahley had gotten up to her guys lower ribcage and Brian had just about finished his, he had been wearing a helmet along with the sword and armor, definitely a soldier.

"Kim Hanley called me last night to catch up," Stahley said, "She asked how you were doing and said to say hi."

"Did she ask how I was doing as in, boy I miss ol Brian and wish I'd gotten much closer to him while we were all together or, as in, yeah, Brian's there with you, is he still around?"

Stahley sipped her water and looked off across the dig for a moment. "You know," she said finally, "the 'I'm just a perpetually horny young guy and isn't that cute' thing begins to get old as you approach your thirtieth year, as you yourself will be doing soon."

"Do you think?"

"I do."

"Ok, good safety tip, thanks."

Stahley shook her head and took another sip of water.

"So what else did Kim have to say? Anything juicy going on with anyone we know?"

"Remember a few weeks ago we were talking about Cleo?" Stahley asked.

"Sure," Brian said, "The mad scientist, is Kim dating him?"

"He's back in Boston, she mentioned that she'd seen him walking through the Common about a week ago, he's living in his parents' townhouse on Beacon Hill."

"Life is tough for some of us isn't it," Brian snorted. He looked at Stahley, "were you thinking about calling him or something?"

"No, I wasn't, he's not going to tell me anything more than he already has, not without something to hold over his head and I don't have anything that fits that description."

"I don't know Cleo all that well, hell I hardly know him at all but I'd be willing to bet that it wouldn't take a whole lot of sleuthing to find something."

"Ah, water under the bridge," Stahley said as she got up and dusted off the seat of her shorts, "you said so yourself."

"I did," Brian stood up too, "but you so seldom listen to anything I say."

"I listen to everything you say," Stahley replied, "I just choose to ignore a good portion of it." She put her lunch stuff away and they headed back down into the pit.

Several hours later Brian was just thinking about quitting for the day when Stahley came past him headed for the stairs. She was almost running.

"Stahl, what's wrong, where are you going, you ok?"

"I've got to go," she said without turning around, "I have something to do." She got to the bottom of the stairs, stopped and turned to him. Brian almost took a step back, her face had gone pale, the tan she'd had since their first week in Italy was gone. "Don't let anyone near my dig," she said to Brian, "I'll be back in a few days and I'm almost done with it. Promise."

"Stahl what's wrong, you don't look very good, are you sick?"

"I'm just not feeling well so I have to go, I'll be back in a few days, I want you to promise to keep everyone away from my dig."

"All right, I promise, not a big deal, can I do anything?"

"Just that, I'll be fine," she turned and rushed up the steps and was gone. A moment later he heard her Vespa start up and tear off down the street. He went back to his dig, wanting to finish with the helmet before he called it a day.

When he got back to their apartment building Brian knocked on Stahley's door and got no response so he went back down to the courtyard to see if her Vespa was there. It was but it was pushed way up into a corner out of the way, not in parking space were Stahley usually left it. He tried her door again later that night with the same result and went to bed. The following morning he tried again and also called her cell which went right into voice mail. So on his way out of the building he stopped at the building managers' office and asked the super if she had seen Stahley.

"She is gone," the old woman told him, "back to America."

"What, when?"

"Yesterday, before you come back, she said she going to Massachets…"

"Massachusetts?"

"Yes, there, she was in much hurry, be back in a few days."

"Thanks," Brian said absently. He went out and got his own scooter and headed for the dig site. As he wound through the streets of Naples he began to get angry. Stahley had obviously gone back to Boston to confront Cleo once again which was fine, it was a waste of time but it was fine. But she could at least have told him before she left instead of just running off. He may have tried to talk her out of it but damn it they were friends and she should have told him. Instead she'd lied and told him she was sick so she wouldn't have to listen to his opinion.

By the time he reached the dig he was really fuming. He said good morning to the Italian students and went straight down to his dig, letting his anger fuel his work. But by noon when he stopped for lunch he'd been going over it in his mind and something didn't seem right. So Stahley had decided to go to Boston and confront Cleo, fine, but why did it have to be in such a rush? She had told him at lunch yesterday that he was back in Boston; she had told him in a kind of offhand way and let it go. Why a few hours later was she lying to him and rushing out of there to catch a flight home? Then he thought that maybe she had gotten a call that had set her off but that didn't work, after lunch she hadn't left the pit all afternoon, until she'd rushed off, and there just wasn't any cell phone reception down here at all, not a single bar, never had been, so that couldn't be it.

He climbed out of the pit and sat down to eat his lunch alone and kept turning it over in his mind. Could she have just let it eat at her all afternoon until she couldn't deal with it any longer and decided she needed to book it back to Massachusetts? That didn't sound like Stahley though, he'd known her for years and that just didn't sound like her at all. She'd been at her dig all afternoon anyway and she would have been concentrating on that instead of....he stopped eating and turned to look down into the pit. Stahley's dig site was on the far side, almost at the opposite pit wall but he could see that she had put a green tarp over it and weighted it down with stones. That was odd because they usually didn't cover their digs like that, just threw the tarp over then any which way because what was a little rain or sunlight going to do to them? And she'd been very adamant about not letting anyone touch it while she was gone but why would anyone? They all had their own digs to work and it's not like any one was better than the others, they were all pretty much the same. He took another bite of his sandwich and chewed while he looked at the green tarp. What could have possibly happened while she was over there that made her rush off like that? He took another bite and chewed and kept looking at the tarp.

After lunch he talked to the Italians for a few minutes then headed back down into the pit. When he reached the bottom he started for his dig. "The hell with it," he said under his breath and turned toward Stahley's dig. When he reached it he rolled the rocks aside and threw the tarp back. It was a skeleton lying on its back and it was almost completely uncovered, only the left arm which appeared to be outstretched was still buried, and the top of the skull. The lower skull and neck were...

His eyes fixed on the neck and everything seemed to go still, the city noises, the voices of the Italians joking at the far side of the pit, it all faded. In the years to come he would remember that moment always as if it had just happened, when he was in his eighties this would still be true. He dropped to his knees and leaned over the skeleton and stared because it was wearing a medallion around its neck, a very distinctive medallion, one that he'd seen before and that absolutely could not be there. The first time he'd seen it was the day that Chris had bought it at a little silver vendor's shop in Tangier. He and Chris and Stahley had been staying in Gibraltar for a few days on their way home from their first dig in southern Europe and they'd taken the day ferry over to Tangier. Chris had bought the medallion along with a second one for Brian and a bracelet for Stahley. Brian's medallion was at home in a bureau drawer, Stahley still wore her bracelet every day, she had been wearing it yesterday, and the day before. Chris had had the silversmith engrave their initials and the date into each of the pieces. Brian was looking at Chris's initials and that same date in the tarnished but still intact medallion around the skeletons neck lying before him. He was looking at a date that had occurred five years ago on the skeleton of a man who had died almost two thousand years ago.

She was screwing with him, that was it, it was a joke. He studied the earth around the excavation and damned if it didn't look just like the dirt around his own hole a couple of dozen yards away. He leaned down and probed it with his fingers and it was solid. The skeleton was also solid, and also looked just like the one he'd been digging, it looked real. And he remembered the look on her face when she'd left the previous day, that had been real too. He slowly and carefully, gently, covered the skeleton with the tarp again and walked away. He headed for the stairs because he was pretty sure that he was done for the day.

He went back to his apartment, took a long hot shower and thought about it. Then he called Stahley's cell again and this time he didn't even get voicemail, the phone was turned off. So he dug out his old address book that he still used because he didn't trust electronic data storage, not at all. Which was good because his address book dated back to his college days and beyond, the number he was looking for would never have made it into his i-Phone. He found it and dialed his cell phone without even thinking about the time difference.

"Hello?" Kim Hanley said in Boston.

"Hey Kim, Brian Carter here, I didn't wake you did I?"

"Hey Brian, long time! No you didn't wake me...its 9 am."

"Yeah, of course it is, I always have trouble with the time zones; I'm in Italy with Stahley you know."

"Actually you were in Italy with Stahley, she's in Boston now."

"That's right, she is, did you see her?"

"No, she called me though, yesterday, she wanted to know if I knew anything more about Cleo, did she tell you I ran into him?"

"She did, he's living in his parents townhouse in Back Bay huh?"

"Yeah, life's tough isn't it, couple of million dollar row house that Homes and Gardens did a spread on a few years ago. It's nice to be rich."

"I wouldn't know I'm afraid. So what did Stahley want to know? All she told me was that she was shooting home for a few days and needed to meet with someone."

"She asked me if I'd seen Cleo again, I haven't, and she wanted to know if he'd ever talked about anything weird while we were dating, you knew I dated Cleo right?"

"Actually I didn't," but it figures Brian thought to himself, doesn't it just, "can't say I really see it either, he's a little off."

"He's more than a little off; he's truly out there, But he was fun too, in a different sort of way, and he did have all that damned money, have you ever been on a yacht?

"I never have," Brian replied, playing along.

"Well it doesn't suck."

"But I bet Stahley asked you about the weird stuff right?"

"She did, she asked if Cleo had ever talked to me about all the shit he was messing around with."

"And did he?"

"Sure, guys don't leave much out in post coital conversation Brian, nothing loosens their tongues like a good tumble, you should be careful with that. We talked about all sorts of things."

"Of course you did," Brian replied, trying not to let the image of Kim and Cleo making the beast with two backs seep into his head. If it did it would be there for days. "Was Stahley interested in anything in particular?"

"Time travel of all things, and I had much to tell her, that was one of Cleo's favorite subjects, where he'd go, what he could see, on and on and on. Then he'd start spouting quantum physic formulas or other such shit and that's when I would start to reevaluate our whole relationship. If I had a time machine I'd go back to 1910 and buy all the Coca Cola stock I could lay hands on."

"Thanks Kim, if you talk to Stahley again ask her to call me, her cell phone is off and I really need to speak to her about the dig we're working on here."

"I will if I talk to her but I have a feeling that I won't, I wanted to get together for a drink while she was here but she was in a huge hurry to talk to Cleo and then go back to Herculaneum. "

"Then I'll probably see her soon, thanks Kim," she said goodbye and he broke the connection. Then he sat back to think; so Cleo was interested in time travel, he had all the money in the world to indulge his interest, not to mention time, and while he was an extremely strange guy he was also brilliant. Stahley had been right on the money about Cleo and the genius insanity thing.

Hunger finally drove him to the tiny kitchen to make something for dinner then he realized that he never made dinner and didn't have any food in the apartment anyway so he picked up the phone to call for takeout.

Four

He was at the dig at the usual time the following morning even though he hadn't slept all that well. He fell asleep turning what Kim had told him over and over in his head because he had this niggling feeling that he was missing something, something huge. He'd thought about it getting ready this morning and on the drive over, he'd thought about it when he'd walked over to Stahley's dig, threw the tarp aside and looked down at the skeleton still unable to believe that it was Chris. He finally returned to his own dig to finish it up and was almost done when it hit him; it landed on him like a wall.

One of the last things that Kim had said was that Stahley had told her that she needed to go back to Herculaneum...not Naples, not Italy, but Herculaneum, the town that had existed on that spot two thousand years ago, until Vesuvius had erupted and buried it under forty feet of ash. It was a hot windless day down in the pit and yet Brian suddenly went cold, so cold that he shivered.

He rose slowly from his dig, walked over to Stahley's, and stared down at it again. He would uncover the outstretched arm, that was where he'd start. Stahley hadn't bothered with it, she had stopped once she'd found the medallion.

He started at the elbow and worked outward toward the covered hand, not worrying about preserving anything, or documenting anything, just working as quickly as he could to uncover the arm. It was outstretched straight away from the body and tilted slightly downward and as he worked feverishly to uncover it Brian became sure that he didn't want to see what was at the end of the arm, but he kept working, increasing his pace, because while he didn't want to see, he knew that he had to. And he thought he already knew, he thought he was pretty sure what he was going to find at the end of the arm

The Italians yelled goodbye to him as they left for the day and he barely registered it, just raised one hand in response, because he was almost there, he was at the wrist now. The wrist was bare; Chris had often worn a metal Fossil wristwatch but must not have been wearing it that day. Or maybe he'd lost it and it was buried in the ground somewhere nearby. He was halfway down the hand when he noticed the extra bones, smaller, much more delicate finger bones underneath and mixed in with the man's finger bones.

He made a small sound in his throat and stopped. He sat back and looked around. He was alone in the dig now, the sun was going down behind the city and shadows were puddling in the corners of the pit. In an hour it would be dark where he was and he suddenly did not want to be there when it got dark. He looked up at the spot near the top of the stairs where he and Stahley always ate lunch, looked at it for a long time, not wanting to let that go, then finally leaned back over the hole and started working again.

There was a much smaller hand, a woman's hand, entwined with the male skeletons hand. It was a right hand so he knew. As he reached the end of the male skeletons fingers he reached the wrist of the smaller hand and it was there as he knew it would be, Stahley's silver bracelet, the one she'd been wearing when she'd left the day before, the one she'd worn everyday of her life for the past five years. He could see her initials engraved in the top and he knew that if he freed the bracelet from the soil it had lain in for two millennia there would be a date engraved on the inside, a date from just five years ago, but he didn't do that, he stopped digging and sat back again. He looked down at the bones of his two best friends and wondered what the hell he was going to do.

Reeling in the Years

One

At 37 Carl Hughes was too young to be dwelling on the past which was why when someone told him about Highschoolchums.com he told them he'd never heard of it. His high school yearbook was packed away in a box somewhere, right next to his college yearbook; he couldn't remember when he'd last looked at either one. He still had a couple of friends from college and just one from high school. He couldn't tell you where the rest of his friends from Wharton High School were now if his life depended on it which was fine with him.

One day though, slow day at work, he'd gone on the website and started tooling around and before he knew it an hour had passed, and then two. There was a list of all the students he'd graduated with along with their graduation photos, a lot of them also had current information next to the names; where they lived now, what they did for a living, married, single, some even had current photos. Carl had to admit that it was kind of fun to check out what had happened to people, which ones had done ok, which one's had done really ok, and which one's had done absolutely nothing with their lives. It seemed most of them fell into the first group.

He was trolling down the list of names looking for ones he wanted to investigate further when his hand froze on the computer mouse...

Nancy Anderson

Just the name, no contact info next to it and no graduation photo but then there couldn't really be a graduation photo could there, because it was never taken. Nancy Anderson hadn't been around to have one taken. And she shouldn't be listed as a graduate because she'd never graduated; she'd never even made it to senior year. He looked at the name for a long time; someone must have posted it on the site as a sort of memorial to Nancy so she could be included with her friends. And that's when he decided that he'd gone far enough down memory lane for one day and clicked away from the site.

Two

The thing was, now he couldn't stop thinking about her. So a few days later he went

Down into the basement of the little house he'd bought after his divorce and dug around in the pile of old boxes in the corner until he found a shoe box and a manila envelope. He brought them back upstairs with him and sat down on the sofa. His ex-wife had had many faults but jealousy had not been among them, she had never cared that he kept a bunch of stuff left over from relationships with old girlfriends. Of course it occurred to him now that the reason she hadn't cared about *that* was because she hadn't really cared about *their* relationship.

He opened the shoe box and went through the stuff inside and it was the usual stuff, a couple of ticket stubs to concerts they'd gone to together, or in a group. A weird troll doll she'd bought him as a gag gift on his birthday, he'd never really gotten the humor behind that one. A wristwatch she'd gotten him for his next birthday, Timex, the kind of watch a high school girl can afford to buy for someone when they're working part time at an ice cream stand and even then it would have been a rather large purchase for her. Then at the bottom of the shoe box, a framed photograph of them together at a party, hugging and smiling at the camera. The photo had been taken by Billy Westfall, real photo, no digital crap back then, Billy Westfall, who four years later od'd in a shitty little apartment in the city. It occurred to him that of the three people involved in that photo he was the only one still around, Jesus what a depressing thought. There was a second picture, stuck into the lower left corner of the frame was a small photo of her by herself, taken in one of those photo booths they used to have at the mall. He'd always loved that picture of her; she was looking straight at the lens, just the hint of a smile on her face, her blond hair falling down over her shoulders. She was impossibly beautiful and impossibly young.

He only had those two pictures of her, just those two. In all the years since he'd always been sorry about that and he'd wish that on just one of the days they'd spent together he'd thought to bring a camera along to take just a few more pictures so he'd have them now.

He pushed the box aside, opened the flap on the manila envelope and let a pile of notes and cards cascade out onto the coffee table. She'd been a great one for passing notes between classes in high school, and he'd saved every damned on of them. He read a few of them then stopped and put everything back into the envelope. It had been years since he'd taken them out and read them and he wasn't ready to go down that particular road again that night.

He got his laptop out and booted it up on the coffee table. In no time at all he was back on Highschoolchums.com. He scrolled down the list of names and there it was, Nancy Anderson, and next to it was a graduation photo.

Three

He grabbed his cell phone and called Frank Bower, the one friend he still had from high school and good ol Frank picked up on the second ring. Frank was married, to his college sweetheart no less and they had three kids, Frank could usually be found home in the evening these days...

"Hughes, what's up buddy, it's been a while."

"It has at that Bowser, how are your wife and my kids?"

"God," Frank moaned, "you've got to work on some new material buddy, my dad used to say that for shits sake. And don't call me Bowser; I'm 37 goddamned years old."

"Your dad was a very intelligent and witty man, I have always said that."

"Yeah well he always thought you were a bad influence on me and that you would never amount to anything."

"Well it's still early; he may be proven right yet. Have you ever seen a web site called Highschoolchums.com?"

"I haven't, is it time for another frigging reunion? Not sure I'm up for that Hughes, the last one was beyond surreal."

"No, well I don't know, haven't heard anything. It's just that someone at work told me about this site and I've been tooling around on it a bit and Nancy's name is on it, with a graduation picture."

"Nancy Anderson?"

"Yeah."

"That's impossible man, she never had a graduation photo taken, and she sure didn't graduate, you know that better than anyone."

"I do, but it's there, first her name the other day and now her graduation photo, today."

"Does it look like her?"

"It is her."

"Hold on," the phone jostled a bit as Frank moved, "ok, what was the site again?" he said after a pause. Carl told him and heard him typing it into his computer. He waited with the phone up to his ear hoping that in a minute Frank would tell him he was losing his mind because neither Nancy's name or photo were on the site. Instead Frank said, "Shit, she is on here, and that does look like her, how the fuck is that possible?"

"You got me," he replied, staring at the wall of his living room. "You think it's someone's idea of a sick joke?"

"Even if it is, that's still her in that photo man, how did someone manage that? They go out and find another knockout seventeen year old that's a dead ringer and take a picture of her?"

"The thing is," he replied, "I remember that blouse she's wearing; I took it off her enough times in the back seat of my car, and the necklace, the sea shell necklace? I gave her that for Christmas."

"Ok, so wait then," Frank said, "when did we have graduation photos taken, it was in September right?"

"Yeah, September, after she was gone."

"Well could she have sat for hers earlier for some reason? Maybe she wanted to get it out of the way and just went and had it done."

"Without telling me? She would have showed it to me Frank, and they would have put it in the yearbook, maybe not with ours, but somewhere in the yearbook, don't you think?"

"Yeah, they would have," Frank agreed. "But that has to be it buddy, there's no other explanation. Maybe she wanted to surprise you or something and...never got the chance. And so now one of her friends or her mom posted the photo on the site in memory of her. I'll bet that's what it is, it makes sense."

"Yeah, I guess it does, nothing else does. I wish I knew who did it though."

"I still talk to a few people we hung with back then, I'll ask around and see if I can find out."

"Thanks Bowser, sorry to creep you out before dinner."

"Hey, as if my wife's cooking doesn't already do that, later man." Carl heard Frank's wife yell something at him as he ended the call and smiled.

Four

He was busy at work the following day which was good because he didn't have time to check the web site again even though he wanted to. When he got home that night he made dinner, ok, actually he got dinner out of the freezer and put it in the microwave. Later he was planning on watching hockey, the Big Bad Bruins were playing Montreal at the Garden and while the Big Bad Bruins were way way out of first place at the moment he was not a fair weather fan. Besides, it was frigging Montreal.

He managed to get through the first quarter before pulling out his laptop and booting it up. He opened the site and scrolled down the list and now, along with her name and photo was an address. It was an address he knew very well because it was the house she'd lived in in their home town, the house she'd grown up in. He had been to that address many times twenty years ago and not once since. He thought about calling Frank but didn't, anyone who had a graduation photo of her that he'd never known existed would certainly also know where she'd lived. The address wasn't nearly as weird as the photo. He navigated over to Google Maps and entered the address then zoomed in on it with the satellite view. The street looked the same, so did the yard around the house although the above ground pool Nancy's dad had put up in the back yard was gone which made sense, he'd gotten it used somewhere and the thing had been ready to collapse the day after he'd put it up. There was no street view available because the house was on a small cul-de-sac and whoever had been driving the Google car apparently hadn't thought it important enough to drive down. He exited maps and googled the address itself and several entries popped, all having to do with the fact that the house, and pretty much all of the handful of others on the cul-de-sac, had been foreclosed on, Nancy's old house over a year ago. It didn't look like anything had happened with it since then, whoever held the paper on it was probably backlogged with foreclosures, a sign of the times, and hadn't gotten around to dealing with it yet.

It was half way through the second period now and Montreal was beating the Bruins like a rented mule. He turned off the TV and went back to the high school web site and just looked at Nancy's photo. He'd told Frank that he remembered the blouse she was wearing and he did, because it had been one of her favorites, she'd worn it a lot. Once when they were in the back seat and his seventeen year old hormones were in overdrive he'd torn the seam on the left shoulder of the blouse taking it off or her. Nancy had laughed and made a joke about him needing to calm down and enjoy the moment because that was who Nancy had been. His ex-wife would have torn him a new one for ripping her favorite blouse, gone into a state of high piss off and told him to take her home. Nancy had sewn the tear and continued wearing the blouse and it was barely noticeable but it was noticeable to him because he knew where to look and they would joke about it, about was an animal he was.

Thing was, he looked closely at her photo on the web site and the sewn tear wasn't there and he didn't know what that meant. It had happened the spring of their junior year and that was way before she would have had a graduation photo taken. Even if she had had it taken early, it couldn't have been that early. So why wasn't the fixed tear there? Then he looked up at her face in the photo, she had that same little smile she'd had in the photo booth, like she knew something that no one else did. She'd always had that look; it was one of the things he'd loved about her. He clicked out of the site and shut down the laptop. He was too damned young to be pining for the past, and staring at a photograph of a dead girl wasn't going to do him any good. He went to bed.

Five

The next day was Saturday and he slept in because he could, no wife bugging him to get up and mow the frigging lawn or some other such shit. As he drank his first cup of coffee, mid-morning coffee, he had to admit that he wouldn't have really minded getting up to mow the lawn or some other such shit if everything else in his marriage had been firing on all cylinders.

He was showered and ready to face the day and actually considering some yard work when Frank called him on his cell.

"I asked around," Frank told him, "but nobody has any idea who put the info up on that site, sorry man. It was probably one of her old girlfriends feeling nostalgic and wanting to have people remember her. That's who would probably have her photo too after she'd had one done."

"Her old address is listed now too," Carl replied, "saw it last night."

"Really? Well anyone who went to school with us would probably have known that, it's not a big deal that someone remembers her address. We lived in a very small town."

"Guess not."

"Have you been back to the old home town lately buddy?"

"I haven't."

"Don't bother; it's depressing as all hell. There's even less in the center than there was when we were there, most of the houses down where Nancy used to live are in foreclosure or just abandoned, it's grim."

"I guess you can't go home again," he replied.

"No but you can shop there," Frank replied quoting an old movie they both liked. "Later man."

He did some yard work, not a lot but some, then he took another shower. He was sitting on his tiny back deck with a beer when something occurred to him. He got his laptop and loaded the site. Scrolling down the list of names he came across the one he was looking for and there was an email address next to it. He sent an email then went about the rest of his chores for the day. He was just finishing dinner when his phone rang."

"Carl Hughes as I live and breathe," a woman's voice said.

"Hello Karen, that was quick."

"Not often that a blast from the past like you sends me an email, and a mysterious one at that, so what's up? How have you been for the past oh twenty years?"

"Married, divorced, no kids, you?

"Pretty much the same actually, I did have one child but I was married to him so not sure he counts, his real mom got custody in the divorce. Do you know that you're the seventh person from school who 's gotten in touch since I put my name on that site?"

"Really, anyone good?"

"Remember Tom Roscoe? He wanted to get together for dinner and whatever, that's how he actually phrased it, "dinner and whatever", I passed. I can't believe he didn't OD years ago. So is that what you're interested in Hughes? Dinner and whatever?"

"Maybe some other time I would be but for right now I just had a question."

"Ok, shoot."

"Have you gone through the rest of the list for our class on that site lately?"

"You want to know about Nancy."

"You were always very direct Karen, I remember that about you."

"I didn't post her name or picture if that's what you were going to ask me."

"Any idea who did? And did you know that she had a graduation photo done because I didn't, she never said a thing to me about it."

"Why does all this matter to you now," She asked him, "I would have thought you'd spent the last two decades trying to forget it, and her, considering how things went. I guess not huh?"

"I hadn't thought about it in a while," he admitted, "until I went on that stupid web site. Now I can't stop thinking about it. You were her best friend Karen, did you know she had the picture taken."

"She never said a word to me about having her graduation picture taken, and she would have if she'd done it. She told me everything Hughes."

"Then how do you explain that photo on the site? It is her."

"Yeah, it is, no doubt, and I wish I had an answer for you but I don't. I would say maybe her mom but she passed away five or six years ago. I have no idea who else it could have been. Maybe

Nancy had some kind of premonition about something and decided to sit for her graduation photo early then left it with someone other than you or me, who knows?

"Doesn't that bug the shit out of you?" he asked her.

"Apparently not as much as it does you," Karen replied. "She really loved you you know," she added softly, "You're all she talked about, which got really tedious for the rest of us by the way. She told me once that you were her soul mate and that you were going to be together always. Didn't take her too seriously considering that fact that we were sixteen at the time and you were her first boyfriend. It was puppy love Hughes, if she'd lived you both would have gone off to college and drifted apart and that would have been that. It's how those things work."

"Not always," he replied after a moment, "It's not always how they work." He felt like he had a lead ball in his stomach.

"Well it doesn't matter now and you should let it go, I can't believe you need to be told that after all this time," she hesitated for a moment, "Unless its guilt, did that ever occur to you?"

"Every day for ten years," he replied tightly, "and again the past few days. But that's not what it is."

"Ok, if you say so."

"You think it is."

"Hey look Hughes, we haven't seen each other in twenty years, I don't even know you. All I can tell you is that I didn't put her name up there and I've never seen that photo of her before. If you want to get together some time and talk about old times be happy to but not about this. I loved her too but taking a grim trip down memory lane with you isn't my idea of a fun night out."

"Yup, always very direct," he said, "always liked that about you Karen."

"Sorry if I've pissed you off but that's how I feel. You need to let it go, sincerely you do."

"I do, you're right. Just seeing that photo that I never knew she'd had done bothered the hell out of me, and made me start thinking about everything again. So I will take you up on the walk down memory lane sometime soon, and we won't talk about this."

"No you won't, "Karen replied, "and that's ok too because I'd probably just remind you of Nancy anyway. But it was nice hearing from you after all this time; maybe I'll see you at the next reunion."

"You actually go to those things?"

"Never," she paused for a moment, "Nancy's gone Hughes, you're not, you survived that night and she didn't, so take care of yourself ok." With that she broke the connection.

Six

He watched a movie on TV that he'd seen before then decided to hit the sack. Then he decided that one more look at her picture before bed wouldn't hurt and he was back on the site in three minutes. He scrolled down to her name and now there was a telephone number, right below the address. He stared at it for a moment then without giving himself time to think picked up his phone and dialed it. He didn't really have to look at the site to do it either because he still remembered the number, it was her old number and in another life he'd called a thousand times. He also knew who was going to answer and he almost broke the connection, he almost hit the button and let it go at that...but he didn't and she answered on the second ring, as if she'd been waiting for his call.

"Hello Hughes," she said and for one insane moment he was going to ask her if she had caller ID. It was her voice; the memory of it came rushing back in on him like a waterfall. He hadn't heard that voice in over two decades and it suddenly seemed like all those years between then and now were a dark tunnel full of dead leaves and cobwebs that he'd had to stumble through to make it to this day.

"Tell me who this is," he said, surprised that he could speak at all.

"You know who it is, that's why you called me."

"How are you here Nance, how are we talking right now."

"Does it matter?"

"I don't know, but I think so, I think it matters."

"It's been a very long time and I have so many things to say to you Hughes but the first is that I still love you. You weren't sure about that."

"I'm not even sure yet who I'm talking to, you need to say something to me, something that only Nance would know."

"That's easy, my pet name for you penis was Howard as in Howard Hughes, do you remember?"

"Yes," he said softly.

"Or this," she continued, "on the night I died, just before, you and I decided that we were going to apply to U-Mass together and not go if the other didn't get in, would anyone else in the world know about that Hughes?"

"No," he replied and his voice cracked a bit. He started to say something else then stopped.

"I'm me Hughes," she told him softly. "And there's a very simple way to prove it."

"There is," he asked but he knew, he knew what it was and part of him was giddy with the idea of it, the rest of him was terrified.

"Of course silly, its Saturday night isn't it? Don't you always pick me up on Saturday night? How many Saturday nights have we missed being together. I want to fix that Hughes, I want you to come and see me. We have a lot to talk about."

"You're at your house," he said simply, it wasn't a question.

"I am, I'm back and I'm waiting at my house for you, just like I always used to be."

"I live in the city now; it will take me at least three hours to get there."

"I'll be waiting, just like I always used to be."

"Nance, I never got a chance to talk to you about that night, that's bothered me every day since, I need to tell you how sorry I am."

"I've always known that Carl," she said softly, "you didn't need to tell me, I knew it then and I still do. Come and see me tonight my love and we'll put it all right. I'm really here and I'm waiting so hurry, I've waited so long for this." The line went dead and he sat there for several moments still stupidly holding the phone up to his ear. Finally he lowered it and started at the photo on the web site, a photo that shouldn't exist, of a long dead girl that he'd just spoken to on the phone. He raised the phone and hit redial and got a recording telling him that the number was not in service.

So he sat on the sofa looking at her picture for a long time and wondered if she was really there, at her house, right now, waiting for him. Then he wondered what was at her house, waiting for him. But what if it *was* her, really her, did anything else matter? Fifteen minutes later he was on the Mass Turnpike headed west.

Seven

He made it in two and a half hours because the Pike had been nearly deserted once he got out of the metro Boston area and he hadn't run into any troopers. By the time he reached exit 2 near the New York border the highway was incredibly dark and deserted. He'd lived in the city for years; he wasn't used to this kind of absolute darkness anymore. Considering where he was headed this wasn't the most disconcerting item of the evening...but it didn't help much.

He got off onto exit 2 then turned onto Route 20 South which skirted the town of Lee then plunged into the night, a two lane road bordered by old growth forest on both sides. He passed through the deserted center of the tiny town of Tyringham then was enveloped again by stygian darkness. He hadn't seen another car since getting off the turnpike; his high beams provided the only illumination, the forest plunging back into darkness after he'd passed.

It struck him for the hundredth time that he should have waited until morning and then thought about stopping the car and turning around all the time knowing that he never would. He had always come when she'd called before, except for once, except for that last time...

Just before he reached West Otis which was nothing more than a wide spot in the road he turned left onto a narrow side street. He didn't have to slow to look for it in the darkness, he'd come this way many times before and even though that last time had been two decades ago it didn't matter, he took the side road, called West Center Road, with barely a thought.

Just over two miles on he came to another side street on the left and he stopped in the middle of the road and just sat. Hop Brook Road, the left, would take him into the village of Hays. If he went straight on for another mile or so instead he'd get to Hays Pond, and if he drove around the pond, past the few run down summer homes on its southern shore, to the north side of the lake, he would reach the little strip of sand they used to laughingly call a beach, and the marshy island out toward the center of the lake that acted as their private clubhouse in summer and a base for skating parties in winter. He had no intention of driving to the lake though; he had no intention of ever clapping eyes on the lake again. He swung the car onto Hop Brook Road and gave it a little bit too much gas.

West Otis was a wide spot in the road but it was a thriving metropolis compared to Hays. Downtown Hays consisted of a gas station, a convenience store and a feed store; all were dark and shuttered at the moment and as he passed he saw that for the feed store it was permanent. There wasn't a soul in sight and he assumed the residents of Hays were all home in bed because everyone knew that nothing good ever happens at 2 o'clock in the morning. There was a single street light that weakly illuminated the intersection at the center of the village, Carl glanced at the empty lot by the convenience store where they used to hang out because they had nothing much else to do then he passed straight on through the intersection.

If he'd wanted to go to his house, the house he'd grown up in, he would have turned right at the intersection and driven a mile or so down until he reached a dirt driveway on the right. But he hadn't come all this way in the middle of the night to visit the old family homestead, both his parents were gone and besides, the house had burned down not long after he'd graduated from college. He's always suspected that his father had done it for the insurance but had never asked him. He didn't go to see where his house had been and he had a very strong sense that he didn't belong here, that he was never meant to come back here and he almost turned around to go back to his life, his life now, but he didn't, he couldn't.

So he continued on down Hop Brook Road as his headlights caught things that he knew by heart; a twisted oak tree, a slat fence bordering a field that had gone to wild years ago, a large boulder at the edge of a dirt road up which a friend once lived. In the past he'd driven this road with anticipation because Nancy was waiting for him and she'd been the only bright spot he'd ever found in this forgotten place. And now after all this time he was driving it again, and apparently she was waiting for him again, and he was terrified.

He reached her street on the right, the street light that used to mark it was either gone or just burned out but it didn't matter, his hands turned the wheel without his head even having to consider the movement. The road ran on for a quarter mile or so into a cul-de-sac with half dozen houses on it, a micro-housing development that had been built back when some fool thought this part of Massachusetts was about to take off. He passed the first two houses on either side and both were dark and run down. He knew from his internet surfing that both, along with every other house on this street, had been foreclosed on. It was a dead neighborhood. Once upon a time he'd known the people who'd lived in these houses but they were all gone now, moved on to parts of the world that were still alive, that still had a pulse.

And then the beams of his headlights picked up her house, a small ranch on the right hand side of the road just before you reached its end. The lawn had gone to weeds and the driveway was cracked and buckled from the frost heaves of winters past. And the reason he could see all of that so clearly was because the light next to the front door was on. He doubted there'd been power on this street in years but the light next to the front door was on because she had always left that light on for him when she knew he was coming.

He pulled over to the curb in front of the house and started to put the car into park then stopped. And he sat there. And then he noticed something else; Nancy hadn't owned a car, she borrowed her parents Impala from time to time or he drove her but sometimes she rode her bike, to her job at the convenience store he'd just passed, or to his house, wherever. She rode her bike a lot, the bike that was now leaning against the side of the house by the driveway, the bike that looked exactly as it had the last time he'd seen it.

The only light was the one by the door, the windows were all dark, except that he thought he could see a faint glow coming from somewhere deeper inside the house, on the left side, where her bedroom had been. He put the car in park then back into drive again. And he sat there...

The beginning of the summer before their senior year, there hadn't been any spring that year, typical for New England, they'd gone from damp raw weather to 90 degrees and sunny with no stops in between. And they'd all spent a lot of time at Hays Pond, on the island if they felt like swimming to it, or on that tiny strip of beach if they didn't. And at night they drank there, after driving into Otis to score some beer, or tango, or whatever they could get. Usually there'd be at least eight or ten kids there partying, or breaking off into smaller groups as Nancy had liked to say.

One night in late June, a hot sultry night, he and Nance had gone to the lake alone, very late after she'd snuck out of her house. They'd been hanging with friends all day and Carl was drunk enough that when Nancy reached his car where he'd parked it at the end of her street to wait for her she'd insisted on driving. They drove to the little beach and Carl was still drinking and when they got there they went skinny dipping and that sobered him up a bit but not much really. And then he'd wanted to make love and she said no because someone might come along, they weren't the only ones who used the beach late at night. So he'd come up with the idea of swimming out to the island and doing it there and Nancy told him he was drunk and the water was cold and it was a stupid idea but he started out for the island anyway and he knew she would follow him, she always did, even though he was being stupid, because she loved him and she didn't want to disappoint him and she saw it as her job to take care of him. And he heard her swear at him as she began swimming behind him toward the island and he'd smiled.

The water was cold, it was a spring fed lake. When he was halfway to the island she still hadn't caught up and she started yelling something at him but he couldn't make it out and he kept on, determined to reach the island. She yelled again and he thought he heard something about him stopping and her going back but he kept on anyway and he finally reached the islands muddy shoreline and dragged himself up onto it because he was tired, and drunker than he'd thought. He heard her again, one last time, heard his name and the word please and then he passed out and when he woke up she wasn't there and she wasn't on the beach because she'd drowned and was dead at the bottom of the lake.

At Nancy's funeral he had been standing there thinking about how she'd looked when they got her out of the lake and wondering if he could live with that when her mother walked up to him and slapped him across the face, hard. She didn't say anything, she just walked away and that was ok because she didn't need to say anything. Nancy's family moved away not long after.

He sat there in front of the house now and thought about all of it, really thought about it, for maybe the first time in a decade. Not because he was callous or didn't care but because to think about it made him think about suicide sometimes and who the hell needed that? Because you see he had always been there for Nancy, he loved her more than anything in the world and it was his job in the world to protect her. And when she was drowning in that cold muddy pond and calling for him to save her he was lying drunk in the mud not more than fifty feet away. Because when he did think about it he wondered what her last thought had been; that his stupidity had killed her? That he had let her down when she'd needed him most? That if she'd never met him she wouldn't be sinking into the stinking mud at the bottom of a deserted lake now, killed by a cramp? That he stole her life?

He sat there in front of that house that he never thought he'd see again, in the same spot that he'd parked in a thousand times, and part of him wanted to rush inside and tell her how sorry he was, tell her all the things he never got to say to her back then, tell her how much he loved her still. In the months and years right after the accident he would have given anything to have that

chance. But now he sat in his car with the engine running and did nothing because he was terrified. He was terrified of what was really in that house...and of what it might want.

He put the car into park and turned off the headlights then turned them back on because it was way too dark without them. He wondered if he sat there long enough would she come out to him? He looked at the front door then at the window to its left that had been her bedroom back then and wasn't now. He thought he saw movement inside the room. He put the car in drive then back in park...and he sat there...

The Internet May Be Hazardous To Your Health

1.

The office, on a Friday afternoon in July; deserted hallways, dark offices, silent phones, the only email he'd gotten all day had been from his wife, he was just waiting for 5 o'clock and the weekend to begin. In short, Fred Mitchell was bored out of his tiny little mind. He checked his email for the hundredth time, made some notes for a meeting he had coming up...in a month, and then finally gave in and went on line to surf the web for a while, as in for the rest of the day. They'd all gotten an email from the 20th floor a few months ago warning them that the IT Department would be monitoring their computer usage and that they should all restrict said usage to work purposes only. Since their IT Department consisted of two guys who couldn't even keep up with the day to day technical demands of the office he seriously doubted that they had time to give a thought to employee computer usage much less monitor it. Not that he'd ever sit at his desk happily looking at porn all day but as far as a little harmless surfing went...he was willing to risk it.

Sites that were among his favorites to kill time on were the ones that showed you satellite images from anywhere in the world. It was very cool that he could go down to street level in one place then pull back and skip to a spot half a world away and do the same thing, looking at stuff at street level from the other side of the world without ever leaving his chair. That day his first stop was San Diego, the Gaslight District, a favorite of theirs and someplace they hadn't been in a while. That particular sites camera car had apparently been tooling around there during Comic Con because there were some very oddly attired people roaming the streets, it made for awesome viewing.

From there he jumped all the way back across the country to someplace very close to home; Martha's Vineyard, a perennial favorite of theirs. He zeroed in on Oak Bluffs, specifically the deck at Nancy's restaurant right next to the harbor. One of their first stops when they went to the island was always lunch on Nancy's deck. He brought the satellite image in as close as it would go which was pretty damn close and began tooling around.

And then he stopped and stared because he was looking at him and his wife sitting on the deck eating lunch. He could even recognize the shirt he was wearing; it was one of his favorite golf shirts. He looked down at the bottom of the screen to check the date of the image and saw that it was listed as being from September of this year. But that wasn't right because he and his wife hadn't been to the Vineyard since last summer; they were actually doing their annual trip right after the Labor Day weekend when the hotel rates were cheaper and the crowds smaller. And besides, it was July, September was two months away. The image must be dated wrong; it must be from last summer when they were there. He checked the date again, yeah, definitely wrong; it had to be from September of last year not September of this year. But then he went down to street level, to Lake Avenue which ran right by Nancy's deck, and zoomed in and he saw that his wife was wearing her white straw beach hat, the hat she had just bought at the beginning of the summer, *this* summer. He stared at the image for a while, leaning forward over his desk with his face right up to the monitor and there was no doubt, that was the hat. He glanced down to check the date again to be sure he hadn't read it wrong and it still said that the images were from September of the current year...in July.

He sat back and then something else occurred to him; they always stayed at a little hotel right around the corner from Nancy's and he always parked his car in a space at the side of the building. They brought their car to the island because it was cheaper than renting one when they got there but they wouldn't have needed it to drive one block from the hotel to the restaurant so it would, or should be parked beside the hotel. He stayed in street level and navigated down Lake Ave, turned left onto the Circuit Ave Extension and up to and just past their hotel then north onto North Bluff Lane. All the guests cars were angle parked along the side of the building but his wasn't there which made no sense because they always took his SUV to the island and he always parked right there. His grey Isuzu SUV definitely wasn't there but then he zoomed and panned to look at the license plates of the parked cars that were there and he found his plate, attached to the back of a black Audi Q5 SUV.

His phone rang and he almost jumped out of his chair. He looked at the screen and saw that it was his wife;

"What do you want to do for dinner?" she asked him when he picked up.

"I don't care, it's Friday, want to just go out? Or get takeout?"

"Was hoping you'd say that," she answered, "I really don't feel like cooking."

"Darcy, when we were on the Vineyard last year, we took my Isuzu right?"

"We did, we always do, why?"

"We didn't rent an Audi SUV and it just slipped my mind."

"I think I would remember if we had rented an Audi SUV, and anyway, why would we?"

"I don't know. One more thing, that straw beach hat you have, you just bought that in June right?"

"Yeah, at TJ Maxx, why, and what does my hat have to do with renting Audi's?"

"Not a damn thing that I can think of."

"Are you all right Fred?"

"Yeah, just bored and waiting for the bell to ring, see you at home."

He looked at the image on the screen for a while longer then had a thought. He exited out of the site then shut down his browser then restarted his computer. When it was up again he re-opened the browser, then the site, then went back to North Bluff Lane and the goddamned Audi was still sitting there with his goddamned license plate on it. Back around the corner on street view and he and Darcy were still sitting on the goddamned deck eating lunch. He also noticed this time that Darcy was smiling but he was looking right at the camera car, and he had a bandage on the last two fingers of his left hand. He got out of the site and the browser and decided to go home early.

2.

They got Chinese takeout for dinner then watched the news on TV then Fred wandered into his home office while Darcy watched some show about housewives who lived in California, or someplace with palm trees. The Tour de France had started the previous week and he'd intended to watch the coverage of that day's race but of course as soon as he'd shut the door he booted up his laptop and was back on the site. Audi still there, ditto him and Darcy.

He thought of something else and put in his brother's address in Connecticut. They were supposed to be out there for Thanksgiving and he was curious what the site was going to show him because if it could show him a vacation that hadn't happened yet why not a holiday that hadn't happened yet too? His brother and his family lived in an upscale development with big houses set on big lots of land. He zoomed down to the house and noticed that the trees were bar and there was a dusting of snow on the ground. He glanced at the image date; November 26th, the date that Thanksgiving fell on this year. Then he noticed all the cars parked in the big circular driveway and on the street out front and he recognized most of them because they belonged to family members and friends. He didn't see the Audi though so he zoomed in closer to look again and instead he spotted Darcy's sedan parked in the driveway. He looked at it wondering why they would take Darcy's car to his brothers; they always used his car for trips, not hers. So they suddenly have a brand new Audi and they don't take it on a road trip? Did it break down? Was it stolen? He stopped and shook his head, he was speculating about a car he didn't even own. And it didn't explain why they hadn't taken his Isuzu to Connecticut, not to mention how the frigging site was displaying an image from four months in the future. He thought about showing it to his wife and thought better of it though he wasn't sure why. Maybe by showing it to her he would be legitimizing it, making it real while now he could just write it off to his being overworked or just tired, or imagining things. As long as it was just him seeing it then it might not be real. He shut the laptop down and went to bed.

3.

Two days later on his way to work he got t-boned in an intersection by a construction worker driving a pick-up truck who was speeding because he was late getting to a job site. Fred walked away with cuts and bruises but the Isuzu was toast. The construction workers insurance carrier not only paid book value for the Isuzu but settled with Fred for pain and suffering, mental anguish and lost wages. Turns out the construction worker had already had two accidents that summer along with several moving violations and his carrier, which cancelled his policy a short time later, was afraid that Fred was going to sue them...and win.

Armed with a butt load of insurance money Fred and Darcy went out car shopping and Darcy suggested that since Fred seemed to have Audi's on the mind lately, and they had the money, they could at least look. So they did, and Darcy fell in love with the Q5 and so they bought one. And that was how Fred ended up with the car he'd already seen with his license plate on it during a vacation that hadn't happened yet. At first he was reluctant about the purchase, bad Ju Ju and all, but he really did love the SUV, and maybe the images on the web were meant to tell him to buy an Audi, and he'd insisted on dark blue instead of black so that was ok. He was actually more concerned about the Thanksgiving picture because it may mean that the Audi had broken down just a few months after they'd bought it and was in for repairs.

In any case, he loved the new car, he was very careful at intersections now, and he hadn't been on the web site in weeks. Until the day he came out of a store and walked across the parking lot toward the Q5. The SUV was parked in the sun against the side of the building and Fred stopped in his tracks because in that light his dark blue SUV looked like a black SUV.

He was back on the site that night studying the image of the Audi parked on the Vineyard and he thought it did look kind of blue around the edges. He checked his brother's house again, still just his wife's car in the driveway then he thought of something else he could check; he entered the address for a hotel a couple of towns away that they were supposed to attend a wedding at in three weeks. It had a big open parking lot out back and he should be able to spot the Audi there because there was nowhere else to park. He hit enter and the image came up and instead of the hotel he saw a huge whole in the ground where the hotel should have been. He checked the date and it said the image was from three weeks in the future, the date of the wedding. It spoke to how much he was becoming accustomed to this phenomenon that he let that go and just stared at the photo. No hotel, just a parking lot and a big black hole.

He backed out of the map site and went to the hotel's website and it was there, all nice and normal and accepting reservations. Just to be sure he called the Concierge and spoke with him briefly.

He in no way sounded like he was standing in a big black hole and Fred was fairly sure it was something that he would have mentioned during their conversation.

A week later the hotel burned right down to the ground and the only thing that kept Fred from feeling guilty about keeping his mouth shut was that everyone had managed to get out. And he was still left wondering why the shiny new Audi wasn't parked at his brother's house for Thanksgiving.

4.

They went on their trip to Martha's Vineyard as planned, and they took the Audi and parked it by the side of the hotel, and they ate lunch of Sandy's deck and just as they were finishing lunch Fred watched the camera car for the map website drive by and Marge was wearing her white straw beach hat and he was wearing one of his favorite golf shirts, he hadn't even realized the significance of that particular shirt when he'd gotten dressed that morning.

For the rest of the week he kept looking for the damn camera car and didn't see it which shouldn't have been surprising because he'd checked everyplace they ever went on the Vineyard on the map site at least twice and seen not hide nor hair of him or Darcy, or the Audi anywhere else on the island. Darcy asked him a few times if he was all right and he said he was. Then she asked him if he was looking for his next wife and he said he was.

He finally started to relax and enjoy himself, something it's hard not to do on the Vineyard. They had a great time and left the island sunburnt, tired and happy. When they got home it looked a bit shabby to them simply because there was no ocean anywhere in sight.

Fred went back to work the next day and while he was eating his lunch at his desk he went back onto the map site and checked Nancy's deck and there was the image of them from last week, eating lunch and enjoying the first day of their vacation. Back to his brother's house and there was Darcy's car in the driveway and no sign of the Audi. Then, just for the hell of it he punched in their own house and hit enter. Darcy's car was in the driveway in that image too, there was no Audi but there were plenty of other black cars there, including a hearse parked right out front at the curb. He just looked at the image for a long moment while a large ice cold lump of dead weight grew in his stomach. He didn't want to look at the images date, didn't want to acknowledge that or deal with it. Finally he dropped his eyes to the bottom of the screen; the image date was exactly one week away...one week. They wouldn't be holding a wake at their damn house, he was pretty sure that was illegal, against the zoning laws or some such shit. He typed in the name of a funeral home not too far from their house, his fingers felt numb, they felt like overstuffed sausages and he had to type the address in three times to get it right because he knew, he wasn't sure how he knew but he knew.

He looked at the image date first and it was from the same day, ninety minutes later than the one from his house. The cars were all at the funeral parlor now, except for Darcy's, and he knew that they were the same cars, and there were people coming out of the funeral parlor and walking in different directions and then he saw the coffin being wheeled out of the church and he went down to street view and Darcy was walking behind it dressed in black and with her hand resting on one corner and then he knew why her car wasn't there, her car wasn't there because she'd rode in the limo. It could have been one of her parents except they were both deceased. It could have been one of their children except they had none, it could have been anyone but it wasn't, it was him. He looked at Darcy's image for a long time and he found that what really bothered him wasn't that he was the one in the box, what bothered him was that she was alone.

He shut down his computer and called his wife, just to talk to her, because he could still do that.

5.

His money was on a heart attack, that's what had killed his father, and his grandfather, and probably his great-grandfather. He made an appointment with his physician and by pushing hard got it for the next afternoon. He wasn't sure it would matter but he wasn't going down without a fight. Then he sat down and created a Word document for Darcy outlining everything she might need to know should the fight be lost. He printed it out and left in on his desk in a sealed envelope with Darcy's name and "personal" on it. He also thought about talking to her about it but decided not to because he didn't want to scare her if it was nothing and, truth be told, deep down inside he still believed that it was nothing. What he didn't realize, and have never been told, was that pretty much the hardest thing for a person to visualize was their own death. Otherwise it would be a hell of a lot harder to get most soldiers to stand up and run directly at the enemy.

The following day he left work early to go to the clinic where his doctor's office was, he'd decided he was going to tell his doctor he was having chest pains even though he wasn't because that would light a fire under their asses to run all kinds of tests. And maybe in doing that they would find something that *was* wrong with him, no matter what was on the internet he wasn't going to just frigging drop dead, something would have to cause it and maybe they could find it and fix it before it killed him and then fuck the internet, the pictures would change.

Half way to the doctor's office, at the very same intersection where the Isuzu had been totaled he got t-boned again, this time by a delivery van with a dozing driver behind the wheel only this time the hit was on the driver's side not the passenger side and even the brand new Audi's ten airbags couldn't save him.

The Serenitatis Purge

Chapter One

Ben Baker was just finishing his lunch when the woman began to scream. She was a couple of tables away from him sitting with two other women who looked scared as she just stood up and began screaming. No discernable words at all, just really terror filled screams which might have struck Ben as odd, a woman just beginning to scream in a quiet lunch room, if it weren't for the fact of where the lunch room was.

Neither of the woman seated at the table tried to stop their friend from screaming which told Ben that they were either casual acquaintances, like the people at his own table, or that they were just too frightened to do anything. Either was a viable possibility considering the setting. And then two security soldiers appeared as if by majic and started toward the woman. Alec had been telling them since they'd arrived a week ago that there were secret tunnels in the walls of the facility that the security soldiers used to move around and that was how they always managed to just appear when their presence was required. Sitting there Ben saw the panel in the wall slide open and the two security soldiers step out and approach the woman. He hated it when Alec was right about anything.

The two SS guys didn't even try to calm the lady down and judging by the level and intensity of her screams it probably would have been an exercise in futility but still, Ben thought they should have at least tried. Instead they simply walked up to her and hit her with their stun sticks, one in the chest and one in the head which caused the woman to drop to the floor like a rag doll. They flex cuffed her hands and feet then picked her up and carried her out of the dining hall, an electric cart had magically arrived at the rooms entrance to take her away.

"What was her story," Raymond asked as he sat down at the table with his lunch, "didn't like the meatloaf?"

"They're not serving meatloaf," Ben replied absently as he watched the cart roll off.

"It was a joke," Raymond replied, "it sounded good, it wouldn't have sounded good if I'd asked if she hadn't liked the re-constituted alarmingly colored protein potash. Besides, when was the last time you actually saw meatloaf?"

"Where do you think that cart is taking her?"

"To the med center I would assume, shoot her full of downers. Don't think she's going to pass her screening now though, tell you that for nothing. Pretty sure she's going to be taking up permanent residency here."

Ben turned back to the table, "Alec was right about the wall tunnels," he told Raymond, "the two SS guys came out right over there by the soda dispenser."

"Well, even an asshole's right once in a while," Raymond replied.

"Makes you wonder what else he's right about," Ben said.

"Nothing, he probably saw them emerge from a tunnel at some point since we've arrived and didn't say anything about it to make us think he knows all the deep dark secrets about this place when in fact he doesn't know dick, he's full of shit up here, just like he was full of shit on Earth."

"You're accepting the fact that there are deep dark secrets about this place then?"

"I've never doubted it." Raymond replied and started eating his potash.

Chapter Two

After lunch they wandered aimlessly around the corridors of the facility for a while making small talk. Small talk was big at the facility, it not only helped pass the endless hours filled with nothing to do, it was also an attempt to give them all a sense of normalcy that none of them really felt. Ben finally ran out of small talk so he turned to Raymond and asked a very non-small talk question.

"Do you think they have the corridors monitored? He asked. "That they're watching us all of the time, they have been since we got here, and that that's part of the whole thing?"

"Alec tell you that too?"

"I heard a couple of people talking about it in the rec center yesterday. They said that you shouldn't wander aimlessly around the facility like we're doing now, because they were always watching and it didn't look good."

"What the hell else would they expect us to do?" Raymond replied, "There's only so much virtual reality you can stand and besides, it's not even very good here and the rec center is always crowded. It's not like we can go for long walks outside."

"I guess," Ben agreed, "but we could be in the data center studying, or in our rooms studying."

"Studying what? There's nothing to study! The whole idea is to be yourself and just do the best you can. What exactly did you want to study?"

"Just general stuff, just to widen our horizons so we'll be more knowledgeable about things so we'll look like we're taking an interest in the world we live in, that's got to be important to them."

"Believe me," Raymond said, "at this point your horizons are as wide as they're going to get."

"So you're not worried about any of this then?"

Raymond shrugged, "It will be what it will be, nothing we can do about it." He turned and looked at Ben, "you're a good person Ben, so am I, so are Bethany and Cassie, we're all going to be fine. All this is not for us, it's for guys like Alec, he's the one who should be worried.'

"He doesn't seem to be at all," Ben said.

"That's because he's egotistical and narcissistic and sociopathic. His entire world revolves around him; he's the center of his own universe so he can't imagine anything bad actually happening to him in it. He's going to keep looking at this whole exercise in that way right up until they land on him like a wall."

"So you really think he won't be going back with us?"

"There's no way he's going back with us, this entire thing was designed with guys like him in mind. With his history of offenses and his personality, his outlook on life? They are just lying in the weeds waiting for him to walk through their door, believe me. I for one will barely notice he's gone."

"Still, it'll be something if we have to go back without him."

"Why, because we're from the same grid and we all went to school together? Sorry if I sound cold hearted but it is what it is, you'd better start getting used to the idea."

"I guess so."

"Enough gloom and doom," Raymond said, "Alec's doom anyway, where are the girls?"

"They're in the gym, at least that's where they told me they were going."

"So let's go get them and think of something to do."

"You go ahead," Ben said, "I'm going to go by the data center and grab a few discs for later, I'll catch up with you."

Raymond slapped him on the shoulder, shook his head, and started off then stopped and turned back, "if you happen to run into Alec you might want to go the other way," he said. "Just in case they really are watching us, you're judged by the company you keep and all that…" he turned and headed off in the direction of the gym.

Ben started toward the tech center then turned down a narrow hallway instead. It was a small out of the way passage that most seemed not to notice but it dead ended at a shimmer wall so he came there every day. He stopped in front of the wall and waved a hand in front of it causing the dull steel to ripple and slowly turn transparent. The effect was actually breathtaking, the wall seemed to be gone, floor to ceiling and in front of Ben was the stark lifeless surface of the moon and beyond that, floating against a black void, the warm blue and white sphere of the earth. Ben had stumbled across the narrow hallway with the shimmer wall the day after he'd arrived and had returned often since then to gaze at Earth and wonder if this was as close as he would ever be to it again.

Chapter Three

It had begun as a grass roots movement kept alive on social media, started by a man in Cupertino California who had lost two family members to violent crime. Just an insignificant blog really, it languished in anonymity for over a year before finally going viral. From there it had been picked up by several regional governments and finally by the world governing body after legislation had been filed by multiple regional representatives but strangely enough not by the one from California.

The world governing body initially put it on a back burner. Their reluctance to deal with it was understandable; it was a rather large undertaking after all and the legality of it was problematic to say the least. The moral and ethical implications were even more troublesome. The matter may have remained like that indefinitely, everyone talking about the merits of the idea but no one willing to actually take that first step...and then the riots of '55 happened. Civil unrest in major cities across the globe, fueled partially by overcrowding and unemployment and prodded on by international gangs, exploded into conflagrations of looting destruction and death. The riots eventually ended, the fires were extinguished, buildings repaired, victims buried, and most of the gangs were hunted down and eradicated but none of that mattered to the citizens of the planet, they'd had enough, and once the politicians saw which way the wind was blowing they pushed the legislation through in record time. So it began, and once it did it gained momentum at a truly alarming rate until it reached the point that no one could have stopped it, had anyone even tried. No one did.

The facility had started out as a small mining colony in the lower right hand quadrant of the Mare Serenitatis or, the Sea of Serenity. It wasn't far from the Apollo 17 landing site, a protected historical site now and accessible by pre-arranged and supervised sightseeing trips. Just beyond that was the Mare Tranquillitatis or, the Sea of Tranquility, both names Ben, in his present circumstances, found to be ironically and sadly humorous.

When things got underway the powers that be decided that the mining colony suited their purposes nicely and the small outpost quickly grew into a massive facility that now sprawled halfway up to the huge Posidonius crater in the upper right hand quadrant of the Mare. Because of the facilities location the program quickly became known, unofficially, as the Serenitatis Purge. Ben had heard that they were breaking ground on a new and even larger facility to the west, somewhere on the Mare Imbrium; they were certainly going to need it.

Chapter Four

They all ate dinner together that evening in the dining hall, something they had started to get away from the past few days. When they'd first arrived at the facility they had stuck together in everything, as if had they separated some of them might vanish. They would never be comfortable while they were there but as they became more accustomed to the place they had begun going their own ways now and then. Also, Raymond and Cassie had decided that the less they were all seen with Alec the better. Ben still did things with Alec though because he didn't want to just abandon him and because Alec seemed to know things the rest of them didn't. He had been making other friends though, Ben saw him with them from time to time around the facility. Some of them were all tatted up and wore their hair in the spiked style of Outrunners, a risky thing to do since the riots of 55, and even riskier thing to do considering their current location. Alec didn't seem concerned and when Ben has asked him about them he'd shrugged it off saying they were just some guys he had met.

One advantage to eating dinner together was that they could have an entire table to themselves instead of sharing it with strangers. Ben was getting tired of trying to make idle conversation with people he didn't know, wasn't going to get to know, may never see again, and who were usually so on edge they were ready to jump out of their skin. He'd found that even attractive women at the station, and there were a lot of them, didn't hold his attention for very long...he had other things to occupy his thoughts.

"They're vulnerable my friend," Raymond had said to him a few days earlier, "they're scared and wound up and bored all at the same time and they're looking for distraction as much as we are. They're looking for some good old fashioned human contact, take advantage of it. There's nothing wrong with a little extracurricular activity to pass the time you know. You will never have a better opportunity than you do here, or more willing partners."

"I don't think I could get it up right now if there were a dozen naked dancing girls in front of us." Ben had replied.

"They have pills for that," Raymond had laughed.

So that night even Alec was at the table with them and he was being unusually quiet which made Ben think that maybe he'd finally realized that he an innate ability to rub Raymond and Cassie the wrong way. Or maybe he was just hung over, Ben couldn't tell.

"Just a few more days," Bethany said to them all, "I almost wish it was tomorrow, get it over with one way or the other."

"Shit I wish it had been today," Raymond replied, "wandering around this place with nothing to do is killing me."

"I'll wait thanks anyway," Cassie said quietly.

"Me too," Ben said because he thought he should at least give an opinion. Truth was he wasn't sure what he wanted. At least the longer you waited the longer you could avoid the outcome.

"What about you?" Raymond looked at Alec, "what do you think?"

Alec didn't look up from his plate; "I don't really care one way or the other," he said, "It'll happen when it happens."

"I would think you'd want to get it over with," Cassie commented.

Alec looked up at her, "Why," he asked, "because you don't think I'll be going home?

"I didn't say that," Cassie replied stiffly, "I just meant that you never seem to be able to sit still for a moment, this place must be driving you crazy."

Alec gazed at her for a moment and Ben got the impression he was going to say something to her then he changed his mind and went back to his food.

"It is not what I meant," Cassie repeated.

"Its fine," Raymond said, "we're all on edge, why wouldn't we be."

"I'm not on edge," Alec replied, "I'm examining all the angles, that's all. Something you all should have been doing since day one."

"We don't need any angles," Raymond replied, "we'll be just fine, and if you do end up staying it will be that exact way of looking at things that does it."

Alec laughed and shook his head at his plate. They all sat quiet for a few moments, picking at their food.

"Anyway," Bethany said finally, "I'm glad it's almost over."

"For some of us," Alec replied.

Chapter Five

Once the plan was agreed upon, by unanimous vote of the world governing body, they had to settle upon the rules, the parameters by which the program would operate. In the end those rules turned out to be very simple and were agreed upon in less than two days...two days to decide the fate of a world.

The harder part came after that; the rules were easy enough to come up with, finding a way to achieve the goal set forth by the rules was a different matter entirely. Multiple tech firms were invited to bid on the contract, some declined outright without bothering to give a reason, others begged off citing an imaginary lack of expertise in the field, which left just a handful to attempt construction of the device requested. Of those only two managed to produce a viable prototype for testing and in the end the governing body decided to go with both. The thinking was that two separate protocols would give the appearance of fairness, and that not knowing which device would be in use at any given time would dissuade any attempts at cheating, not that cheating would be possible in any event, not with the procedures they were intending to use. When the devices had been tested and deemed ready, and the expansion of the base at Serenitatis was complete, they had announced the rules to the world. They were chillingly simple;

Over the next several years the entire population of Earth would be transported to the base at Serenitatis to undergo a series of evaluations; evaluations that were not concerned with physical attributes, or social ones, or a person's place in society, evaluations that simply measured a person's psychological makeup, the wiring in their head as many people on Earth chose to put it. The devices built to the governing bodies specs would measure and evaluate a person's psychological profile and decide, bloodlessly, dispassionately, if that individual was a normal, well-adjusted member of the society of Earth. If they were deemed to be so then they were on the next shuttle home, that very day...if not, then they never left. They were given two options, to self-terminate, with assistance of course, or to remain on the moon, accept whatever job was given to them, and live out the rest of their lives there.

So far it was running about 70/30 in favor of becoming a permanent moon resident. This was creating a bit of a housing problem; the governing body had thought it would be closer to 50/50.

The rules regarding exclusion from the program were just as simple; children up to the age of eleven were excused, as were the elderly beyond the age of 70. Other than that everyone went, absolutely everyone, and everyone rolled the dice.

Chapter Six

Ben was scheduled to begin his testing two days after they'd all had dinner together for that final time. For the past two days, the closer they'd gotten to actually walking into the testing center, the more they'd seemed to drift apart. It was as if they each wanted to be alone with their own thoughts and fears.

On the last night Ben was standing in front of the shimmer wall looking at Earth when Bethany appeared and stood beside him. He hadn't thought that she'd even known about the tiny hallway and the wall. They both stood for a long moment looking at Earth.

"Cassie's time got moved up," she said finally, "So we're all going tomorrow."

"Why did they do that?"

"They didn't say, but I heard a rumor that someone who was on the list for tomorrow managed to open an airlock and step outside this morning so, I guess there was an opening."

"Shit," Ben said under his breath.

Bethany was still looking out at Earth, or at the barren lunar surface below it, Ben couldn't tell which.

"What if we don't get back there," Bethany said softly, "what if we have to stay here for the rest of our lives."

"That's not going to happen," Ben told her.

"But what if it does, have you thought about it?"

"A little, but it's not going to happen Beth, none of us are the kind of people they're looking for. We're all upstanding members of the community; we contribute, we have worth. We're all going back, trust me."

"Even Alec?"

Ben turned back to the window without answering.

"He's not even a little bit scared," Bethany said, "and I don't understand that because he *is* the kind of person they're looking for, we all know it and he does too. Raymond thinks he killed that man in Grid 8 last year you know."

"Raymond should learn to keep his mouth shut," Ben replied, "there's no way he could know that, he just doesn't like Alec, never has." He glanced quickly around the little corridor then added, "And you should be careful what you say around here, you never know…"

"Even if he didn't, he's done lots of other stuff, we all know that. He's been that way since we've been kids Ben, you know he has." She paused for a moment then shook her head, "but even so, I don't want him to have to stay here either, I don't want anyone I know to have to stay. I just want us all to go home and get on with our lives." She wrapped her arms around herself and stopped looking out through the shimmer wall.

"We are all going home," Ben said, "you and me and Raymond and Cassie. If Alec doesn't then he has no one to blame but himself, there's nothing any of us can do to help him."

"Then you do think he could stay."

"Maybe," Ben said, "even though I'm pretty sure he never killed anyone." He put his arms around her, "anyway, by this time tomorrow it will be over, tomorrow night we'll be sleeping in our own beds again."

She didn't speak for a while then finally; "so you don't really think about it, staying here? You don't have any kind of plan if that's what happens? If they send you to another colony to work the rest of your life at a job they pick for you?"

"What good would it do to think about it," Ben said.

"You have to consider it," she said softly, "you have to have some kind of plan."

"Do you?"

"Yes."

"What is it?" He asked her even though he thought he knew.

"It will vary depending on the circumstances," she said, "if I can't manage to open an airlock I'll have to think of something else." She reached out and waved her hand over the wall to make it solid again because she suddenly had the feeling that looking at Earth any longer just then would be bad luck.

Chapter Seven

The testing centers were located in the restricted wing of the facility. The far side of the wing led to either the shuttle ports, for a ride home, or the rover bays, for a ride to the induction complex a few kilometers away, depending on how you did in the testing centers. There was also an unmarked door before entering the wing, for those who didn't care to take a ride in a Mars rover. They didn't want those tested walking around in the rest of the facility, no matter how they did.

As instructed Ben had packed up the few belongings he'd brought with him and proceeded to the center with the others. None of them had much to say. He noticed that Alec wasn't carrying a bag.

"Having them send your stuff directly to the rover bay?" Raymond asked Alec, "That's smart, saves you the trouble of carrying it."

Alec looked at him and smiled faintly, "I didn't bring anything with me I cared about taking home," he replied, then, "you've always taken a perverse pleasure in others misfortune Ray," he added softly, "I've always noticed that about you...it's not a character trait that would endure you to others you know."

"Worry about your own character traits my friend," Raymond said. "I'll worry about mine."

"I really don't need to listen to this shit on my way to the frigging testing center!" Cassie said and they stopped talking.

Chapter Eight

Ben was leaning against the curved bulkhead trying to breath normally and wondering if there was anywhere he could get a goddamned drink of water when Bethany walked up to him. She didn't say anything but simply hugged him and kept hugging him. A moment later Cassie was standing next to them, and then they were all hugging. They were in the concourse leading to the shuttle ports.

"We should just wait here for Ray," Cassie said finally and even though they were going home she had a blank shocked look on her face.

"It was really fast," Bethany said, "did you think it was going to be that fast?"

"My machine was humming really loudly," Ben said, "I thought it was broken."

"No, mine was doing that too," Cassie said.

"Mine too," Bethany said, "it made it hard to hear the questions."

"I have a feeling the questions didn't mean anything anyway," Ben told them.

On the far side of the huge room someone, it sounded like a woman, started to scream. They all looked that way then quickly looked away. They saw security personnel going in that direction... after a few moments the screaming stopped.

"Is there anything to drink anywhere," Cassie said finally, "my mouth is really dry. Then she grabbed Ben by the arm, "Holy shit guys, there's Alec!"

They all turned to see Alec walking toward them wearing a grim little smile on his face. They looked behind him for Raymond but didn't see him.

"Don't all look so surprised at once," Alec said when he reached them. "I'm happy to see all of you too."

"We are happy to see you," Bethany said. "Now we can all go home together, the same way we came here."

"I don't think so," Alec said, "I was in the last group out the doors so everyone who's going back is here." He gestured toward the end of the bay, "They're already starting to load the shuttles."

The all started looking around the room for Raymond and as the groups began to thin out, as more people made their way onto the shuttles, it became very apparent that he wasn't there.

"No," Cassie said, "That's not possible, it's a mistake, he'll be out in a minute, he's just late that's all."

"Everyone's out Cassie," Alec said, "they secured the doors behind my group. He's not coming."

"Well fuck that," she replied, "it's a mistake! Who do we talk to about it because I'm not fucking leaving without him!"

"You can opt to stay here with him, I think they let you do that," Alec told her and Ben thought he saw a tiny hint of the smirk again. Cassie turned to him, her face kind of blank for a moment, then she lunged at him and he and Bethany had to hold her back.

"You think this is funny you piece of shit?" she screamed at Alec, "You're standing here with the decent people while Raymond is back there with your friends? This whole thing was about getting rid of losers like you; it was about getting all of you off of Earth just like scraping shit from the bottom of our fucking shoe!"

"Well apparently they've come to the conclusion that Raymond is the shit to be scraped," Alec replied calmly, "and I'm not. He always was a superior and judgmental asshole and apparently they hold that against you, who knew?" He turned and walked away from them toward the shuttles.

"We have to go too Cass," Ben said numbly, "we can't miss our shuttle."

"We can't just leave without him Ben, I'm not doing that!"

"You have to," Bethany said to her and began crying quietly, "we have to go now; you can get in touch with him when we get back and we can try to figure it out."

"It takes a year or more just to get a call through to someone up here, they told us that," Cassie said. "He's right on the other side of that wall, I want to talk to him now!" she started to sob and they took her arms to lead her toward the shuttles. Ben saw a med standing close by with an injection gun, he shook his head and the med moved away, someone else had started to shout in another part of the bay.

The three of them sat together on the shuttle and didn't speak. They were almost the last to board and they all looked once more around the cavernous launch bay but it was empty. Just after launch they were offered a sleep aid and they all took it, it was easier.

Chapter Nine

There was one final processing station after they arrived back on Earth and they passed through it quickly. They'd missed the monorail by a few minutes and the next one wouldn't arrive for 30 minutes so they sat down to wait and they still didn't speak. Around them were the other shuttle passengers, back home again, and most of them weren't speaking either. They were sitting quietly staring straight ahead at nothing. Ben saw Alec sitting by himself on the far side of the room; he walked over and sat down beside him.

"Careful," Alec said to him, "Cassie might cut you loose if you talk to me."

"She's upset."

"It never even occurred to her that Raymond wouldn't be coming back did it."

"It occurred to you?"

"It did."

"Care to tell me why?"

"You've known him as long as I have, you tell me."

"No mood to play games," Ben replied. "Just tell me."

"He's judgmental, he has a superior attitude, meaning that he basically thinks he's better than everyone else, he's changed career paths how many times because he can never seem to get along with his superiors? Basically he's just an asshole and I guess they're looking to get rid of as many assholes as possible."

"So how'd you slip by?"

Alec glanced at him for a moment then laughed. "Don't think I should be here?" he asked.

"I've known you since we were kids Alec, you've been in trouble with enforcement I can't remember how many times, you've never had a real job, even though it always looks like you do, who knows how many scams you've run over the years to make a living, including some things that I suspect may have involved violence, you associate with a lot of questionable people, you were even doing it up there this past week. Do you want me to go on?"

"No," Alec smiled, "I get the gist and you're right about all of it."

"So I'll ask again, how is it that you're here."

"Those questionable people you mentioned, my shady friends, they do have their uses. And you'd be badly mistaken to confuse shady with stupid"

"What does that mean?"

"Thing with them is that not all of them are underachievers like me, some of them have major careers, cutting edge stuff...like with the companies that made the machines the we all sat in front of today."

"The machines are fool proof, "Ben replied, "That's why they removed the human element from the exams."

"Yes, they removed it from the exams but they couldn't remove it from the machines themselves could they. Humans had to design them and build them. Those humans would know how they worked... and how they didn't."

"You're trying to tell me that you found a way to fool the machine, that you cheated, that's not possible."

Alec showed that little grin again, "If you say so," he said and raised both arms, "and yet, here I sit. There's always a way Ben, always, and someone will always find it. Raymond would have done well to realize that don't you think?"

"You cheated," Ben said slowly, "my God! How many others Alec, do you know?"

The monorail pulled into the station and Alec stood up, he looked down at Ben and smiled again. "Welcome to the new Earth, our utopia" he said and started to walk away then stopped and turned back, "You really shouldn't expect too much from it."

Riding the Train; Part Two

The 5:40 to Worcester

One

Jillian Flint tried never to fall asleep on the train, partly because the last time she did she had woken up two stops past the stop where her car was parked and partly because if she was asleep one of her lovely fellow riders could reach right into her purse and help themselves.

On that Monday the 5:40 to Worcester wasn't five minutes out of Boston's South Station when her Kindle dropped into her lap and she fell dead away into a deep sleep.

Two

She woke up slowly and looked around. Her Kindle was still in her lap so that was good but her train car was completely empty and that wasn't. She sat straight up and looked down the length of the car, she like to sit in one of the single seats at the end of the cars so no one could sit next to her and the second level on her car was most definitely empty. She put her stuff away, got up and went down the stairs to the first level and it was empty too. If they had forgotten about her and left her sound asleep while they did their entire run then returned to Boston and parked the train with her still in it she was going to have someone's balls for it.

She pulled open the door to the outer vestibule meaning to check the car behind hers but ran into a problem because there wasn't one. The opening at the end of her car was covered over with a heavy curtain or tarp or something. The vestibule also had doors on either side giving access to the outside so she turned to the one on her left. All she saw beyond the window was darkness. They had done it, they had never checked the train after their run and now it was parked in the shed and everyone was gone and all the lights were off, motherfuckers! She reached up above the door and yanked down on the red emergency handle then shoved the door open. Beyond the door was blackness so absolute that it seemed like a physical barrier to her. She put her stuff down, held both sides of the door frame and leaned out then quickly pulled herself back in and backed away from the door.

When she'd leaned out the air had suddenly gotten colder and her spatial orientation had gone nuts on her, dizziness, a sense that she was going to fall, it seemed like there was nothing out there, when she leaned out the door there was nothing, no light, no solid ground just…nothing. She approached the door again, carefully, and put her head out again, just her head, and fought the immediate feeling of nausea to quickly look both ways then she withdrew back into the middle of the vestibule. She had been able to see the entire length of the double-decker car she was on but beyond it was nothing, no lights, just nothing. The same when she looked in the other direction; a couple of feet to the end of her car then absolute stygian blackness. And cold air, cold air that had a stale smell to it.

She reached into her carry bag and rooted around for a few moments until she found what she was looking for, a chemical light stick like you could buy in the dollar store or a drugstore. She had a handful of them in her bag for "just in case". She was very big on "just in case", as had been her mother. You just never knew when the poop was going to slam into the paddles and you needed to be prepared that was all. And Jill Flint prided herself on being prepared for anything. She snapped the light stick to activate it then tossed it out the open door. It flew beyond the door then was just…gone, just blinked out as if it had gone through a black curtain. She thought about trying again but decided to hold onto the rest of the light sticks because you just never knew.

She walked down the center aisle of the first level to the opposite end of the train and still nobody. She went out into the vestibule and looked out those windows and it was the same, no lights, no nothing.

Then behind her someone said hello and she almost jumped right out of her fucking skin.

Three

She spun around and there was a guy standing on the stairs from the upper level and she knew him. Well, she didn't know him, he was one of the train people she saw every day because they rode into work and home on the same train she did. Some riders became "train buddies" with people they rode with every day, sat with them, talked, and even brought one another snacks and coffee sometimes. She herself didn't have any "train buddies" and didn't want any because why in the world would you want to talk to total strangers just because you rode the same train with them? She knew this guy though, he wore kind of work type clothes, not a suit or anything like that and he carried a lunch pail and was a little rough looking. Manual laborer she guessed, probably never went to college and made shitty money at some menial job in the city. She was surprised he could even afford a rail pass. It was kind of a shame that professionals like her had to share the train with laborers like him; they should have their own train or something.

"Hi," he said again and smiled, "I thought I was the only one here."

"So did I," she replied stiffly, "Where were you? I just checked the entire car."

"In the head," he replied, apparently unaware that the very thought of using the bathroom on a commuter train was akin to rolling around in a pile of toxic waste. She wasn't surprised though. "I woke up and everyone was gone and I figured we were parked in one of the sheds so I thought I'd use the facilities before walking out to find someone. I didn't see you either."

"I was in the other vestibule," she told him, "And we're not parked in the shed."

"Ok," he said, "then where are we?"

"I don't know, haven't you looked outside?"

"Haven't had a chance, I came out of the head and heard someone down here so I came this way. How do you know we're not in the shed?'

She turned and pulled open the door to the outer vestibule and went out assuming he'd follow which he did. She pulled the emergency handle and opened the outside door then motioned to him to look for himself. He went to the door and started to step out.

"I wouldn't do that if I were you," she said to him, "just lean out first and look around."

So he did then pulled back quickly just as she had, he reached out to hold onto the car bulkhead. "What the fuck was that?" he said.

"I would appreciate it if you wouldn't use that kind of language in my presence," she said. Then she took out another of her light sticks and showed him that part of it. She had four light sticks left.

He stuck his head, only his head out again just as she had then backed away from the door and turned to her. "So where in the hell are we?" he asked her.

"How would I know," she replied, "I fell asleep too, I woke up and this is where we were."

He went back to the door, got done on his stomach on the floor which she found almost as disgusting as his using the bathroom, and slid forward until just his head and shoulders were outside the car. He leaned forward for a few moments then looked right and left then pulled himself back in, stood up and slid the door shut.

"There's nothing underneath us," he told her, "the wheels are sitting on tracks but there's nothing under the tracks and they just end a foot or so beyond the car." He moved to the center of the vestibule and pulled open the canvas covering door that should have offered access to the next car in line, nothing there but more blackness. He turned back to look at her. "I have no idea where we are or what's going on but I don't think stepping off this car would be a good move."

"Obviously," she replied. "We'll just wait here, someone will come eventually."

"What would make you think that exactly?"

"We're on a train car, "she responded as if explaining something to a child, "the train car belongs to the transit authority, sooner or later they're going to come looking for it aren't they."

"Lady, I don't know where we are but I have a sneaking suspicion that it's not anywhere that the transit authority is going to find us."

"If you don't know where we are then what are you basing your sneaking suspicion on?"

"The fact that there's nothing 'out there' that the rest of the train is gone along with all the passengers, and that 'out there' feels really wrong."

She frowned at him, "what do you mean; feels wrong?"

"You stuck your head out there too, you know what I mean. Oh, and I forgot the little fact that we're sitting on train tracks that are themselves sitting on nothing."

The sliding door from the vestibule to the interior of the car was still open; she stepped through it and sat down on one of the jump seats along the wall of the inner vestibule. He came to the doorway and leaned against the door jamb.

"I know you," he said, "you're always on the 7:20 coming in and always on the 5:40 going home, you used to always ride with that tall pale dude but lately you've been alone. You get on and off at Wellesley Hills."

"What have you been doing, watching me?"

"Well I will admit that you're easy on the eyes but no, I haven't been watching you, after a while you just notice the other people on the train that's all."

She snorted at that but didn't respond. Let him think whatever he wanted to. It did bother her though that he had been watching her and knew where she parked to catch the train.

"What happened to pale guy?"

"That isn't any of your business is it?"

"Just trying to make conversation, that's all, so what do you do in the city? For work I mean."

"That also isn't any of your business."

"Ok, fine lady, jeez, just trying to lighten things up and take our minds off our problem here. Since we're stuck in this mess it may be good to get to know one another a little better."

"Why?"

"Because that's what people do, they get to know each other. It's not like we have anything else to do."

"Is that an obtuse way of saying that we *should* have something else to do?"

"I'm not following you."

"Oh I don't know, we're stuck here together, it's a stressful situation, maybe we could relax a bit and pass the time by having sex."

He looked at her for a long moment then smiled, "Are you for real lady? Seriously?"

"Well you seem to know all about me, when I get on and off the train so you've obviously been watching me, and now you're hinting that we're here all alone and should get to know one another, to relieve the tension. What else could you possibly mean? The answer is no by the way, you're really not my type."

He looked at her for a long moment then laughed, "You are something aren't you. I was just trying to make conversation lady, that's all, really. And you're not my type either."

"Oh I'm sure, if I gave you the go ahead you'd be all over me like a shot. That's how guys like you are isn't it?"

He was still leaning against the door jamb but now he was looking at her a little like she was some kind of strange creature he'd never seen before. "And who exactly are guys like me?"

"You know, out with the boys every night, pounding beers, looking to score then brag about it with your friends later. Believe me; I know all about guys like you."

"Lady, I'm really beginning to think that you've never even met any guys like me and that it's too bad because the experience would have done you some good."

"And how's that? I need a real man to show me what I'm missing, throw me on the floor and jungle fuck me?"

"I thought we weren't allowed to use that word."

She looked at him for a long moment and he suddenly realized that she was on the edge; she was scare shitless and was covering it up by being a bitch, or being more of a bitch than usual. "Are you making fun of me?" she asked him.

"I am not, and I'm not interested in having sex with you, not that you're not very attractive because you are, but I kind of have other things on my mind right now and I think you do to. We have to figure out what we're going to do here."

"I already told you, we're going to wait until someone comes looking for us."

"And what if they don't?"

"They will."

"Ok, they will, in the meantime, could I have another one of those light sticks, I wanted to try something."

"I only have four left."

"Were you saving them for a 4th of July party or something?"

"I may need them if the lights go out."

That stopped him. He looked around them at the interior of the car...the lights indeed were on, all of the lights were on, and the ventilation system was working, they were so used to the background noise of it they hadn't noticed but it was working. He looked at her again.

"How are the lights on if the car's not connected to anything?" he asked.

"Doesn't it get power through the rails?"

"No, that's a subway car, train cars get power from the engine but there isn't an engine, so how is it that the lights and air conditioning are still working?" He looked around the vestibule and found a couple of access panels in the bulkhead. He tried to open one but it was locked so he pulled a pocket knife from a pants pocket and began trying to jimmy it.

"That's Transit Authority property, you could get in trouble for that," she told him.

"They left us in the dark on a deserted rail car," he replied, "I'll take my chances." He couldn't get the door open by prying it so he started on the lock itself with the knife blade.

"Why aren't I your type," she asked him.

He turned to face her, "What?"

"You said I'm not your type either, why not?"

He thought for a moment then shrugged, "You look like your high maintenance, like you would want someone to spend a lot of money on you and kiss your ass while they're doing it, I wouldn't go for that."

"You're very insulting do you know that? And you don't know me at all; I think you just feel threatened because I make more money that you do."

"How do you know you make more money that I do?" he had gone back to working on the door lock.

"Isn't it obvious?"

"Not really."

"The way you dress, the way I dress, the way you talk, the way I talk, all of it."

"My mother taught me that you should never judge a book by its cover."

"My mother taught me that if it looks like a duck and quakes like a duck it's usually a duck."

"My mother taught me never to get involved with anyone whose problems are greater than your own."

"What does that mean?"

"I think it's fairly obvious isn't it?"

"I don't have any problems, my life is just fine."

"Oh yeah, then where's tall pale guy?"

"Go fuck yourself."

"Wow, that's not very sophisticated language is it, and I'd like to point out that so far you've used that word twice as much as I have."

"But you'd really rather screw me wouldn't you," she said is if she hadn't heard him.

"Oh god, are we back to that again? You have a very high opinion of yourself you know that? And it seems to me that you're the one with sex on the brain not me. You're the one who keeps bringing it up."

"Because I know what's going to happen here, the longer we're here the more tense it's going to get, the more isolated we're going to feel, and sooner or later you're going to decide that if we're stuck here like this you might as well have some fun. In desperate situations people always revert to their animal instincts."

He stopped working on the lock and turned to face her. "Have you had some experience with that kind of thing?"

"No, I have not! But I know how things go. I know what you're thinking even if you don't yet."

"You don't know shit lady, what's your name?"

"You mean you don't know it? You seem to know everything else about me."

He sighed and tried again, "look, you're upset and scared, I don't blame you, this is a very strange situation that we're in. But we're in it together and we should try to get along and solve it together. You continuing to accuse me of things I haven't done, or even thought about doing isn't helping."

"Now you're just being mendacious to get me to relax and lower my guard."

"I have no idea what that word means."

"See what happens when you don't get an education?"

He shook his head and turned back to the access door. He made a couple of halfhearted stabs at the door then turned back to her;

"I wanted the light stick to try something different outside," he said, trying to diffuse the conversation. "I was going to lean out and toss it parallel to the tracks and see what happens, maybe the rest of the tracks are still there but we can't see them."

She looked at him for a moment then reached into her bag and took out a light stick. She stood up and handed it to him.

He took it and went back to the outer door; she followed him out into the outer vestibule and stood behind him. He leaned out the door but not very far and faced forward in the direction that the rail car ended just a few feet away. Even though he was barely out of the car he started to become disorientated again. He got ready to toss the light stick straight ahead in the direction that would be up the tracks if the tracks were still there. She moved into the doorway behind him so she would also be able to see where the light stick went. He tossed it underhand as hard as he could and in doing so his other hand slipped off of the metal doorframe. For a moment he thought he was going out of the car, he bumped right into her, his arms wind milling and she started to go out instead. He turned and got a hand on one of the grab bars inside the vestibule then reached out for her but she had already grabbed the door jamb and yanked herself back into the vestibule.

She retreated to the other side of the small space, breathing hard, her eyes wild. He was breathing hard himself; almost going out of the car had scared the shit out of him. He held onto the grab bar and tried to catch his breath. He was about to ask her if she was all right when she screamed at him.

"YOU TRIED TO PUSH ME OUT OF THE CAR!"

He frowned at her, "What? I didn't, I lost my balance and accidently bumped you, that's all. I reached out to try to grab you once I got my balance."

"THE FUCK YOU DID, YOU BUMPED ME AND THEN WHEN I DIDN'T GO OUT YOU TRIED TO PUSH ME!"

He reached out and slid the outer door closed then turned back to her, "Lady, I swear I didn't, I tried to throw the thing too hard and lost my balance, that's all."

She was still breathing hard, she was staring at him and he didn't like the look in her eyes. If she had any kind of weapon in that bag he could be in trouble here.

"Why would I possibly want to push you out of the car?" he asked her. "Think about it."

Her breath slowed down a bit but nothing else changed, she was looking at him like he was a wild animal that had suddenly found its way into the car. And when she spoke she'd stopped yelling but just barely; "Because I insulted you, because I don't want to have anything to do with you, because you're jealous of me and don't like me because I'm better than you. Because I won't have sex with you! Take your pick you asshole! And I remember you from the train too! You're one of the ones that are always pushing your way past people to get a better seat and rushing other people to get out of your way, oh I remember you all right. AND YOU JUST TRIED TO KILL ME!"

"You know what Lady, and at this point I don't really give a shit what your name is, you are bat crap crazy. I understand we're in a strange situation here but you have gone completely around the bend."

She started at him for a few more moments before she spoke. "I want you to get away from me," she said finally, "I don't want you anywhere near me anymore."

"I'm all for that," he replied, "the sooner the better. Where do you suggest I go?"

"To the other end of the car, you stay down there and I'll stay down here. I don't want you coming past the halfway point. And when we are finally rescued don't think I'm not going to tell them about this."

"You tell them anything at all that comes into your head," he said and picked up his lunch pail. "The bathroom is down at my end of the car, if you need to use it just yell and I'll move to neutral ground."

"Like I would ever use the bathroom on a train," she snorted.

He shook his head and started down the aisle, "maybe you can just hang your butt out over the door sill," he said over his shoulder and then he was gone.

She stood there and listened as he moved down to the other end of the car and then waited for a few minutes to be sure he wasn't coming back. Finally she sat down on one of the jump seats and stared at the darkness on the other side of the windows.

Four

She was tired and she wanted to sleep but she was afraid to because something might happen and she'd miss it or *he* might come down to her end and she wouldn't know it. She got up a couple of times and went into the outer vestibule but being out there alone made her nervous so she returned to her jump seat, making sure the sliding door was closed tightly behind her.

So she sat there and thought about it. Why had just the two of them still been on the train? What had happened to everyone else, when she'd fallen asleep the car had been full, there had even been passengers standing where she was now because there were no more seats so where were they? She had been asleep when whatever happened happened, maybe he had been too. He'd told her he had been but he didn't seem like the type to sleep on a train and she didn't believe him. So why didn't he tell her what had happened? He'd been awake when it happened so he must have seen something, he must know something, but he never said. She really started to think about that and suddenly it made sense, he had been awake so he knew how they got here but he never told her, and why was it just the two of them, why was that? And why hadn't he just told her what had happened instead of all the stuff about looking outside and under the car and all, why hadn't he just said Jill, we were rolling along and suddenly the train stopped and everyone got off and then we were here and.....she stopped because that was it, they had stopped and everyone had gotten off except her because she was asleep and him because he saw that she was asleep and instead of waking her up had stayed behind with her so he'd have her alone on the rail car, so it would just be the two of them here. He didn't *want* her to know what happened because he wanted her here with him so he could do whatever it was that he wanted to do with her. She stared out the window and listened.

He may even be responsible for all of this, how did she know. He may be play acting and pretending to be helpful when he's really not. What he's really doing is trying to break her down and get her to the point where she'd dependent on him and willing to do whatever he wants her to do. But what if that doesn't work, what's his plan then? She thought she knew...

Suddenly a bunch of banging started down at his end of the car and she jumped straight out of her seat. She hunched over so she could look down the length of the lower aisle but she couldn't see him. Then she climbed halfway up the stairs to the upper aisle and looked but still couldn't see him. The banging stopped for a moment then started up again then finally stopped for good. She watched both aisles for a while but didn't see him. She began looking around the vestibule and noticed that the access door he'd been trying to open earlier looked like it was ajar. She went over to it and slid her fingers in behind the door around the locking mechanism and managed to pop the door all the way open. She pulled it open just as the banging started again down at the other end. She glanced over her shoulder then looked inside the compartment and saw a long cable with big sockets at each end and one big wrench. She reached in and grabbed the wrench, it was big, probably two feet long and it was heavy. She took it back to her seat with her, sat down and laid it across her lap. She sat there and listened to the banging and after a while it stopped again.

Five

At some point she dozed, her head dropping onto her chest, both hands holding onto the wrench. The banging had stopped for good a short time before. She dreamed that she was falling through the darkness outside, that she had woken up with the urge to pee and unwilling to go down to his end had taken his advice and hung her butt of out the door, holding on to the doorjamb with both hands. She'd been fine until she tried to stand back up, that's when she lost her balance and tumbled backwards into the abyss. All because *he* had taken the end of the car with the bathroom.

She came awake with a start, her heart racing and grabbed the edge of her seat because she still felt like she was falling. The wrench clattered onto the floor and she heard him, yelling to her and running down the lower aisle toward her. She got down on her knees and looked down the aisle and he was almost to her, running, with a long metal pole in his hands.

She grabbed the wrench and got to her feet, staggering back against the sliding door just as he vaulted up the steps from the lower level.

"I need your help," he was shouting, "I need you to come with me, I found somethi....." She swung the wrench from right to left, two handed grip, she swung from the toes and caught him just above the ear. The blow sent him across the vestibule and against the bulkhead and he stumbled but he didn't fall even though there was blood gushing from his head so she swung again, this time up over the top of her shoulder and brought the wrench down hard on the center of his forehead. He went down then, the bar he'd been carrying to hit her with clattered to the floor and he fell back against one of the jump seats and his eyes were open but she could tell he was dead.

Six

She was sitting in the jump seat looking at him. She'd thrown her scarf over his head so she didn't have to look at his eyes and now it was drenched with blood and completely ruined. She was thinking about what she was going to do, what she was going to say when she was rescued. He had attacked her, there was no doubt about that of course but, she didn't have any cuts or bruises to display to the police, there were no signs of violence in the rail car except of course for his head. Then it occurred to her that she wouldn't have to say a damn thing, she wouldn't have to account for anything.

She got up and crossed over to him. He was still in kind of a sitting position against the jump seat, slumped over to one side. She leaned down, grabbed his ankles and pulled until he was flat on the floor. Then she knelt down next to him and fished his wallet out of his back jeans pocket because later maybe she could check him out, she was sure she'd find that he had a record. She opened the wallet and saw almost two hundred dollars in it which surprised her. She saw the edge of a driver's license in a slit pocket and pulled it out; Jason Barry, he was 36 years old and lived in Cochituate which surprised her too, it was a nice town, near where she lived. Then she saw the edge of another card that had been behind the driver's license and pulled it out.

It was a faculty ID card for Professor Jason Barry, Suffolk University, Boston, his picture was on it, he looked a little younger in it and of course his head wasn't bashed in. She looked at it for another moment then put both cards back in the wallet, there were photos in there too but she didn't look at them, she put the wallet back in his pocket. She grasped his ankles again and began pulling him toward the door and Christ was he heavy. She stopped to catch her breath and slide open the door to the outer vestibule then continued until she had him completely in the outer vestibule. She went to the same door they'd opened earlier and looked out, still nothing but black. She reached up and pulled down the emergency handle again and shoved the door open and stepped back as the feeling of disorientation came rushing back. She managed to push and roll him toward the open door, always keeping him between her and the opening, until he was lying at the threshold on his side, back to her, in kind of a fetal position. She thought about retrieving her scarf, maybe she could salvage it, but she didn't want to touch it. She sat down on the metal floor, grabbed something on both sides of the vestibule, a grab bar on the left and some type of valve pipe on the right. Then she placed both of her feet on his back and shoved him out of the car. She turned around and, on hands and knees, hair hanging in her face, she went carefully to the open door and looked out; nothing, just blackness. She backed away a bit to get to her feet then slid the door closed, went back to the inner vestibule and slid that door closed too. She got a brush from her bag and fixed her hair.

Seven

She'd decided to move down to the other end of the car, when she got there she found his lunch pail on one of the seats. She opened the inner door, went out to the vestibule, pushed aside the canvass covering the opening meant to go to the next car and tossed it out.

She was closing the inner vestibule door behind her when she noticed that he had managed to pry open two access doors in the bulkhead. One was the very same one she had gotten open at her end but there was only a big hose inside, no wrench. The other was completely empty. There was also a section of railing missing from the lower stairs, the longest section. He had apparently torn it off and that was what he was carrying when he had come to kill her. And then she noticed a third panel hanging open, it was located in the bulkhead just inside the door. She had never noticed a door there before on any of the rail cars and she was sure there wasn't one at her end of the car. Inside was a small square compartment with a bright yellow T shaped lever, the head of the T pointed up toward the ceiling. After just a moment's hesitation she reached out and pulled the lever down. The right hand door in the outer vestibule slid open and sunlight flooded into the train car. She heard voices too, and a car engine. She let go of the handle and rushed toward the outer vestibule and the door slid shut. When she got to it there was nothing beyond the window but blackness. She pulled down the emergency lever, slid the door open and poked her head out. She looked all around for as long as she could before the nausea got to her and she pulled her head back in and pulled the door shut. There was still just nothing out there, just blackness.

She went back to the yellow handle, it had snapped back into the up position, and pulled it down again, this time leaning as far as she could toward the open inner door. Once again the outer door opened to admit bright sunshine and again she hear people talking, someone laughed, and another car engine. She could stretch out just far enough while still holding the yellow handle to see a sliver of the open doorway but all she could see was what looked like a parking lot. She let go of the handle and rushed the door again but it closed before she could get there and when she did; back to blackness outside.

She spent the next hour looking for something to wedge into the little opening to keep the yellow handle in the down position but nothing in her bag worked, the handle always snapped back into the up position. Then she looked for something to tie it down with but realized that there was nothing near it to tie something to that would keep the lever down. Then she tried pulling the handle down, reaching out and tossing the wrench at the door to block it open, after numerous tries in which the wrench just clunked down on the floor in the outer vestibule she finally got a good throw, the result of which was the wrench sliding out of the car through the open door and disappearing.

She sank down into one of the jump seats and cursed, kicking her foot against the seat base. Then she thought of the pole that he had torn off the stairs, the one he had intended to hit her with. She got up and went back to the other end of the car and retrieved it and brought it back with her. She looked at it and thought; it wasn't long enough to reach the door from where she was while holding the handle down, it wouldn't have been for him either. So she tried laying it down on the floor where she could push it toward the open door while holding the handle down, maybe the pole would block the door open but it turned out that didn't work either, she managed to pull down the lever and kick the pole so it's end blocked the outer door but as soon as she let go of the lever the door slammed shut, shooting the pole back into the outer vestibule. It came back so hard that she stumbled over it while she was rushing for the open door and she fell to her knees in the vestibule. She stayed there for a time, head down, hair hanging in her face, cursing at the door, the pole, the train car, and the commuter rail operator.

Then she thought of something else, she pulled the lever down again but this time braced one end of the pole against the lever and the other against the ceiling, the ceiling was mostly smooth but she discovered that there were seams that she was able to brace the edge of the pole into. Once she had it set she let go of the pole and the lever and turned to go out the door. She was willing to bet that if he had discovered this method he would have just left without her. She got two steps into the outer vestibule, far enough to see more of a parking lot and an actual tree and then the door slid closed again. She screamed at it and went back, the fucking lever was down! She reached out and grasped it to be sure the pipe was keeping it all the way down and the door opened again. She rushed toward it and it closed. She screamed again and kicked the metal wall of the vestibule until her foot ached, then she kicked it some more with the other one.

She finally went back inside and collapsed onto a jump seat and tried to think. So the yellow lever only worked when someone was actually holding it down, someone had to be touching it, pressing down on it, just bracing it didn't work for whatever reason. Maybe it was body heat from her hand, or maybe it only operated with a biological signal or something like that and it didn't really matter fuck all did it because she had no way to hold it down and get to the door. And then she thought about him and what if he was still there? But she decided it wouldn't matter because even if one of them had held the lever down and kept their hand on it the other one could have stepped out the door but wouldn't have been able to hold it open long enough for the first person to reach it. When she'd managed to get the pipe into the doors track it had closed so hard it had sent the pipe, which was pretty heavy, shooting across the outer vestibule. And she'd heard the door slam closed each time she'd tried to reach it. No, you'd need to have one person hold the lever down while the other used something substantial to brace the door open, at least for a few seconds. Something like...she looked down at the pipe lying on the floor at her feet. Something like a steel pipe set lengthwise into the door track so it was jammed against the edge of the door and the door frame. Yeah, that would probably work wouldn't it? And you'd need two people to do that wouldn't you?

So then she thought about him running back toward her end of the car holding the pole; 'I need your help, I need you to come with me, I found somethi...', that's what he'd said wasn't it? He'd found what? That the two of them, using the pole, could have gotten out of the car, gotten out from wherever the hell the car was now to that sunlit parking lot with the people and the cars driving past? He was a college professor after all, pretty smart guy, and probably not a killer. And she'd been right in a way too, there had been a way out of their predicament hadn't there? It was just that they had to save themselves, both of them. College professor, really smart guy...

She let her head fall back against the window behind her seat and she closed her eyes. "Son of a bitch," she whispered to herself because there was no one else there to hear her.

Epilog

They were standing on the platform waiting for their train when Arron said; "did you just see that?"

"See what?"

"Just on the far side of the tracks, about six feet off the ground, there was a shimmer or something."

"A what, a shimmer, what's a shimmer?"

"Like a shimmer in the air, like when there's a heat wave, I saw it twice."

"Jeez, I told you we should have stopped for coffee."

"Jessica, I saw something, it was the weirdest thing."

"Well where is it now? I don't see anything."

"It's gone."

"What did it look like, just wavy air?"

"Yeah, kind of, but there was something else in it, it was kind of like an old under exposed movie reel."

"Of what?"

"I'm not positive, but it sure looked like a train car door opening and closing."

For God and Country

1.

He got on the train at South Station with a bunch of other people who were trying to stay as far away from him as possible. He wasn't sure why he got on the train, maybe it was because he was tired of sleeping on the streets of Boston, or trudging to the nearest shelter when the weather got too cold to bear, like it was now, and sleeping on a cot with strangers on either side of him who smelled worse than he did. He had walked onto the train loading platforms from the street, if he had come in through the terminal he probably never would have reached the trains, the transit cops would have bum rushed him on sight, and none of the events that followed would have happened.

But he did reach the platforms and there was a train there just getting ready to pull out so he got on and took a seat right by the door. There were five other seats in the little vestibule area by the door and they were all empty. This was because it was the middle of the day and the train wasn't crowded but it was also because he looked, and smelled, like what he was, a homeless guy. No one wanted to be sitting anywhere near him.

The conductor didn't come around checking tickets until after the second stop so by the time it was determined that he didn't have a ticket and didn't have any money to buy one the train was almost to its third stop; South Weymouth, and so that's where he was put off.

He stood on the empty platform for a few minutes looking around; the parking lot was full of cars that belonged to people who were in the city working, making money, living lives, people who knew where they were going to sleep that night. Only one passenger had gotten off the train there, a woman who had taken one look at him then hurried to her car and driven away and that was ok, he was used to it. He walked down the short driveway to the station entrance and stopped. To his right was a busy road with stores and stuff, to his left were woods and fields and open space. He stood for a moment in contemplation and then made the second decision of the day that would end up having a profound impact on his life; he turned toward the open space and walked on.

He passed two old abandoned buildings on his left then rounded a curve in the road, which looked new he noticed, and a condominium complex came into view. As he got closer he saw that the condos were more like townhouses than apartments and they looked new too, they looked like a nice place to live. They also looked like the kind of place where someone would call the cops on him pretty quick. Across the street from the complex was a huge open space that finally ended at a far tree line. Down the middle of it was a wide strip of concrete with faded whites lines painted down its center that stretched into the distance. It took him a minute to realize that he was looking at a runway, a big one that came right up to the edge of the condo complex. Its surface was cracked and speckled with dead weeds and it was obviously abandoned. Past the condos and to the left of the runway in the near distance was a cluster of sorry looking buildings dominated by a large airplane hangar. There were jersey barriers running alongside the new roads of the condo complex but he simply stepped between them and headed out across the uneven ground toward the buildings. As he got away from the condos and into the open space he noticed that the wind had picked up which in turn made him notice that the sky was gone a flat gray color, a storm was coming, he thought by nightfall at the latest. It had been cold when he'd left the heated interior of the train but it seemed a lot colder now, maybe because there was nothing here to shelter him from the wind.

It took him about five minutes to walk to the hanger because on the way he had to go around a couple of rusted and collapsing chain link fences and lots of uneven pavement and debris. When he finally got to the hanger it was pretty big, big enough to put maybe two airliners inside it nose to nose. It had been built with steel girders and panels most of which were rusting; the top half of one side was all windows of which half appeared to be broken. On the other side was an attached industrial style wing that didn't seem to have any doors.

He circled the hangar looking for a way in and finally found it on the far side at an access door that was slightly ajar. He slipped through it into the cavernous interior and stood looking around in awe. It was one enormous room, the roof sixty feet above him and an immense concrete floor. The only thing that broke the symmetry of the space was a small office huddled against the far wall in the center of the hanger. He crossed the hanger and checked the office but there was nothing there, stripped clean. The wind was still building and was whistling in through all the broken windows along the wall. Not much shelter available there so he crossed back to the access door and stepped back outside.

There were quite a few more buildings further on and he headed toward them. They were all boarded up, at least at ground level but, the two story buildings upper windows had been left alone. This had obviously been some type of military base but he cared not at all about that at the moment, he needed to get in somewhere out of the cold and the coming storm.

He passed a large building that looked like a power plant and another with oversized garage doors. Like everything else he saw they appeared to be boarded up tight. He came to another road, this one much older, uneven and worn that the first and he stopped. To his right past the power plant building there was wide open space. To his left were more buildings and trees that would at least shelter him from the rising wind. He turned left.

He passed two overgrown tennis courts on his left and a group of maintenance buildings on his right, then up ahead he spotted a chapel and he headed toward that. It turned out to be boarded up tight too. Directly across the old road he saw a pair of long narrow buildings running parallel to the road, one behind the other. As with the other buildings the first floor windows were boarded over but he crossed the road anyway to look them over. The wind was starting to bite through his cloths now even here where he was sheltered by trees and buildings. As he reached the first of the long narrow buildings it began to snow, not hard, just flurries, but still, it wasn't good.

The two long buildings looked like living quarters, barracks or maybe officers housing, from back when there were officers here. He circled the one furthest from the road first and had no luck, boarded up tight. But then he noticed something with the second one, the one next to the road; the door on ground level at the very end of the building wasn't boarded over. He crossed the area between the two buildings walking across an old basketball court, the two backboards still standing but tilted at crazy angles and rimed with rust, and then a small parking lot that was actually pretty clear, just a few weeds coming up through cracks in the pavement and an occasional piece of debris, a chunk of concrete or a length of steel piping. Behind the parking lot were an old decrepit maintenance shed and a larger concrete building then a solid line of trees.

By the time he reached the door the snow had given up all pretense and was coming down hard and fast, blown almost vertical by the still rising wind. He tried the door and of course it was locked. He studied it for a moment, his head bent against the driving snow, it had a standard commercial steel lever handle with an internal lock and above that a dead bolt set into the door. The deadbolt had a lot of rust around the edges of the drum lock and he guessed it hadn't been turned in a very long time.

He stepped back off the concrete step and looked up at the second floor because he had pretty much decided at that point that he needed to get in somewhere fast, the weather would probably kill him if he didn't. The windows were large sliding casement windows with the exception of four smaller windows at the center of the building that he guessed were a bathroom. Even if he could find a way to get up there they were probably all locked and casement windows were almost impossible to force open and the bathroom windows were too small for him to fit through. The only broken windows he'd seen so far were in the hangar, it was obvious that someone looked after this place from time to time or that it just didn't get any visitors or vandals. A broken window would be asking to be noticed.

He circled around to the front of the building where he found another door. This building was situated at an angle from the road and this end was the one furthest from it. Plus, there was a group of overgrown evergreen trees at this end that effectively blocked the last thirty feet or so of the building from view. This door had the exact same set up as the last one except that when he studied this deadbolt he noticed that it was in much better shape than the one out front. The stand of trees that crowded against this end of the building had sheltered the door from the weather which was probably why this lock had aged better. He studied it for a moment then returned to the rear of the building and crossed the old parking lot to the maintenance shed and looked at that door. It was locked but it was also about ready to fall off its hinges, he simply forced it open and stepped inside. The walls of the building were worse than the door, he could see daylight through them and he hoped the whole thing didn't come down on his head while he was inside. As he'd suspected, some things had been left behind here, not much but there were a few broken tools, nuts and bolts, and something he could use, an old oil can sitting far back on a wooden shelf. The can was so frigging old that someone had opened it with a church key but that didn't matter, he took out his pocket knife, small enough not to get him charged with carrying a concealed weapon but big enough to come in handy, and cut the can in half. At its bottom was a residue of motor oil, not much but enough for his needs. He took the bottom half of the can and left the shed, walking back into what was quickly becoming a no shit snow storm. When he'd crossed the parking lot to the shed he could see the cracked pavement and faded white lines that once delineated parking spots but now a film of snow covered everything.

He got back to the door and it was a bit better, the building and the evergreen trees offered some shelter from the wind. He put his pack down against the door then reached deep into an inner pocket of his ragged coat and came out with a small cloth bundle. He unrolled the cloth to reveal an assortment of old fashioned metal lock picks, possession of which was a felony in Massachusetts by the way. He chose two of them from the collection then rolled the cloth back up and returned it to the pocket. Kneeling down in front of the door he ran both picks around in the bottom of the oil can to coat them with what as much oil residue as he could then he inserted them into the deadbolt lock, working them in slowly then moving them around inside to spread the oil. He withdrew them, re-coated them from the can then repeated the exercise. He did this until he wasn't able to scrape anymore oil from the bottom of the can then he positioned the two picks to go to work on the lock, hoping the oil had loosened it up enough for its guts to work and not just break his picks. He positioned on pick at the bottom of the drum, using it to put pressure on the drum to turn to the left. With the other curved pick he delicately began working the tumblers inside the lock, trying to push them up and lock them as a key would have done. He did own a pair of ratty old gloves, they were in his pack, but picking a lock was a delicate task and he needed his hands bare for it even though they were beginning to really stiffen up from the cold. He kept working the lock, probably four tumblers inside, an old lock, and finally he felt one snap as it locked, then a second and a third. The final one took him some time and he wanted badly to stop and blow on his hands to warm them but he didn't because the first three tumblers would have probably dropped back down and finally the last one snapped into place. He slowly put more pressure on the drum, hoping that the oil had loosened it enough to let the frail little pick he was using move it. He applied more and more pressure, the pick started to bend, in a moment it would break in the lock and that would be that. As he knelt there the wind was beginning to pile up little drifts of snow around his legs and the bottom of the door.

The drum wasn't turning and he braced one elbow against the door handle and tried to jar the door a bit. Suddenly the cylinder turned and he heard the deadbolt slide back. He removed the picks from the cylinder and stood up. The door handle itself was still locked and that lock was small and primitive, much harder to pick under the best of circumstances never mind under these particular ones; snow whirling past his face, hands going numb...but that didn't matter because lever door handles had a fatal flaw and it was called a torque attack, a torque attack meant that if you simply applied enough downward pressure on the handle the torque produced would case the locking mechanism to fail, the handle would operate and the door would open. The companies that made these handles had eventually corrected this by installing a clutch lever which caused the lock mechanism to disengage when someone tried to force it but these were obviously old handles and he was willing to bet that they were not so equipped. He put his right hand on the lever which was pretty fucking cold at the moment and slowly applied pressure, putting his weight into it until the lock snapped, the lever swung down and the door swung open with a loud screech of protesting hinges. He picked up his pack, stepped inside, closed the door against the storm and re-locked the deadbolt behind him.

2.

After the wind outside it was eerily quiet inside the building. He was standing at the bottom of a stairwell; to his left was a door that he assumed led into the first floor which he ignored for now because with the windows all boarded up he wouldn't be able to see shit anyway. So he went up the steel stairs to the door at the top which was open a few inches, letting a weak stream of light into the stairwell. The stairs themselves were dusty and there was some paint peeling from the walls but there was no debris and he noted no footprints in what was a pretty heavy layer of dust. The building was made of concrete and seemed solid; he couldn't even hear the sounds of the storm outside while he was in the stairwell. Once he pushed the door open and stepped into the second floor hallway there was plenty of light and the sound of the storm came back, muted but definitely there, and sounding like it was still getting worse.

He was standing at the end of a long hallway running from one end of the building to the other which had to be the length of a football field. Wooden doors ran along either wall interrupted about halfway down by two large openings on the left hand side that he assumed were the bathrooms. It had definitely been a barracks of some kind. The floor was white linoleum and other than dust it was in good shape, the walls were concrete, also white and here the paint was beginning to peel at a good clip all up and down the hallway. He walked down to the first door, on his right, and pushed it open. The room was bare, same linoleum floor, big casement window that still had its plain white curtains overlooking the back parking lot and the basketball court. The next room was the same, and the one across the hall, on the front side of the building. The fourth room he checked still had two metal bedframes in it, the kind that could be used alone or as bunk beds. He was re-thinking his theory that this had been officers' quarters, not with bunk beds, probably housing for enlisted personnel.

He had gotten half way down to the bathrooms when he poked his head into a front room and got a surprise; two metal bed frames that both still had their mattresses. He entered the room and checked out the mattresses, a bit musty but not bad, the building was shut up tight and it was obvious that no critters had ever gotten in so the mattresses where in good shape. He continued on and in the remaining rooms before the bathrooms he found a third mattress, an area rug and a plain wooden night table. He went past the bathrooms for now and checked the rooms on the other side of the building where he found another small rug and three honest to god blankets, like the mattresses they were musty but in one piece, light gray with USN stenciled at one corner. He took everything with him to the room with the two mattresses then went to check out the bathrooms.

They were large dormitory style bathrooms which clinched the enlisted man's barracks theory. Each had a high center island with a row of sinks on each side, toilet stalls running along the wall to the left and shower stalls along the wall to the right. He walked up to the sink closest to the door and turned both faucets, nothing of course. He tried one of the showers too, still nothing, and noted that the toilets were all dry. He did find two towels, white, with USN stamped on them. He checked the second bathroom, mirror image of the first, and as he returned to the hallway he noticed a bulletin board on the wall between the two bathroom entrances, had walked right by it before without noticing it. There were still several thumbtacks stuck randomly in the cork, not push pins, he was pretty sure this building pre-dated push pins, and one brittle sheet of paper that had once been white held crookedly to the board by a solitary thumbtack.

It was a base closure notice stating that Weymouth Naval Reserve Air Station would cease operations permanently on September 30, 1997. It went on to notify all personnel that as that date approached they were to take the following steps to assist in the base closure followed by a list of various housekeeping tasks. He remembered something about the place now; they used to fly fighters and sub patrol aircraft out of here, and every once in a while they had airshows, with the Blue Angels even making appearances. So the base had closed 18 years ago and other than the condos he'd seen earlier at the bases perimeter the rest of the place had just been sitting here, slowly deteriorating.

It was obvious though that there were caretakers around somewhere, trees were beginning to encroach on the buildings and some of the parking areas and common areas were overgrown but the grass was being mowed around the buildings and the road outside was in use, at least sporadically because he'd seen a couple of cars pass by while he'd been up near the hanger. If the Navy still owned this part of the base they would have to put some effort into it he supposed. Or maybe whoever owned the condo's at the far end of the base owned it all and had plans for the rest. Either way he was going to have to keep his head down a bit because this place probably wasn't as deserted as he'd first thought.

He brought all his found treasures back to the front room with the two mattresses and sat down on one of the beds. This room, like most of them, had long plain white curtains on the windows. Beyond the windows the wind was still building and the snow was coming down fast in big fluffy flakes. He got

up and pulled the curtains closed then sat down again. It was still damn cold but he was out of the

weather and that should be enough to keep him alive through the night. He thought about checking the

first floor but with everything boarded up he wouldn't be able to see shit so instead he fixed up his

room; the mattresses were old and thin so he put another one on top of the one he'd been sitting on.

He took the two towels he'd found in the bathroom and rolled them up together to make a pillow, he

took his battered old sleeping bag out of his pack and stretched it over the bed and finally, he took off

his boots and jacket, wrapped himself in the two blankets and crawled into the sleeping bag. The

blankets were made of rough wool, military issue, and had a dry musty smell but he didn't care because

they would help keep him warm. In a few moments he was sound asleep.

He awoke once in the middle of the night and lay listening to the storm raging outside. It was

warm in his sleeping bag but he had to pee so he climbed out, bracing himself against the cold. There

were streetlights on outside on the old road, a few anyway, enough to cast a muted glow into the

building which he used to pad down to the bathrooms in his stocking feet. He peed into one of the dry

toilets then hurried back to his room and crawled back into the sleeping bag, pulling it and the blankets

up around his head. He was asleep again in minutes.

3.

He awoke the next morning to the storm still raging outside, he lay in his sleeping bag and

thought about being out in it, sleeping out in it, he would have been dead by this time most likely. It was

still cold in the little cinderblock room but it was inside and it was dry and it could be much worse. He finally, reluctantly, got out of the bag and pulled on his boots and coat. He parted the curtains to look out at the road and it was gone, covered by at least a foot of snow. The chapel across from his building was barely visible through the storm.

He sat down on the bed and rummaged around in his pack for a box of granola bars he'd bought a few days earlier. He ate two of them then made himself stop, saving the rest for later. Next he produced a bottle of Pepsi and took a couple of swigs of that. He'd been nursing the bottle for a few days now and so it was flat but he didn't care, it was still goddamned Pepsi wasn't it! After breakfast he got to his feet and watched the storm out the window for a while then left the room to explore the rest of the building.

Whoever had boarded the place up had done one hell of a job, the plywood sheets covering the doors and windows were tight but a little bit of light still got through around the edges and he found that after he let his eyes adjust to the gloom he could see pretty well. The first floor was laid out exactly like the second with two exceptions; at the center of the building, across from the bathrooms, was a fair sized dining hall and next to that what must have been a lounge or TV room. Both rooms were completely empty but when he got into the kitchen he found a couple of heavy white china dinner plates with chipped edges and two white china coffee cups, one with the handle broken off. Also, a pile of old rags; two steel pots and a steel frying pan, all dented to various degrees, a little pile of silverware stamped USN, and finally a battered stainless steel water pitcher. Further down in the rooms he found a couple of pillow cases, another mattress, two old sheets, and three more towels in the bathrooms. In one of the rooms there was still an old pin-up taped to the wall, it looked like one of those cheesecake drawings from World War Two that they would paint on the sides of airplanes. In another room he found a centerfold from a men's magazine on the wall, judging from the woman's hairstyle and makeup (she wasn't wearing any cloths) he thought it was probably from the 60's. He used one of the pillow cases to pack up all of his finds and left it by the bottom of the stairs. Then he descended into the basement level of the building where the gloom intensified to the point that he could see next to nothing. There were small windows scattered around but the combination of the plywood and the fact that they were recessed into the building's wall made them all but useless as a light source. He finally gave up and returned to the second floor which seemed downright bright and cheery to him now.

He arranged his room a bit, setting up the night table next to his bed which he had along the right side wall as you entered the room. He propped the third mattress he'd found up against the wall next to his bed to shield him a bit from the cold cinderblock wall. He positioned the other bed against the opposite wall and laid out his new finds on it, all the stuff from the kitchen. Then he stood at the window and watched the storm. The wind had died down but the snow was still coming down hard, must be two feet out there now. He was interested to see if anyone would be by any time soon to plow the road. Right now not a thing was moving out there. It occurred to him that it would be a perfect time to go out and hit some of the other buildings and see what he could find. And he needed to think about food too, he didn't have much with him and he couldn't stay here long without it. He dug his gloves out of his backpack which he was taking with him anyway, just in case he had to move on quickly, then he headed for the door he'd come in the previous day.

He threw the deadbolt and eased the door open and the cold hit him right in the face. He'd thought it'd been cold inside the building but outside was much worse. He steeled himself and stepped out into the snow pulling the door shut behind him but leaving it unlocked. It was a heavy steel door; he didn't think the wind would blow it open. His first stop was the larger maintenance building behind the second long narrow building. It was a low concrete building and it turned out that it was locked up tight but directly behind it was a rusting old Quonset hut that he hadn't noticed the day before. He went to it and saw that the door was padlocked but there were several windows along both sides that were flimsy enough for him to force open. He dropped into the hut and saw that it apparently had been a depository for all the crap they hadn't wanted to remove when the base closed. There was old equipment scattered everywhere and he spent some time going through it all only to realize that unless he was building a jeep from scratch or laying in some plumbing there was really nothing he could use. Just as he was leaving though he did see something he most definitely could use; a new/old deadbolt lock with the key stuck in it. He scooped it up along with a rusty screwdriver and the only pair of pliers he could find that wasn't broken and climbed back out through the window.

After making sure the lock worked he changed it out with the one he had picked the day before, that one he tossed into the snow on the far side of the basketball court or rather, where he remembered the basketball court had been before the snow then locked the door using his new key which he pocketed and moved on. He walked out to the street and looked both ways. Beyond the chapel he could just make out a one story wooden building then the road curved around the trees. To his left though was where he'd seen most of the buildings on his way in so he turned that way and started wading through the snow where he thought the sidewalk was. The wind was all but gone now and there was that strange blanket like silence that only came with a heavy snow fall so he figured he'd hear a snowplow coming from a very long way off.

The first building he came to on his side of the street looked like an old wooden dining hall and it wasn't boarded up at all so he let himself in and found absolutely nothing. It looked like it hadn't been used since long before 1997 when the base closed, before he left he found a wall calendar in the stripped kitchen that was from 1982 which confirmed his suspicion. Across the street was a much more modern looking building that was still labeled as the Athletic Center and it looked like it may still be in use so he passed it by. Further up on his side was a scattered bunch of maintenance and service buildings of various size and construction; some looked fairly modern but a few looked like old movie sets depicting World War Two. The first was a long narrow building with loading docks that was boarded up but turned out to be easy to get into. Inside was a large empty shipping/receiving area, stained concrete floor, some wooden shipping pallets scattered about, not much else. Against the front wall was a one room office that contained a battered steel desk that the Navy obviously hadn't thought was worth moving, and a steel filing cabinet in the same shape, it's drawers all hanging open. There was a telephone on the wall and for shits and giggles he picked up the handset to check for a dial tone...nothing, he moved on.

Next was one of the war movie buildings, a rusty old Quonset style building that was constructed of blue metal siding and looked like it had been there for a hundred years. The windows were too small to get through but that was all right because the doors at either end weren't boarded over and one look at them was enough, he had the lock on one of them picked in under a minute and once inside he struck gold. Among a clutter of old office furniture, tucked into a corner, was an ancient propane gas heater with a propane bottle still attached and another lying on its side next to it. From the weight he thought both bottles were still at least partially full. The thing was going to be a bitch to carry but he didn't care because if he could get it going he would have heat. He carried the heater and both propane bottles to the door and left them just inside, he'd be back for them later, then he continued his exploration. There was a small office in this building as well, it contained an old wooden desk that fit right in with the World War Two theme of the building, a wooden ladder backed chair that reminded him of grade school, and a little wooden table under the window with the remnants of a long dead potted plant sitting atop it. He sat down at the desk to check the drawers. The skinny drawer above the knee well held a couple of rubber bands that crumbled when he touched them, two pencils and a piece of paper with a note scribbled on it;

New billet, Corpus Christi, report by Sept. 1.

No year included which was too bad, the piece of paper was old and yellowed, he was guessing it'd been there a long time. He checked the remaining three drawers and in the top one found a half used pad of note paper and more pencils which he left in place, in the bottom drawer he found a stack of old paperbacks, battered and dog eared. There were a couple of Louis Lamoure's and three crime novels, all went into his backpack. He sat at the desk for a few moments looking out past the dead potted plant, the snow was still coming down at a pretty good clip, he supposed he should schlep the heater and gas bottles back to his building while the snow was still falling to cover his tracks. Wouldn't do to have whoever watched over this place to see footprints leading right up to a bunch of abandoned buildings would it. He got out of the chair and returned to the door to study the heater. It was really nothing more than a metal cylinder on a stand enclosing a heating element. Sticking out of one side was a connector for the propane bottle. It was a bit rusty but the connection for the bottle was brass and it looked tight. He used the sleeve of his coat to wipe it off and look for any defects. Once he was satisfied he hefted the heater and found that it wasn't that heavy, the bottles were what were heavy. His backpack had straps on both sides which usually secured his sleeping bag; he used them now to tie one bottle to each side of the pack then he hefted it onto his back, definitely doable. Then he picked up the heater itself and left the building.

On his way through the snow to the street, or where the street used to be before it was buried under a foot of snow, he noticed another small old building behind the one he was leaving. He figured one more wouldn't hurt and headed for it. It turned out to be an old warehouse building and it was wide open, one of the sliding bay doors was hanging off its hinges. He didn't expect to find anything useful but he was there so what the hell. He stepped carefully into the building because the cracked and stained concrete floor was covered with junk. He threaded his way around piles of rusty piping and bent steel brackets and was about to turn around when he spotted something in a corner and made his way over there. In a wooden box on the floor were three old kerosene lanterns like the one he and his dad used to use when they went camping. These ones weren't red like the one they'd used; they were a mixture of black paint and rust. One had a broken glass chimney but the other two looked serviceable. He searched around some more and couldn't find any kerosene so that was a problem; lamps weren't much good without it. He took them with him anyway and headed back out into the storm.

He was carrying quite a load now so he turned right and started back toward his building. The snow was tough to move through so he stopped every few minutes to catch his breath. When he finally got to the door he used his key to open the lock then got inside. It didn't seem any warmer inside the building and he couldn't wait to get the heater going, if the heater would go. Once in his room he cleaned off the connections with a rag then connected one of the propane bottles to the unit, opened the valve and hit the striker built into the heater. There was a marginally loud pop that scared the living shit out of him and then the element in the heater began to heat up, in no time it was glowing happily and throwing a surprising amount of heat into the room. He got up and shut the door to keep the heat in then checked the heater to be sure everything was operating correctly. If he gassed himself to death he supposed it wouldn't be a great loss to anyone but he intended to avoid that particular outcome if he could. It occurred to him that it was a concern the he wouldn't have had a year ago. The room began to warm up fairly quickly, more so than he would have thought, and after fifteen or twenty minutes he was able to take off his coat at least. He took the paperbacks out of his pack and stacked them on the nightstand then put the two kerosene lamps on the spare bed. They both had wicks and were in working order, all he needed was some kerosene. He looked out the window again, the snow was still coming down and he supposed he could make one more foray to try to find some. He would also have to deal with the matter of food before very long. He didn't have a lot left in his pack and while he did have a small amount of cash, walking all the way back past the train station to the main road in this storm would take hours and could very well prove fatal. With that thought he ate one more granola bar from his pack, he now had three left. So he would go out again, while the snow was still falling to cover his tracks. He lingered in the warming room for a while longer than reluctantly shut down the heater and headed back out, closing the door to his room behind him. He stopped in the bathroom to relieve himself in the same toilet he'd used the previous night and that was something else he was going to have to figure out soon, or the whole floor was going to start getting odiferous in a hurry.

Back out in the storm he turned left again because that's where the majority of the buildings were. As he reached the warehouse he'd been in earlier he noticed that the building across the street looked like what he imagined a dining hall should look like so he crossed over to it. The front windows weren't boarded over and several were cracked but none were broken so he wasn't getting in that way. The door was locked and before he tried his hand at it he circled around to the rear of the building where he found a couple of loading bay doors and a side door, it had an old drum lock in it that turned out to be child's play. He entered into an industrial kitchen; everything was stainless steel and still pretty shiny. This kitchen looked much newer than the one he'd found in his own building. There was nothing in the kitchen he could use and the dining area was completely empty save for a single table by the windows with a couple of coffee mugs sitting on it gathering dust. He let himself out by the same door then moved on to the next building up. Like all of them this building had a square of wood attached that was painted dark yellow with a red X on it which meant that the building was condemned. He found this a bit odd in relation to this building because when he looked through the windows there were two very serviceable looking pickup trucks parked in the two bays at the front of the building, one with a snow plow attached. He guessed that this building was used by whoever was looking after the closed base. This was confirmed when he walked around to the street and noticed that the next building up had a weathered wooden sign on it that read; *Caretakers Office.*

He was going to have to be careful here, both buildings were empty at the moment but they were obviously being utilized. Up until now he'd only taken things that had been left behind by the Navy, the government, whoever, when the base was shut down. But these buildings were still occupied and he couldn't let whoever was occupying them know that he'd been here. And because they weren't abandoned taking anything from them felt more like stealing to him, he'd been homeless for some time and he was a lot of things but he wasn't a thief.

The building holding the two pickup trucks had several doors; he picked the lock on the one at the rear (his lock picking skills were definitely being honed to a fine edge) and went in after cleaning the snow off his boots. He was in a short hallway that led down to the bay that held the two trucks. Off of the hallway was a small storage room lined with shelves, he would return to that. In the bay itself the rear wall was lined with tools and such and looked pretty orderly, whoever had kept it that orderly would probably notice if anything was missing so he moved on. At the right rear of the bay was a narrow staircase leading up to a second floor and another storage area. Among other things was at least one of the things on his Christmas list, kerosene. There were four five gallon cans of kerosene lined up against one wall. He checked them and none of them felt like they were full; he also noted that the tops of the cans were dusty. He had no idea what use the caretakers had for kerosene but he did know that he couldn't just walk off with an entire can when there were only four of them because someone would notice that. He would need something to use as a container. He looked around the rest of the storage room and finding nothing that fit the bill left without the kerosene.

Back on the first floor he checked the small storage room off the hallway and came up empty for useful items, the room held mostly automobile related items for the trucks out front. A final door off the hallway revealed a small dirty bathroom. He left the building but didn't try to relock the door, something that would be difficult with a set of picks anyway. He didn't want to push his luck by messing around in the caretakers building and beyond that building was a large power plant building that he thought he'd leave for another time. He'd passed by a large building twice now that was identified by a large sign as the base fitness center and he hadn't bothered with it but now he thought he'd have a look because it actually looked like it was still at least partially occupied. He got in and saw that the old lobby/offices section of the building was being used as a museum/memorial to the airbase. Beyond that the rest of the building apparently wasn't in use at all. He crossed the hallway then went through a set of double doors and found himself in a huge high ceilinged gym, two full basketball courts lined by wooden bleachers and a work out area at the rear. There was a row of narrow windows high up by the ceiling and they threw a diffuse milky light into the space. He walked slowly across the parquet floor that was buckling in a few spots but overall looked in pretty good shape, someone could play a game there tonight. His footsteps echoed across the dusty floor and he wondered when the last time anyone had been in there. He crossed to the rear wall then through a door where he found a locker room, rows of metal lockers the doors left hanging open on most, a bone dry shower room with empty soap dispensers on the walls. There were a few small windows in here so everything was dim and indistinct but he did find four musty bath towels and a pair of old sweat pants and a sweat shirt hanging in two different lockers, into his backpack. Next to the locker room was office, picked clean, and then a small kitchen/eating area. There was a Coca Cola vending machine that Coke had apparently forgotten to come and retrieve when the base closed. He couldn't tell if it had anything product in it because he couldn't get it open. Anyway, he wasn't too sure what a seventeen year old Coke would taste like.

There were still salt and pepper shakers on the half dozen small tables in the eating area and the kitchen still had some utensils in place, it seemed that the last people out of here hadn't tried too hard to clean this building out. There was a fine coating of dust on everything so he was sure no one had been in here in some time. He found two canvass sacks in the kitchen and used one to pack up a couple of steel bowls, two empty plastic milk jugs and a plate he'd found. There was a small walk-in cooler in the very back, the door standing ajar, he stuck his head in to check it and sitting on a steel shelf by the door, as if someone had put it there meaning to come back for it then never had, was a box of MRE's, military rations, "Meals Ready To Eat". He just stood there looking at it for a moment, not believing his luck; the he began pulling the pouches out of the box. There were twelve of them and they all went into the canvass bag. He checked the rest of the kitchen and was on his way out when he spotted something else he could use; tossed in a jumble in one corner were a bunch of plastic five gallon water bottles meant for use with a water dispense. There was no dispenser in sight so someone must had taken it and left the empty bottles behind. He stuffed four of them into the other canvass carry all and that was it for the gym.

When he got back outside the snow was still coming down at a steady clip and it was about up to his knees now. It was still covering his tracks but it was also getting harder to walk through, especially carrying a bunch of stuff. He went straight back to the building with the trucks and let himself back in. He used the dirty little bathroom to relieve himself then flushed and went back up to the second floor store room. Taking some from each of the four cans he filled two of the water bottles with kerosene then stuffed rags into the necks to stopper them, the world's biggest Molotov cocktails. He lugged both back downstairs and realized he needed another plan to get them back to his building. He went back to the first floor storeroom and found a couple lengths of rope and a roll of duct tape; he didn't think anyone was going to miss those. He taped the mouths of the water bottles to seal them further then tied one end of the length of rope around the neck of each He looped the rope across his shoulders and slowly straightened up. Then he hoisted the rest of his shit and left the building. He put everything down to relock the door then loaded up again and started out. He got more than halfway back to his building before he had to stop. He ended up dragging the two kerosene/water bottles the rest of the way. By the time he let himself back into his building he was cold and wet and sore.

4.

The heater was humming along nicely, he had taken one of the bath towels he'd found in the locker room and stuffed it in the crack under the door to keep the cold air out, the drapes were pulled across the windows, and now he actually had to turn the thing down to its lowest setting because the room was getting hot. One of the kerosene lamps was on the night stand, also burning nicely and he was lying on his bed reading one of the mystery novels he'd found in the old desk. He was in the high clover.

When he'd finally gotten back to the room and gotten the lamp going he realized that it was no good because it would be visible from the road. Someone seeing a single window lit up in a building abandoned decades ago would be very bad indeed. So he'd moved everything across the hall to a room that looked out onto the old basketball court behind the building. He was pretty sure that the court had seen its last game of HORSE. Beyond that there was nothing but trees so everything was good there. Of course at the moment the basketball court was buried under over a foot of snow and the trees were invisible through the dark and the storm. He'd collected snow in the steel bowls and melted it over the heater then poured it slowly into the plastic milk jugs. A second trip out got him more snow and one bowl he'd left on the heater to get good and hot then he'd used it for one of the MRE's; spaghetti and meatballs and nothing had ever tasted so good. After that he was in for the night so he got out of his clothes and put on the sweatpants and sweatshirt he'd found in the locker room, musty but probably a lot cleaner than what he'd been wearing, and the last pair of clean socks he had in his backpack. So now he was lying in bed reading by lamplight while the snow continued to fall outside his window. When he started to doze, it had been a long day after all, he shut down the heater and crawled back into bed, he had used the sheets and blankets to make his bed, his ratty old sleeping bag was stretched across the spare bed to air. He turned off the lantern and was asleep in minutes.

He woke up in the middle of the night again but this time it wasn't because he had to go to the bathroom...it was because someone was coming up the stairs.

5.

The door he'd used to get into the building was at the far end of the hallway, it opened into an enclosed stairway that had doors on each floor. There was another identical stairway at the other end of the building. But there was also a stairway a third of the way along the hallway that was open from the ground floor up to the second floor and was accessed by a door in the front of the building. This stairway was across and one room down from the room he was currently occupying and someone was coming up those stairs, he could hear the footsteps as plain as day. He sat up in bed and his first thought was that it was a goddamned shame because this could have been a good thing for a while, a hell of a lot better than a shelter, so it was too bad he'd been caught so soon. But then as he came fully awake he realized that was bullshit, it was the middle of the night and this building had been abandoned years ago, and that door at the front of the building was boarded over. They he noticed that the door to his room was open which was odd too because he had not only closed it but shoved a towel under it to block the cold air from the hallway.

The footsteps sounded like they had almost reached the second floor. He quietly got out of the bed, the room was still fairly warm but Christ was the floor cold, and moved to the open door. The hallway was dark but his eyes were adjusting quickly and there was light coming in from outside, that odd soft light that seemed to always occur during snow storms at night, so he could see. As he reached the door and looked out the footsteps stopped and...there was no one there. The hallway was empty and when he padded over to check the stairwell it was empty too, he could look over the railing all the way down to the first floor. The only sound in the hallway now was the wind whining around the outside of the building. He went down the stairs to ground level and checked the door, still boarded over, then the length of the building on both floors, ending up back at his room sure that the building was empty and dark. He stood quietly outside his room for a time, listening, then finally went back in, shut the door and put the towel back under it. For good measure he moved the spare bed in front of it. He lay awake for a time listening and that was what he was doing when he finally fell asleep again.

The following morning he checked the building again and found that it was locked up tight. Not only that but he hadn't used the center stairs before last night and he noted that the only footprints in the layer of dust that coated them were his from the previous night. He had just been a little creeped out from being in a big empty building by himself that was all. Which deep down he knew was just so much bullshit because he had heard someone coming up those damned stairs. After breakfast he put his least dirty cloths back on and went down to the basement, he hadn't checked that yet and now with the kerosene lamp he could see although a good flashlight would have been a lot better. Outside the storm had finally stopped but the wind was climbing again, blowing white powdery waves of snow across the open areas of the abandoned base to collect in drifts against any obstacle encountered. Checking out the basement gave him an excuse for not going back outside just yet. It turned out to be pretty much what he'd expected, a long disused basement in a good sized building; hulking old furnace, rusty water holding tanks, lots of piping and wiring, everything old and in various stages of deterioration. He found the main water main into the building and thought briefly about opening it to see if he could get running water but thought better of it, lots of old plumbing that had been bone dry for years, the chance of a burst pipe, or a half dozen of them, wasn't worth the risk. The lamp was less than ideal for the task of looking in and around large machinery in a dark basement but he managed to do a pretty thorough search and didn't find anything useful, the place had been stripped pretty clean. He did find a note pasted to the furnace that showed it being shut down for the final time in 1997.

He left the basement and went back up to his room to grab the two canvass carry bags then headed down the back stairwell to conduct another search. The wind was still blowing at a pretty good clip outside and while he wasn't looking forward to the wind chill it would work well covering his tracks. The road still wasn't plowed so he thought he had plenty of time for another recon of the area. He had reached the bottom of the stairwell and was about to open the outside door when a loud crash sounded from the basement. He turned to the basement door, which he had closed behind him less than an hour ago, opened it and looked in but couldn't see far into the dark space. He went back to his room and retrieved the lantern then returned to the basement and went through it from one end to the other. Everything looked the same to him but there was so much crap in the basement that something could have fallen and there would be no way for him to tell. He took a last look around then headed out for his next shopping trip around the old base.

6.

He was rooting around in the old power plant building, finding nothing useful, when a car passed by on the road outside. He listened only absently, making sure that the car didn't stop, then continued with what he was doing.

They had plowed the road late on the afternoon after the storm and in the three days since then there had been sporadic traffic using it, mostly during the day. It was heaviest in the mornings and late afternoons with commuters from the train station on their way to and from work but even then, it never amounted to more than a few cars at a time. He had also noted activity in the caretakers building on the morning after the storm and the following day, nothing since. He had developed a pattern of making his forays into the old abandoned buildings in the evening hours, after the last of the traffic, light as it was, had ceased for the night. It meant dealing with much lower temperatures but it was worth it to keep his presence on the base secret. Today though he'd changed his routine and come out in the afternoon because it was Sunday, the caretaker building was empty and there was next to no traffic on the road. It would be easy enough for him to avoid the few cars that did pass by.

The power plant building was one of the last, other than a few of the smaller outlying buildings, for him to search and he wasn't having any luck finding anything useful. Not that he hadn't done well mind you, in the past few days he'd found a lot of good stuff including a second propane heater and a dozen or so fuel bottles to go with the heaters, a second carton of MRE's, about a dozen more paperbacks, and a real find; a carton pushed back into a corner of a closet in one of the older buildings containing four brand new Navy bridge coats. They had been in various sizes but luckily one had fit him perfectly and he was wearing it at the moment. He had found the coats in what he believed was one of the oldest buildings on the base. Behind the blue metal Quonset hut where he'd found the first heater where several more old buildings that looked long disused. The one directly behind the blue building was one story, concrete, with something on the roof that looked like the top of an aircraft control tower. The doors in this building were as old as those in the blue building and had the locks to match so he was inside in no time. The interior looked like it was picked pretty clean, not much left but some old wooden filing cabinets, some battered office furniture and that was it. He went through the first floor pretty quickly then up to the little observation area on the roof. It looked like it had been some sort of aircraft control tower room on the inside as much as it had on the outside. One big room with large windows all the way around and a counter under the windows that looked like it had once held all sorts of equipment and in fact still did have odds and ends attached. There was a bank of telephone receivers all hung in a row on hooks that were made of heavy old Bakelite and looked like something right out of the 40's. On another part of the counter was a metal panel that still displayed several old toggle style switches. When he looked out through the big windows in the direction away from the base there was nothing out there but a huge open space covered with snow and a few stunted trees. Off to the right was the road, continuing on out of the base but in front of him was just a lot of nothing, he couldn't tell if there were runways out there because of the snow but he supposed that they used to land something there. The space wasn't long and narrow though, like a runway should be, it was round, a huge round open space.

He left the control room and directly beneath it found one fairly good sized room with several storage areas off of it that he had missed on his way in. It looked like no one had used the area in decades; actually the entire building looked like that, there was a heavy coating on dust on everything, much heavier than what he'd found in the other buildings. He checked the storage rooms which were really little more than big closets and pushed way into a back corner of one was a faded cardboard box in which he'd found the bridge coats. The tag inside each identified it as a navy bridge coat and had a date of 1944 which he found hard to believe but being packed away in a box all this time had apparently left them in almost perfect shape. He'd taken them all even though only one fit him; he would find a use for the others. Also in the box were a couple of wool watch caps, he was currently wearing one of those as well.

All this had allowed him to settle pretty comfortably into the old barracks including one luxury he hadn't enjoyed in a very long time, a bathroom warmed by the second heater to the point where he could sit in a stall all by himself with some reading material and enjoy a long leisurely crap! He actually looked forward to it every day now and he had found that if he just filled the holding tank on the toilet with water it would flush very nicely. Of course it wouldn't fill with water again and he had no idea where it was flushing to but who cared, it worked. And he had found a functioning water tap outside the caretakers building so he had a steady supply of water. It was obvious that no one had been in his building in years (he had not forgotten the footsteps on the stairs but he'd decided to ignore the occurrence) so as long as he kept his head down and was careful there was no telling how long he could stay.

He left the power plant building empty handed and because it was close by he decided to check out the big hanger again. He hadn't been in it since the first day when he'd been rushing to beat the storm so maybe he'd missed something. He made his way across the uneven ground toward the hanger. It was still damned cold but the last two days had been bright and sunny and a lot of the snow had melted away. He went to the same door he had used the first day and it was still ajar. He pulled it open against the snow, here in the shadow of the huge building it was still deep, and stepped through. He pulled the door shut behind him then turned to see two airplanes parked side by side at the far end of the hanger. He just stood there for a moment staring dumbly at the aircraft then he looked all around him and the rest of the hanger was just as he remembered it. He looked at the aircraft again, "get the fuck out of here," he muttered under his breath not realizing that he'd said anything. He briefly considered just going back out through the door and forgetting what he was looking at but instead he began walking across the hanger floor toward the aircraft. He'd already recognized them both, he had built model airplanes as a kid and as an adult, in his old life, he had been interested in warbirds, had even gone to a few airshows in his time. So he knew that the aircraft on the right was a Grumman TBF Avenger, a World War Two torpedo bomber, the one on the left was an F4U Corsair, a Navy fighter from the same era. Both aircraft had their wings folded as they would have for storage aboard an aircraft carrier; the Corsair was parked facing directly at him while the Avenger was at an angle so he was looking at it almost in profile. The rest of the hanger was absolutely empty.

As he got closer he saw that both aircraft looked new, brand new. He hadn't kept tabs on the warbird market, or anything else, for some years now but he knew that a TBF Avenger in that condition would be worth probably between three and four hundred thousand dollars, the Corsair would be well north of a million, maybe even two million. Who in the hell would park aircraft that valuable in a decrepit old hanger on a closed military base. And they hadn't been there on his first visit; he knew that for a fact, so how did they get there? Land on a closed runway that's mostly cracked asphalt and currently under a foot of snow?

He stopped about fifty yards from the aircraft, no longer sure at all if he wanted to go near them. He could no longer hear the wind through the hangars broken windows and it seemed very still all of a sudden. Something was way wrong here. He made a decision and once he had he quickly closed the distance to the Avenger which was closer. When he reached it he touched the left wing with one hand and it was real, it was there, and in the ice cold hanger the metal skin of the aircraft was warm, almost hot to the touch, as if it had just been sitting in the sun. And that was it for him, he turned and headed back to the door, not exactly running but walking damned fast. Before leaving the hanger he turned for a last look and of course both aircraft were gone, nothing but a falling down old hanger with daylight slanting in through broken windows. He turned and got the hell out of there.

7.

On the night after the airplanes in the hanger he was on the very edge of the huge open area where the buildings ended and the tarmac and runway area of the old base began checking out one of the small equipment sheds that dotted the base. After he'd left the shed and began walking back toward the road he suddenly stopped because he realized that he was hearing voices coming out of the darkness out there. He stood and listened for several moments to what sounded like three or four men talking, their voices fading in and out with the wind and he knew damn well that no one was actually walking around out there in the middle of a winter night, in a foot of snow. The voiced faded and didn't return and he continued on back to his building.

That night as he lay in a warm bed in a warm room, his belly full and having just read a couple of chapters of Louis Lamoure he decided that he didn't care if the base was a tad haunted, he could live with it because it still beat sleeping on the street or in a shelter somewhere. He had no idea how long this was going to last, the base had been sitting empty for seventeen years already; it could sit for ten more. He did know that he was going to stay on this ride for as long as it lasted, and then he'd move on to whatever came next. Some weird shit here and there was a small price to pay for these accommodations. Besides, he was having fun going through the old buildings and finding little treasures, the whole place was like a time capsule.

The next day he spent in the old barracks heating up water to wash up and do some laundry in one of the sinks in the bathroom. Late in the afternoon, after the bulk of the vehicle traffic had died down and as it was getting dark he put on the best cloths he had, the Navy coat and hat he'd found and he left the barracks to walk back up to the train station. It was Christmas Eve and he had something he needed to do.

He had remembered that, amazingly enough, there was a pay telephone at the train station; it was probably the last one for miles around. No doubt it had simply been forgotten and he hoped that it still worked. As he passed through the condo complex again he felt a bit more confident than he had that first day, he was more presentable now. When he reached the entrance drive to the train station he kept going past it up to the main road because there was a drugstore there. As he entered he saw a handwritten sign taped to the door telling him that they would be closing at 6 pm, it was Christmas Eve after all. He wondered what time it was then, he hadn't owned a watch in a very long time, but it had to be before six because they were still open. There was only one other person in the store which he didn't like, it would make him stand out all the more, but he continued on anyway. He got a basket and picked up a few things he needed, along with a few snacks and some Pepsi because it was Christmas Eve after all. He tried not to look at the rows of Christmas decorations as he passed by them, or hear the Christmas music playing over the stores sound system.

The clerk behind the counter looked like a high school girl which was good, younger people tended to be less judgmental about how you looked than their parents were, either that or they just didn't give a shit. She smiled at him without really seeing him and he noticed the clock on the wall behind her, it was quarter to six and she was anxious to be out of there and start her holiday. He paid for his items with crumpled old bills then asked her for a bunch of quarters, holding out a battered five spot and she made change without missing a beat, handing him a pile of silver. He wished her a Merry Christmas and got the hell out of there.

The train station parking lot was empty, not a single car left because after all, it was Christmas Eve. The pay phone was right where he remembered it being, mounted on a rusty steel pedestal in an open metal box facing the lot. He picked up the ice cold receiver and fed the phone a quarter thinking there wouldn't be a dial tone and that would be the end of it but there was and so he dialed a number from memory and then fed the phone more quarters.

"Hello?" tiny voice, a little boy.

"Hello, who is this?"

"This is Brian, I'm six now so I'm allowed to answer the phone," Brian said just in case there was any doubt.

"Of course you are Brian and you did a great job – *I'm your grandfather Brian* – is your mom home?"

"She's in the family room wrapping presents," he said this with all the breathlessness that presents caused in six year olds, "I'll get her," the phone clunked down onto something but a moment later Brian was back, "I'm supposed to ask who it is," he said.

"I'm an old friend of hers Brian."

"Oh, ok," the phone clunked down again and a moment later he heard Brian yell because apparently he was much too busy to actually walk into the family room, "Mom! There's a man on the phone for you, he says he's a friend of yours and he's old." He smiled at that as he stood there in the empty station gripping the freezing handset, keeping his back to the wind. He had an image of a warm cozy house with a Christmas tree and a fire in the fireplace and good smells coming from the kitchen because after all, it was Christmas Eve.

"Hello,"

He almost hung up right then, "Hello Beth, Merry Christmas."

"Dad," it was a simple declaration, there was no surprise in it, nor any happiness.

"I just wanted to make my annual Christmas call to you, wish you and Marty all the best, and little Brian too of course."

"It's been four years since your last annual call dad, Brian was two."

"Has it been? I'm sorry, time just seems to pass so fast you know, I keep meaning to call but things keep coming up. How is everything with you guys, Brian sounds like a very intelligent young man."

"You don't get to do this dad; you don't get to just call whenever you're sober enough to remember that you used to have a family. It's Christmas Eve and we're having people over and I don't need this, I really don't."

"I've been clean and sober for over a year now Beth, swear to God. I've got my own place now, I'm off the streets - *not a lie exactly* – and things will be picking up for me soon. Maybe once I get everything settled I can come over and meet Brian in person."

"No, absolutely not, do not show up at my door dad, I mean it. You have no right to do that and you have no right to just call me like this, you gave up the right a long time ago."

"It wasn't easy for me either," he said softly, hunched over the pay phone, the wind was starting to pick up and he thought soon his teeth may begin to chatter, "Did you ever think of that?"

"I was fifteen," she almost shouted and then caught herself. If this had been one of those heartwarming holiday movies were everything worked out in the end there would be tears in her voice about now but there weren't, there was just anger and under that maybe resignation. "You just walked away because you couldn't deal with what you did and you left me to deal with it on my own. My mother was dead and my father was responsible for it and instead of sticking around to own up to it and try to help me through it, help both of us through it, you just walked away."

"I wanted to," he said, "I should have, but you blamed me for it, there was nothing I could do about that."

"I blamed you for it because it was your fault." Even the anger was gone now; all that was left in her voice was resignation.

"I know that," he whispered, "don't you think I do."

"I have to go now, we have guests coming and I have things to do," she hesitated for a moment and he searched for something more to say to her because he knew this would be his last chance but he found nothing.

"I'm going to change our phone number after Christmas," she said finally, "after so long I didn't think I'd hear from you again, I thought you were probably dead and I can't do this anymore, I can't keep...take care of yourself dad," and the line went dead.

He stood there for a few moments hunched over the phone box with the receiver still up to his ear, as if she might come back, not feeling the wind or the cold. Finally he placed it gently back into its cradle and walked away. It was a cold dark walk back to the empty barracks carrying his bag of Christmas purchases.

8.

He didn't see the airplanes again, or hear the footsteps or the voices again. He spent Christmas day, during which the caretakers were absent and there was no traffic at all on the street, going back over old ground just for something to do. In his old life he would have gotten up early with his wife and daughter, sat on the living room sofa drinking coffee and opening presents then moved into the family room with his daughter to watch some holiday movie while his wife made breakfast for them all. That was the quiet before the storm, the part of the day he'd always loved, to be following later by a big family dinner, either at their house if they were hosting, or at another family members house if someone else was. The past few Christmases he'd been too drunk to really remember all that stuff, but he was stone cold sober now, and it was running through his head like a loop of film that he couldn't turn off. Finally, in a who gives a fuck state of mind he let himself into the little museum inside the fitness center and spent the day, and into the evening (how nice was it to read by electric light again) reading about the old base and looking at mostly black and white photos. He stayed well into the night because he didn't want to leave the warmth and the electric lights and return to his abandoned barracks. Finally he caught himself falling asleep in the chair with a book in his lap so he got up, tidied the museum to erase and sign of his presence, and headed out into the cold night.

It took the kerosene heater some time to warm the frigid air in his room so he sat on the bed fully clothed just staring at the wall thinking about the base because he didn't want to think about anything else at the moment. The facility had been built in the early 40's as a dirigible base because back then they used dirigibles, or blimps, to patrol off the coast for enemy submarines. They'd found some too, one had been sunk right outside of Boston harbor. The little control room he'd been in had overseen the blimp landing area which had been the huge overgrown circular expanse he'd seen out the control room windows. Later the base had converted to fixed wing aircraft and three runways had been built. People who'd served here had gone off to war, some hadn't come back.

When the room was warm enough he got out of his cloths and climbed into bed. And that was Christmas.

He woke up in the middle of the night again and again not because he had to go to the bathroom. He woke up because someone was standing in the doorway of his room. He sat up quickly thinking that the jig was finally up and didn't that suck. A man was standing in the doorway which was odd because he was sure he'd closed the door and shoved the towel underneath it. The man appeared to be wearing khaki pants and a short sleeved khaki shirt but it was hard to tell because he was silhouetted against the hallway lights which was even odder because the building had no power.

"You don't belong here," the man said to him, then he turned and walked away down the hallway. He flew out of bed and across the room to the door in time to see the stranger reach the end of the hallway. As that happened it registered that not only where the hall lights on but the hallway itself was warm, bright and clean, walls freshly painted, floor waxed. The stranger stopped and turned at the end of the hall.

"You can't stay here," he said and then disappeared through the doorway that went to the stairwell. He rushed to the end of the hall and threw the stairwell door open and there was nothing there. The stairwell was deserted, cold, dark and dirty, and when he turned back to the hallway it was too. He walked slowly back to his room, his hand out to feel the peeling paint on the wall that hadn't been there a moment ago. Once in his room he closed the door, stuffed the towel under it then moved the spare bed in front of it. He got back into bed because it was cold, but he didn't sleep for a very long time.

The following day he checked the entire building and found exactly what he knew he'd find; nothing, but he had to do it anyway. He then spent some time at the windows of the first room he'd settled in watching the road and the other buildings within sight for any unusual activity and saw none. And all the while he was doing that he knew goddamned good and well that the guy he'd seen last night wasn't a caretaker. The hallway lights had been on and the walls and floor had been spotless, the linoleum floor had been waxed to a high sheen, and it was warm, the building heat had been on. And if that wasn't enough boys and girls, if that didn't tear it, then how about the fact that the guy had simply vanished at the head of the stairs, the door to the stairwell opened into the hallway but it hadn't, it hadn't moved at all, he would have seen it, the guy had simply walked through it and was gone. He turned away from the window and crossed the hall to his room where he lay down on the bed and stared at the ceiling.

Before he'd begun his illustrious career as a bum – sorry – a displaced person, he'd been a college graduate with a degree in business management and a solid career. In college he and three other guys had spent two semesters living in an old Victorian house just off campus. While living there all four of them had occasionally heard footsteps, voices, and doors closing, not all the time but often enough that they became accustomed to them, often enough for their skeptical fellow students to go away believers after only a few overnight visits to the house. None of it was very threatening and with one exception they'd learned to live with it. After all, an old Victorian was a huge improvement over cinderblock dorm rooms. The one exception was their fifth roommate, a guy named Jim who only lasted in the house for about a month before moving out and refusing to ever return. Jim would never tell them exactly what happened to him, he refused to discuss it at all, but his girlfriend had told them that she knew he'd seen something in the kitchen one day but she didn't know what because he wouldn't tell her. Whatever it was had scared him so badly that he'd left the house with only the cloths on his back and had made her go back to collect the rest of his things, he wouldn't even wait in the car on the street in front of the house while she went into the house. The rest of them had never really wanted to know what had scared Jim that badly because they still had to live in that house for another seven months.

So when it came to shit like ghosts this wasn't his first rodeo. But hearing indistinct voices in a back stairwell or footsteps on the second floor when you knew there was no one up there was a bit different then having a three dimensional guy who looked for all the world like a real person but wasn't tell you to leave the place where you were living. That was just on a whole different level than a few things going bump in the night. He could live with the footsteps on the stairs and the planes appearing then disappearing in the hangar and indistinct voices drifting over a deserted airfield at night. The question was could he live with a full-fledged fucking manifestation that actually spoke to him. And what about that? The whatever it was had told him that he didn't belong there and he had to leave. If he didn't leave what came next? If he stayed would things start coming at him out of the dark corners of the building? That would truly suck because one thing this building had was an abundance of dark corners. He didn't think so because the guy last night had looked like just an ordinary guy, he was wearing a naval uniform which made sense for the setting and other than the fact that he was there at all he hadn't been at all menacing. He hadn't screamed at him to get out, he had simply stated it then walked away. He was well aware that he was rationalizing now because if he left he had absolutely no where to go and no way to get there. That alone was motivation enough for him to stick, at least until the next act, if there was one, at which point he could re-evaluate.

So that's what he would do, hang tight and see what happened. It beat packing up and heading out into the snow to who knew what. And with that he fell asleep because he'd been awake most of the night.

9.

He woke up because it was freezing in his room because the propane bottle on the heater had run dry. It was also dark in his room; he had apparently slept the day away. He sat up on the bed and cleared his head then changed bottles on the heater and got it going again, full bore. He also lit one of the kerosene lamps and trudged down the hall to use the bathroom. When he returned he shut the door and sat hunched on the bed waiting for the room to warm up. It was full dark outside but he had

no idea what time it was, he supposed he was going to be up all night now, having slept all day. He also

supposed he could wait up to see if his visitor came back and ask him in for a visit.

When the room had warmed up he heated up some water and made himself an MRE,

Fettuccine Alfredo tonight, followed by a few chocolate chip cookies that he had left over from his

purchases on Christmas Eve. He crossed the hall to his old room to check traffic on the road, in five

minutes no cars passed by so it must be late. He was cold then so he returned to his room and propped

himself up on his bed to read some of his current novel and wait to see if his visitor returned. In fifteen

minutes he was sound asleep again.

He woke up some time later because the man was indeed standing in his doorway again. The

lights behind him were on again and over the visitors shoulder he could see the clean white corridor

walls...again.

"I know," he said to the man, "I don't belong here."

"You have to leave," the man said.

"I can't, I don't have anywhere else to go."

"You can't stay here," the man turned and started off down the hallway just as he had the first

time. He was ready for it this time and was off the bed and out into the corridor in a split second. He

followed the man down toward the stairs and the thing was, he looked real, you couldn't see through

him or anything, he looked like a person. He was thinking about reaching out to try to touch him when

he stopped abruptly by the door at the top of the stairs.

"You have to leave," he said again.

"Why?"

"You don't belong here."

"Is that all you can say? I do belong here, I'm the only one here and I'm not bothering anyone, the building is empty. Why can't I stay?"

The man looked at him for a moment then turned and passed through the closed door. He yanked the door open to follow fully expecting the stairwell to be dark and deserted, paint peeling off the walls but it wasn't, it was just like the corridor. The man was going down the stairs and he followed him, down to the first floor corridor, also brightly lit and warm, and on down to the dining hall. He turned the corner into the room right behind the man and then stopped short. The dining hall was bright and warm, there were tables lined up across the large room, a sideboard with condiments and silverware, and there were people, a half dozen or so sitting at one of the tables talking and laughing, and he could see a couple of guys in cooks whites visible in the kitchen through the serving window. The man stopped halfway to the table and turned back to look at him.

"All ghosts," he said to the man with awe in his voice, "this building's crawling with ghosts."

"You're not going to leave are you?" the man said.

He shook his head and the man turned and continued on toward the table. He followed. When they both reached the table the others turned and looked at him. They were all wearing various versions of naval uniforms; one was wearing a flight suit.

"He won't leave," the man told them.

"Well you're not going to eat with us," the man seated closest to him said, "you smell like shit." The rest of them laughed.

"If you're not going to leave and you plan on sitting here you need to go take a shower first," another of them said motioning back toward the corridor.

He turned away and walked back to the corridor then down to the first floor bathroom in something like a daze. He had to be dreaming. The bathroom was as new and shiny as the corridor and dining hall were and there were toiletries and towels. He reached into the closest shower stall and turned on the water then stripped down. He absently took a bar of soap and bottle of shampoo off the shelf over the sinks and stepped under a stream of wonderfully hot water. He was absolutely dreaming but who cared, he hadn't had a hot shower in weeks and it felt infuckingcredible even if it was a dream. He wanted to stay in there forever but he was also afraid that the guys in the dining hall would vanish so he finished and toweled himself down. Folded on one of the sinks right in front of him was a set of navy khakis complete with underwear, socks and shoes. He put everything on leaving his own cloths on the floor and feeling more human than he had in forever.

When he got back to the dining hall they were all still there plus one or two more. They all turned and looked at him when he came in and it occurred to him that his mind may have finally completely jumped the tracks and right at that moment he was actually strapped to a bed in Bridgewater State Hospital's psych ward, or else standing in the deserted dining hall of a dark empty barracks seeing things that weren't really there.

"Big improvement pal," one of them said as he approached the table. Then he motioned toward the serving window, "you might as well get some chow if you're staying, looks like you could use it."

He nodded numbly, turned and walked across the room to the serving line. There was a stack of metal trays on the counter so he picked one up and went along the line as a guy dressed like a cook silently served him chipped beef on toast, green beans and a biscuit. Last stop was a huge coffee urn and he got it black in a heavy white porcelain mug. When he got back to the table the only chair available was at the head of the table so he sat there. They were all talking and ignoring him so he took a sip of coffee and it was heaven.

"That's real coffee," one of them pointed out to him, "none of that ersatz crap they serve overseas."

He nodded and tucked into the chipped beef and it was actually good despite its appearance. Of course anything hot might taste good to him at this point. He was almost finished when they all finally took notice of him.

"So what are you doing here?" the same guy who'd told him to get some food, he was wearing officers bars on his shirt.

"I guess I'm living here for the moment," he answered. "I'm homeless."

"What does that mean?" from a guy down at the end of the table.

"I don't have a home; I've been living on the streets for a while now."

"So you're a bum."

"You couldn't tell that when he walked in Kowalski?" the officer said, "Christ."

"I'm a bum," he agreed, "and I've kind of settled in up on the second floor. The base has been closed for a long time and the building is...."

"Deserted, we know," the guy who been standing in his door said. "Crying shame is what it is, just leaving all this here to rot."

"How long have all of you been here?" he asked.

"Some longer than others," someone at the end of the table said.

"How long do you plan on being here?" another one asked him.

"I don't know, as long as I can, I don't have anywhere else to go."

"Neither do we," someone laughed.

"That's not exactly true," the officer said. "Some of us do and just don't want to go."

"Finish your dinner," the guy who'd been in his door said, "you're probably not going to be here long."

"It's a miracle he's here at all," someone else said.

He finished his dinner and his coffee and thought about going back for seconds but when he looked up the kitchen was dark, the men there gone.

"Chow's over," the guy from his door told him, "they usually don't hang around."

"Where do they go," he asked and the guy from his door just shrugged.

"They just go," the officer said, "we're going to have to be going soon too. I assume that your intending to stay here then."

He nodded as he drained the last of his coffee, "if it's all right with all of you, this is really a good deal for me right now."

They all looked at each other across the table then the officer shrugged too and nodded his head, "it's all right with us, I'm not sure how you managed to do it but, might be nice to have someone new to talk to around here."

"Does this mean I'm dead?" he asked and they all laughed.

"Not yet," the officer said. The guy from his door stood up, still smiling, "I'll walk you back to your bunk now, we've got things to do."

He rose and started to pick up his plate and mug.

"That's fine," the officer said, "they'll take care of them."

So he said goodbye and followed door guy back up the stairs to his room, walking through a warm, well-lit building. When they reached the door to his room door guy stopped and turned to him. "Maybe I'll stop by again," he said, "the food in the mess halls not the best but it beats the rations you've been eating doesn't it?"

"It does," he agreed.

Door Guy turned to leave and he watched him until he reached the head of the staircase and was gone. Then he turned and went into his room and it was dark with peeling walls and the propane heater was humming away. He turned and closed his door on the dark dirty hallway then went to bed.

10.

When he woke up sunlight was making the closed drapes shimmer and the first thing he noticed was that there was no set of khakis on the spare bed where he'd left them the night before. On the other hand he did smell a hell of a lot better than he had yesterday, he smelled like soap. His own cloths were also nowhere to be found so he bolted downstairs to the first floor bathroom where he found them in a heap on the floor beside the first shower stall. He stuck his head into the stall itself but it didn't look any different than any of the others. He tried the faucets and got nothing. He picked up his clothes and walked down to the entrance to the mess hall and saw one set of footprints in the dust on the floor, starting at the doorway and ending halfway across the empty room. He had the sudden image of himself last night, sitting on the floor in a dark deserted dining hall having a conversation with people who weren't there. But he smelled like soap dammit, and he was clean...

He stood there for a long time looking at the single set of footprints and thinking about his sanity, wondering if he should get the hell out of there and find a hospital somewhere where he could get help, or not but still get the hell out of there. Hearing footsteps and voices was one thing, having a full-fledged fucking psychotic episode in the middle of the night was another. That boys and girls was a whole other ball game.

Finally he went back upstairs and ate something then went and stood at the windows of his first bedroom looking out at the road and counting the few cars that passed by. Somewhere off in the near distance he could hear a snow blower, probably at the condo complex. It reminded him of his old life, their house in the suburbs, working nine to five, barbecuing on the weekends, having his wife to talk to about things, their favorite TV shows. He turned away from the window and returned to his room because thinking about those things wasn't good, because that way lay real madness. He got his stuff on and headed out to do some exploring because he needed something to do, and if someone saw him and he got caught then so be it, maybe it would be for the best. He would take it as a sign that it was time to leave the haunted airbase behind.

He spent the entire day rooting around in old buildings trying to keep busy and tire himself out so he'd sleep that night and only half looking for useful stuff. When he stumbled upon another cache of propane tanks in a small cinderblock building on the edge of the old tarmac area near the hanger he supposed it was good luck and he spent most of the rest of the day lugging the bottles back to the barracks. He stayed away from the hanger.

A few times cars came by while he was near the road but the drivers didn't even look at him, except for one woman who waved, he waved back. The caretakers' office was closed up tight so that was one thing he didn't have to worry about. By the time he got all the propane bottles back to the barracks it was beginning to get dark. For a moment he considered just walking out, heading back to the train station and trying to sneak onto a Boston bound train but he didn't, he stored the propane in an empty room then fired up his heater and lamp and picked out an MRE for dinner.

Later he was lying in bed reading by lamplight when he heard a train whistle off in the distance. The whistles had always been there, sounding as the north and southbound trains passed the crossing next to the station but he'd never really noticed them before. Now he put his book down and listened to the mournful sound as it faded into the night. He had no idea how late the trains ran but it must be until ten or eleven pm, he still had time to pack up and get over there to catch one of them...He went back to his book, a murder mystery, and started reading again.

The middle of the night again and the guy standing in his doorway again and he wasn't surprised in the least. He sat up in bed and looked at the guy and the brightly lit hallway behind him.

"You going to tell me to leave again?" he said.

"Do any good?"

"No, I really don't have anywhere else to go."

"In that case you know where we are,"

He got out of bed and pulled on his shoes, deciding to just go in the sweatpants and sweatshirt he'd found in the gym. After all, in this make believe world the barracks heating system was fully functional. He followed the door guy down to the dining hall again and there they all were, just as they'd been the previous night. He went up to the serving window without being told to because he was hungry. This time they were serving breakfast which made as much sense as dinner had because after all, it *was* the middle of the night. He got scrambled eggs, sausage, toast and coffee and walked over to the table. He noted that the entire room was set up with tables but the one he was headed to was the only one occupied. He sat down in the same chair as before and tucked into his breakfast as the others talked about things he mostly didn't understand.

"The eggs are powdered," one of them finally said to him, "but what are you going to do, there is a war on."

Another one of them chuckled a little at that and the man who had spoken gave him a look. He finished his meal and powdered or not he thought the food was pretty damn good, then again why would you have a dream with lousy food? He sat back to finish his coffee and noticed that once again the kitchen had shut down, and that no one else at the table was eating, they just had coffee. Many of them were smoking though, something that he grown accustomed to not seeing over the past decade or so.

"You ever serve in the military?" one of them asked.

"No, never did," he replied and a couple of them mumbled under their breath. "Something wrong?" he asked.

"You're wearing a sweatshirt that says USN on it," the officer pointed out.

"Oh, sorry, I found it in the gym the other day; I can go up and change it if it bothers you."

"No," the officer replied, "don't bother; it's a hell of a lot cleaner that what you were wearing last time."

"Thanks," he said, "this is just a dream I'm having anyway isn't it."

"What does that mean?"

"This base closed a long time ago, no one lives here anymore, you guys aren't really here. So either your ghosts or I'm dreaming all of this. I'm going with the latter.

"Was the chow you just ate real?"

"It seemed to be, but then again if this is a dream it would wouldn't it?"

"You smell one hell of a lot better than you did when you came in here last night," one of them said, "That a dream too?"

You've got me there," he admitted.

"Why don't you think we're ghosts," Door Guy asked him.

"You look real; you don't look like what ghosts are supposed to look like, so I'm going with a dream."

"Pretty realistic dream."

He shrugged, "I guess it is but sometimes that's how dreams are."

"Do you think you're cracking up?"

"No, not really. Maybe roaming around in this empty old base has had more of an effect on me than I'd thought though. It is kind of a spooky place to begin with."

"We're ghosts," the officer told him.

"If I were dreaming that's what I would expect you to say," he pointed out.

"I'm not a ghost," Door Guy said, "I'm a fond remembrance of my former self."

The officer gave him a look then reached into his shirt pocket, pulled out an old Zippo lighter and slid it across the table. He picked it up and looked at it, it had a Navy crest on one side and it was well worn.

"You keep that," the officer told him, "Not for good mind you but you put that in your pocket and hold on to it until tomorrow night."

He shrugged and put the lighter into a pocket in the sweatpants he was wearing. "So this is going to be a nightly thing then?" he asked.

"We're here every night; it's up to you if you want to join us. You do get a free meal out of the deal after all."

11.

The first thing he did when he woke up the next morning was shove his hand into the pocket and it came out holding the Zippo. He held it up for a long time just looking at it, flipping it open, spinning the wheel and watching the flame flicker and dance, and thinking about how incredibly significant such an ordinary object could turn out to be.

Door Guy didn't stop in his door that night, he simply rapped on the wall as he passed and continued on to the stairs. They were all seated in their usual spots when he entered the dining hall but they stopped him before he could go to the food line.

"If this is going to be a regular thing then you need to shower regularly," the officer said.

"A haircut and a shave are in order too," Door Guy added.

"The living can really stink can't they?" someone at the table said and they all laughed.

He turned and crossed the hall to the bathroom where he saw placed neatly on shelve above the first sink a couple of towels, soap, shaving implements and a pair of scissors. So he took another long hot shower and it was fabulous...again, then he shaved, cutting himself a couple of times because he wasn't used to using a shaving brush and an old fashioned double edged razor. Lastly he peered into the mirror and cut his hair the best he could and actually ending up with it not looking half bad. There was another set of khakis on the next sink down, he put them on and returned to the dining hall where that night they were serving up soup and sandwiches. He sat down at the table and slid the Zippo back across the table to the officer.

"Believe we're here now?" the officer asked him.

"I do. You're name's on the lighter, Vic Taylor."

"Unless he stole it from someone named Vic Taylor," one of the others laughed.

"That's Lieutenant J.G. Taylor to you," another said.

Lieutenant Taylor leaned forward over the table to shake hands, I'm shaking hands with a ghost he thought then but it just felt like an ordinary hand. "Ignore these uneducated enlisted types," Taylor told him. "They're a bunch of wise guys." That brought some hoots and more laughs from around the table.

"I thought these had been enlisted man's quarters," he asked, "The BOQ is down the road isn't it?"

"Yeah sir," one of them said, "what are you doing hanging around our barracks? Don't you have a dinner party or cotillion dance or something to go to?"

"When I reported here for air training in '42 they were using the building here as officers billets because there were so many of us," Lieutenant J.G. Taylor replied. "Of course we had to fumigate the damn place before taking up residence since it had previously been occupied by enlisted men." More hoots and hollers from around the table and they all laughed again. He motioned down toward the end of the table where Door Guy was sitting, "your buddy there is an officer too although he doesn't like to admit it too often, not amongst this rabble anyway."

He shook hands with Door Guy and they introduced themselves. Door Guy's name was Frank Braden and he was a J.G. too. The rest of the men around the table introduced themselves to him too but he knew he wasn't going to remember all the names.

"Don't try to remember everyone's name," Vic Taylor said as if he'd read his mind, "some of them come and go anyway, it's not always this large a group."

"It's not," one of them agreed, "but we couldn't pass up a chance to have dinner with someone who's still actually alive and kicking. It's never happened before."

"So why do you think it's happening now?" he asked them.

Frank Braden shrugged, "maybe because this place has been deserted for so long and now you're living here, you're the first live person who's stepped foot in this building in ten years or more."

"I remember when the last of them finally left," one of the guys said, "they were good guys and the place was always hopping, it got really quiet and lonely after they were gone."

"It did at that," Vic said, "but none of them ever knew we were here," he looked at him, "not like you, must be some reason."

He shrugged as he finished his soup, "I lived in a haunted house in college, maybe that's why, I was more open to the possibility than the next person."

"I take exception to the term haunted house," Vic replied, "Sounds like we're all Halloween characters or something.

"Aren't we?" one of them said and they all laughed again.

And that was how his nightly dinners began with the past residents of the barracks in building 41. Well, almost nightly, on occasion he slept through the night and didn't see them. He asked them if they were there on those nights and they told him they were there every night, and every day. But he only saw them at night, in that small window of time when he was able to cross over to where they were. During the day he was back in his own world, the real world if you preferred, and there was no sign of them. At times during the day he would go down and check the dining hall just in case, poking his head into the big empty room then walking away.

And he grew to really look forward to his evenings with them. It wasn't just the food that, even though it wasn't real he supposed, still filled his belly every night, or the hot showers and clean cloths. It was the company, the camaraderie that he'd never really had with anyone before. He began to understand why veterans spoke so fondly of their military service; it was that camaraderie, the friendships, that they recalled, not the bad things that sometimes went along with service. And Vic had been right, it wasn't always a large group, sometimes there were only three or four guys there but Vic and Frank were always there and Frank always swung by his room to call him to chow. He got to know both of them better and better as the nights in the dining hall began to add up. And he stopped wondering why it was and just enjoyed it.

A hard lesson that he'd learned; there were some things that were impossible to live with, but you could get used to just about anything.

Outside the snow held and was replenished by occasional storms and the traffic on the road remained sparse. He continued his forays around the empty base, looking for useful things but he also fell into a routine, spending the nights in the dining hall then sleeping to compensate for it. Some days he didn't even leave the barracks.

12.

One night Frank banged on the wall as he passed by and he got up and followed him downstairs. When he entered the dining hall Frank was the only one sitting at the table, eating his dinner. He got his own dinner from the cooks then joined Frank.

"Where is everyone?" he asked.

"Looks like it's just us tonight," Frank said, "the others must have someplace else to be."

"Like where? Somewhere else on the base you mean?"

Frank looked up at him from his tray, "places you don't know anything about my friend, and some of them may have moved on, they don't all stay here forever you know. Some do but a lot decide to continue on with what had been their lives."

"You can do that? I always thought ghosts were trapped in one time and place, somewhere that meant something to them in life. I didn't know they could just move on whenever they felt like it."

"Most can if they choose to; others stay in one place, sometimes not by choice, someplace that meant something to them in life, like this base. A lot of boys became men here over the years, some died here.

"So, did you die here on the base, in a training accident or something?"

"I died of a heart attack in Duluth Minnesota in 1989."

"What? I don't understand."

"Not much to understand, I had just left a Safeway and was walking to my car when my heart decided that was the ballgame and down I went, dead before I hit the damn ground."

"No, I mean why are you here then?"

Frank didn't say anything for a moment then just shrugged, "this is where I was happiest I guess, so this is where I ended up. After the war I started a shipping business, built it up into a pretty big company over the years, worked my ass off doing it. I just never had time to get married or have a family, my company was my family. Pretty pathetic I know but when you're doing it it doesn't seem like that, and the time goes by so fast, good Christ how fast the years go by. So, I guess I ended up back here because this was the most important time of my life, and probably the happiest. I was involved in the biggest thing I'd ever see, a world war; it was the single most significant thing I'd ever do. And I was here with a great bunch of people; we were on a crusade, at least that's how we saw it; for God and Country."

"So you died in Duluth in 1989 and woke up back here?"

"'bout the size of it," Frank said. He'd finished his dinner; he pushed the tray away and sat back to light a cigarette.

"Are you trapped here, just reliving this part of your life over and over again?"

"No, that's not how it works, not for most of us anyway. I'm here because I want to be here, I wanted to come back here and relive this part of my life again so I am. Today I trained on a TBF Avenger because that's what I did on this day seventy years ago. I can stay here and keep reliving it or I can keep on and relive each day, up until 1989 I suppose, although I don't think I'll opt for reliving my empire building years again, that's for sure." He barked a laugh and finished his coffee.

"Does everyone do this when they die? Go back to some part of their life and relive it?"

"No, not everyone, some people aren't interested in this and they just move on. And some aren't even given the option."

"Where do they move on to?"

"To whatever the next thing is, I'll find out when I decide to go there."

"When will that be?"

"Who knows, I like it here."

On another night Frank never came by at all but he was awake anyway so he got up and went looking for him. When he walked into the dining hall Vic was sitting at the table by himself drinking coffee.

"Frank never came to get me," he told Vic as he sat down with his meal. He had also noticed that only one guy was working in the kitchen this time. Usually there were two or three.

"He's around somewhere," Vic replied, "we can't all be here every night to sit around with your sorry butt you know."

He smiled and ate his dinner.

"Mind if I ask you a personal question," Vic said after a few moments of silence.

"Why am I a bum?"

"Pretty much yeah, most of the bums I knew back in my day were drinkers, which was how they became bums. But you don't seem to drink at all."

"Clean and sober for over a year now."

"So why then?" he held up a hand then, "If you don't want to say that's fine, it's none of my business anyway and it's probably a long story."

"Actually it's a real short story," he said wiping his mouth with a napkin then pushing his tray away. He sipped his coffee for a bit, staring across the empty dining hall, he noticed that the one kitchen guy was gone and the kitchen was dark.

"Look, forget it," Vic said, "I can tell it's bothering you so let it slide. Like I said, none of my damned business."

"No," he said finally and put his coffee mug down on the table a bit too hard. "I've never told anyone before so I might as well, they say confession is good for the soul right?"

"Depends what you're confessing," Vic replied.

"I killed my wife," he said suddenly then picked his mug up for another sip; thought about it, put the mug back down on the table.

"Ok," Vic was watching him closely now, "How'd you do that?"

"You know what road rage is?" had asked and Vic shook his head. "Yeah, I didn't think so, that particular expression is fairly recent. It's pretty simple actually; road rage is when someone driving a car gets really angry with someone else driving another car and does something about it. It's usually over something really stupid like one guy cutting the other guy off then giving him the finger. That's what happened you see, my wife and I were driving to the movies, just a Saturday night at the movies when someone started tailgating me on the highway then swerved in front of me and cut me off, flipped me the bird, and drove on. Something you should just write off to there being a lot of assholes in the world and continue on with your life. Not me though, I had suffered from road rage for years. I was an angry driver and usually that just meant leaning on the horn or an obscene gesture but not on this night, I went from a nice night out with my wife to a state of total rage in just about one second. I chased the guy and started tailgating him and then he pulled a brake job on me and I almost hit him and it was on. We chased each other down the highway, in and out of traffic, going faster and faster, right by the exit for the movie theatre and all the while my wife yelling angrily at me to stop it, just slow down and stop it. And then she wasn't angry anymore, she was scared, because we were going very fast and getting closer and closer to each other, and then she was crying, and then sobbing, and begging me to stop because she was scared and she didn't want to die. She said that if I loved her I wouldn't do this to her," he paused for a moment and Vic didn't think he'd continue, but he did. "That was the last thing she ever said to me. I did love her, more than anything in this world but by that point the anger was huge, it was all there was and I couldn't control it; I couldn't push it back down and make it stop no matter how much I loved her and then our bumpers touched and at that speed that's all it took. I went off the highway and we rolled and rolled and when we finally stopped I was lying on the ground a dozen feet away from the car and my wife was pinned beneath the car and she was screaming, just screaming and it was the most horrible thing I have ever heard, until she stopped screaming and that was worse."

He picked up his coffee mug again, looked at it then gently put it back down. Vic was just watching him, he didn't say anything.

"I missed the funeral because I was in the hospital. And then I got out and followed up the worst thing I'd ever done in my life with the second worst thing, I walked out on our daughter. I tried for a while to put things back together but I couldn't, there was no way to do that. And she knew, she was a teenager, she knew, and she looked just like her mother, every time I looked at her I heard those screams...until finally I couldn't look at her anymore. So I left her with her aunt and uncle and I walked away, I killed my wife and then I abandoned our daughter." He wiped his hand quickly over his eyes. "And I was a drunk; I drank for years, as much as I could. I didn't have the courage to kill myself you see, I wasn't brave enough to put a gun to my head or slash my wrists so I tried to drink myself to death and it didn't work. I came out the other side over a year ago, started puking it up every time I drank, just couldn't keep it down. So then I thought ok, I'll let the DT's kill me but they didn't either and so here I sit. And I'm still homeless because I have no family and no reason to do anything else and because there's no coming back from what I did, there's no way to make it right or move on from it, ever. As sad and pathetic as it probably sounds to you I'm just waiting for it to be over. Except now that I've been here and met you guys I think that it may never be over, that death won't even end it, that that will be my penance and while it's exactly what I deserve it still terrifies me."

They sat in silence for a few moments before Vic spoke; "Did it help to get it off your chest?"

"No, but it feels better that someone else knows what a piece of shit I am, even if it's a dead guy," he tried to smile and couldn't quite pull it off.

"I had some pretty bad things happen to me in my life," Vic said, "but I ended up back here when I kicked, not reliving any of them."

"I hope your right but if you're not I'll accept it because I own it." He fidgeted with his mug a little, "it makes me think about seeing my wife again too, what if she's waiting for me, to call me to account for what I've done. As much as I want to see her again to say how sorry I am it wouldn't be nearly enough, nothing I could do could ever be nearly enough, and I don't know if I could face her, for her to know that I ran out on our daughter."

"Have you spoken to your daughter, is she ok?"

He nodded, "I called her a while ago, for the last time I think, she doesn't want a thing to do with me and I understand that. But she seems ok; she's married and has a little boy. My wife would have loved to have had a chance to meet him, to play with him." He looked at Vic, "we were just going to the movies," he said dully then lowered his head and put his hands to his face.

A few nights later it ended up just being he and Vic again, Frank started off with them but begged off after a bit to go off and do whatever they did when they weren't communing with the living. A third sailor who he'd seen at the table a few times was also there but just to say goodbye because he'd decided to move on.

So it was just he and Vic sitting at the table drinking coffee, Vic smoking. It was funny because most of them smoked and when he'd first started having dinner with them he'd almost pointed out that smoking was bad for your health, and then he'd realized how incredibly stupid that would have been and how much shit they would have given him for it.

"How are things going in the real world?" Vic asked him.

"No idea, I haven't left the base in weeks."

"Actually I meant with the base. You still roaming around the old buildings picking up junk?"

"Yeah, pretty much, I've hit almost all the buildings by now except for some of the small ones, probably found everything that was worth finding."

"You like it here."

"I do," he replied without taking time to think about it.

"So you'd like to stay here, with us?"

"Sure, I'd love that but I don't think it's in the cards. They'll catch me eventually and throw my ass out," he said, "only a matter of time.

"What will you do then?"

He shrugged, "I don't know, after all of this I don't see how I can just go back to the streets but that's probably what I'll do. It would be great to do something you know? Something at least a little meaningful again but," he looked down for a moment then shrugged again, "I don't think there's much chance of that happening...I think I'm all used up, you know?"

"I may have another option for you," Vic said to him, "if you want it."

"What's that?"

"A way you could stay here for good, or as long as you wanted to anyway.

He looked at him, "and how would that work?"

"You could take my place. You're halfway through already, I mean you hang out with us every night. This would let you go all the way through, it would still be here but it would be *my* here when I was alive."

"How would I do that? I mean, I'd have to be dead right? I have to tell you, if I'd had the guts to kill myself I'm pretty sure I would have done it long ago."

Vic smiled, "you don't have to kill yourself, I'm not talking about you haunting the place like we do, you couldn't do that because you're not dead and you don't have the history with this place that we do. You'd still be alive but you'll be the *me* version of alive when I was here in '42... if that makes any sense."

"I can just do that."

"Not just on your own, you'd need help; you'd need a spot to take here, somebody to give it to you."

"Well where does that leave you then?"

"I'm going to move on," Vic said, "it's time for me to leave this behind and move on to the next thing."

"Do you know what the next thing is?"

"No," Vic looked at him, "Do you?"

"No," he laughed, "but you're the one who wants to go there so I thought you did."

Vic shrugged, "it doesn't matter really, it's the next thing and it's time for me to go, I've been here long enough and I've gotten whatever I needed to get from it. So, you can have my place if you want."

"How do we do that?"

"I think I just leave and you become me, the me that was here anyway, because once I move on I won't need that me any longer, I'll be a new *me*."

"And I can just jump back to 1942 and pick up where you were, just like that?"

"Pretty much, I don't think it comes up often but it can be done, maybe it's something about this place itself, or something about you, I'm not sure, but I know it's possible. You would become me the day I first set foot on this base, September 27th 1942."

"So I'll be Vic Taylor, and I'll have your memories and stuff?"

"You'll be Vic Taylor and you'll have my knowledge, my abilities, to fly a plane and such, but you'll still be you, you'll have your own memories and history and all, you'll just be taking my place. One warning though, you'll have to live the life I lived back then starting with my training here at the base, and on from there. So eventually you'd come to the same end I did, and just because after that I ended up here that doesn't mean you will, you may not. Something to think about."

They sat drinking their coffee for a few minutes, each thinking their own thoughts. Vic knew enough to wait for him to speak first and finally he did; "There's nothing left for me here," he said quietly, "maybe this way I can do something worthwhile, something that in the end will mean something, that will put me in the plus column in some small way again, and let me find some damned peace."

"Maybe that's why you ended up here," Vic replied.

"Yeah, maybe, it's as good an explanation as any." He turned to face Vic, "So when were you planning on leaving?"

Vic laughed and slapped him on the shoulder, "soon," he said.

"How soon?"

"Very soon, why don't we meet here tomorrow night, I'll make sure Frank's here to say goodbye to both of us, one last meal together, and then we'll be off."

He didn't sleep the remainder of that night and couldn't manage anything but a walk around the base the next day. He thought about calling his daughter again, one last time, but dismissed the idea. As much as he wanted to talk to her once more he knew that that door had closed and though it broke his heart there was still nothing he could do about it. So he wandered the bleak, deserted base, still cloaked in winter snow, and waited for night to come.

That night it was just the three of them in the dining hall and the cook left right after they got their dinners. They ate and talked about small things, enjoying the meal and one another's company. And when they had finished they sat drinking their coffee in silence, each thinking their own thoughts.

"Well," Vic said finally, "I think I'm going to get going, no time like the present boys."

"Send me a postcard and let me know how it is," Frank said and they all smiled.

Vic turned to him, "so we're set on how this works, once I'm gone you go with Frank, you leave this building and just keep walking with Frank, and you'll be cooking with gas."

"I've got it," he replied then hesitated for a moment, "One more thing," he said, "what happened to you, and what's going to happen to me, do I die in the war or do I drop dead in Duluth Minnesota like Frank?"

Vic looked at him for a moment and then smiled, "Do you really want to know? Really?"

He thought about it then finally shook his head, "No, I guess I don't. But at least tell me if there's anything that I should look out for, anything I should avoid."

"Sure," Vic laughed, "a girl named Shirley in Honolulu, barmaid at a place called The Rusty Scupper, stay as far away from her as possible and I'm not kidding."

He smiled and nodded, "Shirley at The Rusty Scupper; got it."

Vic held out his hand and they shook, "Have fun pal and give em hell, I damned sure did. For God and Country."

"For God and Country" he said and Vic turned and left the dining hall without looking back. He looked at Frank and Frank was smiling, "I think I might see you back here someday," Frank said to him as they left the dining hall walking side by side.

EPILOG

Josh McCurty and Brain Trask, both employed by the caretaker's office of the de-activated Weymouth Naval Reserve Air Station were working their way through barracks #41, doing an annual inspection to check for...who knew what. The last annual inspection had been six years ago and both doubted that it had involved anything more than someone unlocking the doors and sticking their head in to smell for smoke.

Trask was checking out the second floor bathrooms when McCurty called to him from down the hall. When he got to the room McCurty was standing in he stopped in the doorway.

"What the fuck is all this?"

"Looks like someone was squatting here," McCurty said, "had quite the little set up too. He must have pilfered all this shit from buildings on the base. Christ on a crutch, I think some of those propane tanks are from our own goddamned building."

"You think he's still here?"

"Nah, there's dust all over everything, looks like he's been gone awhile."

"Why would he leave all this stuff behind? There's a backpack right here with personal shit in it, toothbrush, old wallet and some photos of a woman and a little girl."

McCurty looked at him, "You don't think the guy's dead in the building somewhere do you?"

"We started in the basement and worked our way up here numb nuts," Trask said, "We would've found him."

"What about some other building on base, from the stuff here it looks like he's been in all of them for Christ sake."

Trask looked around the room for a minute then swore under his breath, "We're going to have to check them all," he said, "every frigging one of them, because if they find out that this guy was living here right under our goddamned noses we're on the street the next day. If it turns out he died on base and someone else finds him we'll be on the street that very *same* day." He looked at McCurty, "Every single building," he repeated.

And they did just that, they checked every building on the base, they never found anything.

30 Minutes Remaining

1.

There was a small patch of grass outside the door to the old administration building, maybe 12 feet by 12 feet that he had been trying to keep alive and looking nice for no good reason that he could think of. He watered it every morning and afternoon, picked out any stray weeds, even mowed it with a push mower he'd found in an equipment shed. He had to admit that it was looking pretty good and looking at it made him feel good.

Other than his self-assigned landscaping duties there wasn't a lot for him to stay occupied with on the little island. He would putter around the half dozen buildings that made up the camp trying to keep it looking nice and keeping an eye out for anything he could use although he'd pretty much picked the place clean already.

The afternoons were hot as hell so he usually stayed on the porch of his little house, reading and napping. Then a quick dinner consisting of whatever he had put together for that evening and then down to the beach at dusk for the highlight of the day.

When he'd first arrived on the island and realized that he was alone he'd often sit on the beach looking for someone, anyone, approaching the place. No one ever did and he didn't do that anymore.

The generator had still had a bit of gasoline left back then so he'd run that to power the shortwave radio but never heard anyone and no one ever answered his calls. The gas was gone now.

He'd sit on the beach just above the high tide line and watch the sunset and think about how beautiful the place was, how people used to pay a lot of money to enjoy this kind of tropical get-away, to sit right where he was sitting now and watch that sunset.

Once the sun had gone down and darkness came on he'd get out the little personal video player he'd found in a desk drawer in one of the cabins. It pre-dated the smart phones that had been the last big thing by five or six years he thought. It had a tiny two inch square screen but for him, now, when that screen came alive it was the whole world. The owner of the thing, whoever they had been, had had an affinity for travel shows. There had been over twenty of them recorded into the memory, most were episodes of a show about traveling in Europe featuring a bubbly young host that he came to think of as Perky Blond Woman. Perky Blond Woman would enthusiastically take the viewer on a tour of whatever part of Europe she was in for that episode. He greatly enjoyed each and every one of them because Europe was beautiful and he was never going to see it, and because they showed people, lots of people.

The sun dipped below the horizon and night fell quickly as it did in the tropics and he got out the personal video player and held it in his lap. He looked up at the night sky, the stars were already out up there, and listened to the waves break over the sand and he hesitated in turning the device on because this was a special night. Not a special night in a good way, like when he'd managed to find this island after weeks drifting in his little boat, or like when he'd gotten the generator going and had hope that the shortwave radio would connect him to someone, anyone, or like when he'd actually found the little video device and turned it on for the first time and met Perky Blond Woman and heard a human voice again. No, this was a special night in a bad way, like when he'd searched the island and found no one, or when the generator ran out of gas and there was no more to be found anywhere, or when he'd used the last of the toothpaste. Because when he turned on the video player the little screen was going to flash a message telling him that he had 30 minutes remaining before the battery needed to be recharged. A minor inconvenience in the old world, just a little reminder to plug the thing in before you went to bed. Of course now the battery was never going to be recharged which meant that he had 30 minutes remaining to watch Perky Blond Woman frolic around Europe, 30 minutes to see and hear other human beings, and then the little screen would go dark for the final time and it would just be him and the sound of his own voice, the island, and a useless little plastic box full of circuit boards and wires. So it was a special night indeed.

A crescent moon was visible now through the tops of the palms that ringed the little lagoon and he watched that for a while. That would still be here tomorrow night, as would the stars and the sound of the surf but it would be different, it would all be different.

He held the video player in his lap for another few moments and he thought about waiting until tomorrow night to watch his last episode but then he worried that the battery would lose charge by just sitting in the humid air. So finally he turned it on and depressed the PLAY button and there was good old Perky Blond Woman walking along a street in Cornwall England talking about how nice it was and there were people behind her, real live people talking and laughing and being alive. And he was glad that Cornwall would be his final episode because he'd always wanted to go there.

Made in the USA
Middletown, DE
10 December 2016